LOBSTERS WITHOUT BORDERS

LOBSTERS WITHOUT BORDERS

A NOVEL

CAROL CHEN

For Dirk,
so precious and now gone

ACKNOWLEDGMENTS

The poetry quoted in Chapter 21 is from "The Princess" by Alfred, Lord Tennyson.

The poetry quoted in Chapter 53 is from "Song: To Celia" by Ben Jonson.

The poetry quoted in Chapter 73 is from *Paradise Lost* by John Milton.

To all my readers and book people—Cheryl Ayer, June Bower, Brenda "Cookie" Breton, Tom Campbell, Patt Chen (especially Patt!), Teresa Dobbins, Julie Dutille, Terry Gerritsen, Chip Haggerty, Barb Karl, Barney Karpfinger, Dorie Klein, Rick Kot, Kristen Lindquist, Madeleine Martindale, Deborah Oliver, Susan Rabb, Cheryl Rogers, Heather Rogers, Marc Rogers, Mary Ryan, Tim Whelan—thank you for your help!

My gratitude goes over the electromagnetic waves to Bethany Atazadeh and Natalia Leigh for their self-publishing tutorials.

Bravo to Taylor Curry, the photographer, graphic designer, and publisher who made this book cover sing!

My greatest thanks rest with John and Helen Chen. They are not here to read this book, but Mom would probably raise her eyebrows and say, "Oh no, here we go," and Dad would blurt out "AOK!" Generous, quirky, funny, and stable, they were the best parents I could have ever had.

1
April 2019

Harriet Buxton was a generously sized woman of an indeterminate age, with thinning hair the color of chicken liver, and yellow eye teeth she maneuvered like polite fangs. In her capacity as Head of Human Resources, she nestled comfortably in her executive's chair at the Maine State Police headquarters and was just now ripping open a package of Reese's peanut butter cups.

She bit into that delightful moment when the chocolate cloak becomes one with the peanut butter heart and began reading through the employee file labeled "Jane Roberts." Roberts was the newly appointed Public Safety Officer on St. Frewin's Island, and the accounting department had slapped a hot pink sticky over her file that barked "FLAGRANT EXPENDITURES?"

"*Hmm, St. Frewin's—one of our more remote island posts,*" Harriet noted. The employee profile reminded her that Ms. Roberts had been an attorney at a major law firm before she graduated from the Maine Police Academy last year. *Odd career shift, very odd....*

Harriet turned to Ms. Roberts' expenses for the past quarter, the contents of which gave her such a start, she struggled to avoid toppling out of her designer chair. As she was exclaiming "$350.00 for one month of client lunches?" Harriet's full-body shapewear cruised over a bulge, shot up, and bit her in the underarms. She yanked on the feral corset and squinted more closely at the numbers. "Times three, equals $1050.00! Does Ms. Roberts think she's still at her bigwig law firm? This boggles the mind!"

Harriet grabbed her office directory and hit the numbers for Lieutenant Joseph Adderley in Major Crimes Unit. He was Ms. Roberts' senior officer, in charge of island community policing. "To think there's someone lurking out there offshore, hosing the Maine taxpayers. Joseph Adderley is going to have some serious explaining to do if he's signed off on Jane Roberts' spending orgy. They'll both have some explaining to do."

"Lieutenant Adderley! Harriet Buxton from Human Resources. How are you?"

"Oh, Mrs. Buxton. Such a surprise to hear from you. How may I help?" Lieutenant Adderley felt his chest tighten. "Mrs. Buxton"—as she was known throughout the force—held a formidable grip on the hiring spigot at the Maine State Police. No department got but whomever she thought they deserved. On top of that, she brandished a stinging metaphorical whip over every employee's performance.

"Lieutenant, I am reviewing the most recent quarterly report for Ms. Jane Roberts, who is stationed on St. Frewin's Island. I'd like to know what kind of shenanigans are occurring under her command. Surely you reviewed these expenses? Please tell me she isn't out to plunder the Maine State Treasury."

"Why, yes, Mrs. Buxton," Lieutenant Adderley began hesitantly as he pawed at his computer mouse to retrieve the report for a closer look. "I believe Jane Roberts submitted paperwork for, ah, working meals with island residents and some...yes...renovation costs for the Public Safety Office. As well as, I will admit, a rather unusual notice that she has dispensed with the Public Safety uniform for her own choice of cotton T-shirts and army cargo pants."

"And you consented to this?" Harriet asked.

"She does state she's highly allergic to polyester fibers and would feel abnormal in fitted clothing. She believes she can't perform her job properly in the State uniform—hence the need to outfit herself as described."

"Lieutenant Adderley—Joseph, if I may? How can we possibly sit back and let this quarterly report go through?" Harriet grabbed two peanut butter cups. "Jane wants black V-neck T-shirts. Black! V-neck! Imagine that, Joseph! This Combat Jane...G. I. Jane...take your pick...is apt to be flitting around St. Frewin's like she's some kind of foxy femme fatale in a TV series. We are talking about the Major Crimes Unit, Joseph, not a branch office of the Mossad!

"And do we have cleavage issues with Jane's V-necks? Major Crimes Unit requires white button-up shirts for dignity and modesty on the job. Pardon my French, but what kind of an image will Maine law enforcement project if we permit Playmate Jane AND her hooters to be out there pacifying drunken fishermen who are blowing each other's head off?"

"Oh not to worry, not at all...Harriett? ...if I may? No worries in that department. Jane's a lean one, if you get my drift."

"I don't care if she's an anorexic pitchfork, Joseph! I am going to mull over this rogue assault on our professional dress code. We can't have the rest of the force getting a whiff of this. But you're not off the hook, by any means. What about these outrageous lunch expenses? How can YOU and your improvident underling justify her spending over $1000.00 a quarter on fried clam platters? I'll tell you what's going on here, Joseph. Jane Roberts is one conniving tapeworm masquerading as a Public Safety Officer."

Adderley could feel the sweat beginning to steam beneath his shirt collar. "Jane does explain in her submission that quite a few islanders have wanted to have lunch to meet their new PSO and find out what she's all about. She hasn't felt comfortable assuming they would treat her, so she's paid her own way each time. I do agree that forty-two lunches a quarter begins to strain credulity. I will definitely talk to her about this aspect of her policing."

"Stay with me, Joseph. We're not done yet. What about these office renovation expenses? Fifteen gallons of Benjamin Moore superior base paint? Insulated roman shades? A huge white board for conference notes? Does Jane think she's running a Fortune 500 corporation out there? Last I heard, St. Frewin's was just a chunk of granite stuck in Penobscot Bay, home to more lobsters than people!"

"Well, Harriet, Jane notes that she wanted to modernize the office to bring it into the 21st century...paint the walls white, sharpen the décor, and make it appealing for people when they have to come in to deal with their problems, especially during the dark of winter. If I might add, as an aside, Harriet, I understand Jane is in the process of parting from her husband. So I'm trying to give her a little slack on these administrative issues while she settles her personal matters."

"That is absolutely bombastic, Joseph! Why would you ever permit such brazen fleecing of the state's coffers? As for Jane's split from her husband, you know that kind of traumatic life event can unleash compulsive spending in some people. Makes them needy for material things when they're losing a partner."

"I believe Jane reported that she's feeling very realistic about the end of her marriage. I recall her saying that what doesn't kill her will make her stronger."

"Kill her? Well that's all fine and good, Joseph, but what kind of performance can we expect from someone who thinks her divorce is a near-death experience?"

2
Friday, May 24

The tallish, young woman tugging on her black V-neck shirt had the faintest hint of dragon lady in her eyes and cheekbones. It was the sort of face you could inherit from restless tribes colliding over continents and centuries—a little Czech, a little Polish, a slice of Chinese, toss in some Italian, a sprinkling of Russian, Visigoths, Huns, whatever, *confetti*.

At the moment she was seated at her desk and staring hard at her monthly police log, so studded with mundane cases, she had to hoist up each eyelid with a finger to stay alert. She exhaled a huge sigh, let loose an eyelid, and forked in another mouthful of exceedingly tart rhubarb pie.

Much to her chagrin, she was two court filings away from becoming the "retired wife" of her lecherous Putative Spouse. He refused to live out the rest of his married life on a small dot in the ocean. No wonder she was feeling increasingly cranky towards the entire universe and quite a few of her fellow islanders, not to mention the sloppy day trippers who lost their kids and littered debris all over the wild.

Whatever happened to the sweet spot in her career? ...in her life? She leaned way back and pulled down her new roman shade, just for the fun of it. So much for Jane Roberts, now six months on the job as Public Safety Officer/Dog Control Officer/Shellfish Warden on St. Frewin's Island, somewhere in the Atlantic Ocean.

What Jane needed was a murder.

Instead, here she sat, stewing in her cramped side office on a Friday and working late with her staff on their monthly report.

"Zee-eeke," Jane yodeled out towards the outer office. "Awfully sorry I can't read your chicken scrawl to save my life. Are you trying to state Bernie Pushaw's wife wants him to come in for a breathalyzer test once a week? Since when are we an AA pit stop, for chrissakes? And is this Bernie Pushaw the guy who tried to taser his mother-in-law while she was making fruitcakes last Christmas? I need info, pullleeeze."

No answer. She was tempted to dial her dear friend Samantha Lloyd and launch into more venom about Jane's soon-to-be "wasband." Jane couldn't resist. She grabbed her phone and plunged into the diatribe of a woman scorned.

Minutes later came the knock on the door. Office Manager Zeke Pendleton, tall and vaguely handsome, stuck his head of sleek black hair inside her office. He and Jane had finally settled into an affection of friction, but it had taken all her patience to put up with his oddities, including his blasted cockney alter ego.

Jane had to admit. There were endearing aspects to Zeke. He moved like a galumphing lab puppy, had a kind spirit, and there was not one pound of misplaced flesh on his taut body. In fact, she was forced to swat away a momentary fantasy of Zeke beside her...*naked*. Such an excruciatingly bad idea. How would she have ever dealt with those long thighs of his? Like two telephone poles in bed....

"Guv—Can you take a break and nip out here? Maggie Banner from the Grand Harbor Inn is on the telly. She sounds a bit knackered."

"Zeke, get back to me later about Bernie Pushaw, OK? Sam—I have to go. Public Safety needs me. Ciao."

Jane put down the one phone and zipped into the main office to pick up the other phone. Maggie Banner's agitated voice was spilling out. "Jane, the Inn's clothes dryers are on the fritz. I had to hang all the laundry outside. And some dog just ran off with the clothesline pinned with guests' underwear! I really need to get that stuff back *now*."

Why the hell was Maggie calling Public Safety after hours about runaway underpants? "Maggie—Just one question. Can't you get your new assistant India to help you track down the dog? ...What? ...Because I'm the Dog Control Officer? Oh, Lord. I know that, but it's Friday night. ...OK, hang on. I'll be right over."

Jane grabbed her keys, but stopped short to do a glaring double-take at Zeke. He stared at her with the guilt of bright orange dust that had landed in a halo around his mouth. Jane couldn't help but pounce. "God help you, Zeke. You have GOT to recycle the entire contents of those cheese puffs right now and eat an apple or something. You're killing yourself with that crap!"

Continuing to blow off steam, Jane headed for her truck for what she hoped would be her last task for the day. She was still hungry, but as she drove off, she began to ponder tonight's dinner to make herself feel better...maybe some pear parmesan pecan salad and roasted chicken with rice...white rice, not brown. White rice because it was so comforting...the hell with brown rice. Mmmm...she was beginning to feel better already. Even if she was stumbling through her thirties, about to be eating solo for the rest of her life, with no adverse party to hug in bed ever again.

3
Friday, May 24
Early Evening

As Jane drove along the fields of Harbor Road towards the south end of the island, she made sure to bomb past all the speed limit signs. Who was going to stop her...herself? She ignored the miles of velvety green grass that could have been air-lifted from the lawn of an English palace. She frowned at the ancient fir trees, brave and tall in the vast meadows of lupine, deep violet and blue soldiers marching towards the sea. On an ordinary day, the simple beauty of it all could calm her nerves, but no such luck today, and probably not tomorrow.

What is wrong with me, Jane wondered. Why were her public safety duties sending her into such a tizzy? Maybe her divorce was making her brittle about everything. Lately it felt like the tiniest irritation might upend her world. That had to be a sign she was going crazy. That's how she felt. Crazy.

In her deepest moments of self-analysis and honesty (if those were even possible!), she knew cutting the knot from Nick Colin made so much sense, it was laughable. Three years ago, Jane Roberts, the young, budding New York City lawyer, had stormed into Nick Colin's life and badgered him for days, which turned into weeks, which piled up into months, until even he finally thought he really wanted to get married...to Jane, honestly, forever and ever.

But they were so wrong together! The sunny armored tank Nick was, kept crashing into Jane's peppery, combative frenzy. And he drank too much. She tried to keep her dismay covert; she kept thinking she could fix things. She signed them up for the Myers-Briggs personality test, which only sowed more distress and confusion...an I-N-T-J (Introverted-Intuitive-Thinking-Judging) Jane in holy matrimony with an E-S-T-P (Extroverted, Sensing-Thinking-Perceiving) Nick? Doomed combo!

Next they lounged around on puffy, fake leather couches in a marriage counselor's office and quibbled about their Big Five Personality Traits. Who was or wasn't Open, Conscientious, Extroverted, Agreeable, or Neurotic. And why was Jane's inventive, curious, efficient (sometimes), organized (eh...), solitary, reserved, challenging, detached, sensitive (scratch that), nervous self not getting along with Nick's consistent, cautious (hah!), efficient, organized, outgoing, energetic, friendly, compassionate, secure, confident persona? Such a psychological swamp.

It finally took Nick's running off with Jane's paralegal to force Jane to admit to the death of their mismatch. But if anyone was going to whack a chain saw through Jane's wedding vows, it ought to be Jane's decision, right? Not some shiny interloper who probably scored really lousy on the Myers-Briggs test...say a T-U-L-S! Ha ha!!

Thoroughly annoyed that she was coddling these useless memories yet again, Jane shoved the thoughts under her mental rug labeled "Matrimony Baloney." She slowed her truck, and turned into the lush corridor of rhododendron and azaleas leading to Grand Harbor Inn. The final stretch of gravel drive and the entire front portico were smothered in gorgeous mounds of lilacs—shades of lavender, white, and deep fuchsia. Jane breathed in the warm, thick scent as she approached the welcoming entrance of the Colonial Revival façade. It soothed her inner volcano...just a pinch.

In the curve of the horseshoe bend stood a wilted Maggie Banner, fanning herself and her light blue suit. She waved Jane in towards the setting sun, whose vast wings of patchy orange and deepening rose were folding into darkness behind the Inn. No earthly sign of dog or bras.

"Jane, thanks so much for rushing over. I really appreciate it." Maggie crinkled her friendly eyes as she climbed into the truck. "Sorry if I'm kind of grimy. Too much hullabaloo today." She began patting dry her damp dirty blonde hair and sweaty face with a tissue.

Jane could not understand it. Despite the "hullabaloo," Maggie's perfectly balanced features (all of them) in her thirty-something face still looked flawless. Jane had no idea how she did that.

"The dog ran off towards Herinton Point," Maggie said. "OK if we head down there?"

Maggie glanced at Jane's fatigue pants and T-shirt. Though the outfit lent a refreshing hint of seduction to Jane's slightly exotic Cop image, something was haywire with her paramilitary fashion statement. Kind of like Castro's fiancée, but wrong island.

As they started down the road, Jane turned towards her passenger with a "Public Safety Look" Jane had practiced in her bathroom mirror—stern eyes; tight lips. "I have to tell you, Maggie. This is really stretching the limits of my community policing duties. I could be out here all night chasing an AWOL hound who's chomping on some dame's girdle. What's that going to look like in my activities log?"

"Sorry, Jane. Maybe I panicked. But ever since I can remember, we've always called the Public Safety Officer when there was a dog problem," Maggie said.

"What does that mean? 'Ever since you can remember'? How long have you been on St. Frewin's?" Jane asked.

"Well, my family's summered on the island forever. It used to be my second home. Now it is my home."

"So, does that mean you're old money, like 99% of the summer people around here?" Jane said in mock horror.

"You make it sound like a crime, Jane. I take it you're not 'old money'?"

"Hell, noooo. Do I look like I landed on Plymouth Rock in seersucker diapers? Maybe I'm being a hard-ass, but you know what I mean, Maggie. This place is crawling with privileged heirs who can sail, play tennis, and eat finger food all at once. And half the men wear strawberry-colored pants!"

"Jane, that is so overblown. Maybe we should change the subject."

"OK, OK." Jane let it go. Maggie was actually quite easy to be with—calm and level-headed. And there were only so many sane women on this small island. Best not to rock the boat.

"Who are these guests, anyway, whose undies are being dragged all over town?" Jane wondered as the road they were on entered a stretch of dense, boggy patches of upright and fallen cedars.

"They're a curious bunch. Ten young women—I'd say in their late twenties and early thirties...from a high-tech company, and they're running me ragged. I think island life has come as something of a shock for these gals—like all this fresh air might kill them." Maggie laughed and then paused for a moment. "How about you, Jane? How are you doing, now that you've had time to settle in?"

Jane froze momentarily. Maggie's question was innocent enough, but Jane resisted giving a straight answer. "I'm fine. Don't ask for details."

"Jane—I'm sorry. You seem a bit tense. Look...I hope I'm not too out of place bringing this up, but people have said you're leaving your husband. And they're worried the move to St. Frewin's might have been too much for your personal life."

"Leaving my husband, Maggie? That's what you've heard? I am thrilled to hear people think I'm leaving Nicholas Colin. Don't tell anyone it was the other way around, OK?"...*Damn. Did I just say that?* Jane cringed. *Quick! White Out.*

"Ha ha!!—Just kidding," Jane rushed to assure her passenger. "I did leave the bastard. And he's crushed, as far as anyone can tell."

"Well, some day it will all be far behind you. We should sit down for tea later on and talk. You'd be surprised..." but Maggie's comment was cut short.

"Maggie—Look over there. That's the dog, right? A few yards in past those trees." Jane pulled her vehicle over and parked.

"Got 'im!" Maggie cheered. "OK—I have to rescue that underwear. You go grab the dog. I'll meet you back at the truck."

Jane started into the woods, ducking back and forth to avoid the jumble of branches snagging at her clothing. She aimed her flashlight towards the wildly wagging tail and called gently to the dog. "Get over here, you little idiot." She knew she had no reason to feel scared, but something irrational, something vaguely prescient, suddenly covered her arms with stubby goose bumps. Maybe it was the cool damp of the forest sliding under her clothes.

The dog was fixated on a pile of sorts as Jane approached and strained her eyes to see. "What have you got there, you panty thief." He growled bossily when she reached him, and Jane's arms and hands flushed with numbness. On the ground, the thin light from her flashlight trembled over a woman's distorted body, gripped by the earth. Jane was speechless. Despite the dog's persistence, she edged closer and aimed her light directly at the person's face. Jane did not recognize her, but as she leaned down to be sure, she shrieked "Oh my god!"

"What's with all the yelling, Jane?" Maggie came racing over. "You're a public safety officer. Shouldn't you try to hold it together more?"

"Easy for you to say, Maggie. Look at this."

Jane aimed the light so Maggie could see the hideous sight. Jane bent further forward to inspect what appeared to be a dead woman whose mouth was splayed to the point of distortion. The fat, blackish-bronze claws and carapace of a lobster thrust forward from the gape of the woman's jaws. Squirming upon the lobster's shell were tiny white maggots, so petite in size, so revolting. Jane wondered if their sheer motion was what triggered her fear and horror...all that flailing and burrowing into the crevices of the lobster and what little remained of the shredded tongue and cheek walls of the deceased. Whose fatal predicament had suddenly become Jane Roberts' last task for the day.

4
Friday, May 24
At Night

Although it would soon be midnight, Jane's adrenaline continued plowing into those secret parts of her brain that dished out the sauce and sauciness of what it meant to be human. She was very tired and now more than ready to quit this crime scene. The novelty of attending to the slain body had grown stale. The novelty of the night's events, however, kept her feeling edgy and intensely alive.

Once the State team had arrived, Herinton Drive morphed into a glaring, busy hive with the night fog whirling around the official activity. Red, white, and blue car lights flashed repeatedly over the road and abutting woods, like a pop-up disco, randomly lighting up the faces of crime investigators walking by.

Jane was all eyes and bold pulse as she grimaced and watched the State staff moving cautiously in their white monster suits, leaning down towards the corpse to photograph the position of the woman's body and limbs, her mangled face. They peered intently at her skin and clothing and scoured the woodsy turf where she rested.

"Jane, come closer and take a look." Todd Chisolm, the lead crime scene investigator, waved her over to where he was sitting on his haunches. He struck her as a friendly cowboy in the midst of all these New England worker bees, with a long drawl that wrapped itself around her.

"Here's your classic fourth stage of death," he said. As Jane scooched down to join him, she dipped her head so that her eyes were in shadow. Maybe he would not notice how she scrunched her eyes shut...deliberately. This communing with the body to fathom the signposts of death was miles outside Jane's tiny pinhead of a comfort zone.

"You might as well get a good look at some livor mortis in the flesh, versus those textbook illustrations they taught you at the Academy. Here's where the blood settled in her calf, right?" Chisolm put his hand on the dead woman's leg. "When I press on the bluish color, see how it remains bluish? What does that tell us?" he quizzed his reluctant student.

"Ah, I'm guessing she died more than eight to twelve hours ago?" Jane blurted out with bleak enthusiasm, desperately hoping she could go home any moment. It was all too surreal—this hanging out with Death in the fog and the blinking darkness, the investigators' hot spotlights shining smokily on the unknown victim. Whose life was now destroyed and silenced, no chance ever to grow old.

Hours earlier, after Jane and Maggie's shocking discovery, Jane had stationed herself at the roadside to secure the crime scene, while Maggie drove Jane's truck back to the Inn and called Major Crimes Unit to report the death. Jane's securing of the site was engrossing for about twenty minutes. Then it occurred to her she might have something in her truck that she could place near the crime scene...just some tiny token to acknowledge that a life was gone. She would check when Maggie returned with the truck.

In the meantime, Jane paced up and down Herinton Drive in the dark. She began dissecting whether she had made the right decision to abandon her law career and end up alone on this empty road with a fresh corpse. Not that her days as a legal practitioner had amounted to an exemplary law career. "Law Careen" was probably more accurate.

Jane could hardly bear to look back on her downfall as an attorney at the New York City firm, Wild, Gotz &

Mankey. It really had nothing to do with her lawyering skills...it was more a hesitant avalanche of random, botched scenarios that finally buried Jane's Martindale-Hubbell entry for eternity.

Like God only knows how she bungled the emailed dinner order for a dozen roast beef sandwiches and twelve matzoh ball soups during that M&A case she and her fellow associates had been working on. Where did the extra zeros come from? Was she so exhausted when she typed in the order that her finger wandered over to the zero key? Why, oh why, hadn't Sammy's Deli rung or emailed her back to confirm whether it really was 120 sandwiches and 120 matzoh ball soups?!

All the soup and sandwiches brought back the image of that horny paralegal who snatched away Jane's husband, just because she wanted to, on a lark. And off trotted Nick Colin, The Rake, lapping it all up with never a glance back at his beloved up and coming law firm associate wife. What had happened to Jane's Mr. and Mrs.? Who cared if they weren't compatible? Were married couples ever truly compatible? She asked herself those questions relentlessly.

Would there ever come a time when her mind would quit auto-streaming the night "The Nightmare" happened? How abysmal it had been to feel as though her entire being was immersed in a vat of dense, frigid, emotional slush. So shocked, her limbs could barely move, and all her body hair stood up stiff, like a frozen shag rug.

When Nick did not come home that night, Jane began calling his cell phone at midnight; she got no answer. She called and called again and got nothing. The clock ticked on; the cell phone became her enemy.

She called and woke up Nick's best friend, who let spill the fateful beans...Nick was out with some woman he'd met at Jane's office Christmas party; the best friend was not sure who she was. Well Jane was fucking sure it was Jane's paralegal. And that was when Jane headed to her bathroom cabinet and scrounged around until she found the old bottle of Miltown her father had handed her for an ornery bronchial cough years ago. Jane took two of those happy pills to try and muffle her torment, but instead she became hyper aware how ice-cold and caved-in her whole body felt, which did not prevent her from obsessively calling Nick's phone number again, every two minutes, and still no answer.

Impossible to smother the imagination, which started to explode into pain and garbage. Jane saw before her very eyes her husband pulling every inch of fabric off the other woman and rolling in bed with her for hours. Hours!

The worst was that Jane knew what the woman looked like and exactly how she laughed with that low, lazy purr. It was killing Jane. She'd lost control. Nick was gone forever. She was crying gobs and ranting "NO, NO, NO!" until her hoarse throat became seared to her exhausted, burning lungs, and long noodles of snot kept bungee jumping out of her nose.

And then Jane got angry. No, MAD. She went mad, and RAGE took over her body. No way did those ancient Miltown pills shut her down. Her inner Wooly Mammoth slowly but furiously waddled out of its Pleistocene digs and charged throughout the apartment to, naturally, destroy every corporeal thing in sight her husband called his own and that she knew would hurt him. It was very important to hurt him.

She ripped up his Motown fake books and tore through his sheet music; she smashed every last piece of his grandmother's gold-rimmed, flowery 1930s Sebring Royal China (though she held off on that gorgeous oval serving platter, which she was going to stash away and keep for herself—he would never know!). She stomped on his three guitars, she bashed his TV into five-inch size pieces (the hammer shattering the screen felt SO GOOD!), she cracked all his beloved vintage vinyl records.

She threw his computer to the floor and jumped up and down on it, and so forth into the night until finally the dark turned to pale light, and after years of seeing it in documents and discussing it at work, Jane now knew what the word "Plaintiff" felt like and why she would become one. That was the kind of gal Jane was. That was her broken heart defending itself.

Anyway, thank God now for the new life Jane was discovering on St. Frewin's Island. And thank God when Maggie returned to Herinton Drive with food and with Jane's truck—and India, Maggie's assistant, in tow with another car. They brought Jane leftovers from the Inn's dinner, and then Maggie and India headed home. Jane scarfed down the cold steak and potatoes in her truck, which occupied another twenty minutes. It would take altogether three and a half hours for the State crime team to arrive and set up shop.

Jane put her empty plate on the seat and opened the glove compartment. She shoved aside papers and odds and ends and reached into the back. Her fingers found the two small oblong rocks—one gray and shot through with thin lines of quartz, the other a lighter gray peppered with small chunks of volcanic tuff. They were mementoes of a hilarious hike she took a few years back with Samantha Lloyd on Big Cranberry Island, where they discovered a beachful of these wonderful rocks.

Somehow time and the ocean had buffed the rocks smooth until they fit perfectly inside a human fist, with natural impressions for the fingers and palm. Jane loved to feel their cool weight in her hand. She held them both, then chose the best one and walked over to the perimeter of the crime scene. Bending down to pat the rock into the damp earth, she bowed her head. At least the poor woman lying there would have this marker...one simple gift to take with her on her journey to the unknown.

....

"OK, EVERYONE." Todd Chisolm's sharp call drew the crime scene investigators together. "Looks like we've lost our surface evidence due to the heavy rains from Thursday night," he announced. "Let's do one more sweep of the ground around the victim, and then we can wrap her and bag her."

Jane didn't like the sound of that. There was something so profoundly final about zippering a human being into a bag, and hearing the light grind of the morbidly long zipper. The "Bag of No Return"..."The Last Bag"...you name it. And in this sad case? No mother or father, no sibling or loved one to kiss the woman goodbye forever. It didn't get emptier than that. Jane felt uncomfortable and a bit smothered when one of the investigators put the right hand of the corpse into a small paper bag and then tied the bag snug with string. Same for the left hand. Same for the head. God. Like some butcher wrapping a ham roast.

5

Saturday, May 25

When Public Safety Officer Roberts reached her office the next morning, she stood at the front door and looked up at the beautiful, beautiful, bountiful sky. Would there ever again be a day like yesterday? Thank you, thank you, you sweet, adorable, forgiving, caring, possibly ancient Greek gods, for coming down and handing me a corpse! And Jane kissed her stale little shoe box existence goodbye.

That dead body the State had hauled away after midnight was going to be Jane's guaranteed passage into the Homicide Hall of Fame. Overnight, she had thrown off the suffocating weight of the murder, seized her drooping psychic clay, and molded it into the new Jane Roberts—Plucky Jane Roberts!—steady at the helm, resilient and serene even in the face of gruesome slaughter. Here she was, about to soar on the Wings of Fate into the Pantheon of Public Safety...all thanks to her corpse. And Jane was determined to try and dress the part for her professional ascent, proudly garbed in the Maine State uniform with all its buttons, tucks, and darts.

But as Jane thrust open the door with a firm hand, the memory of that lobster blocking that poor girl's mouth flew straight into Jane's own throat...*incomprehensible, mind-blowing pain.* Same old, same old Jane Roberts began stomping with glee on perfectly sculpted Plucky Jane Roberts, and Plucky's gritty new backbone collapsed in an uproar. Jane took one look at Zeke and Helen Orbeton, the office receptionist, and felt her bravado vaporize. "Can you believe this? A murder? Right here on St. Frewin's. It's shocking!" Then she wheezed and she gagged. Helen stepped towards Jane and put a calming hand on her arm as she handed her a mug of tea. "Brace yourself, Jane. You can manage this."

Helen's supportive words scarcely reached Jane's reddening ears. All Jane could do was babble on, coughing and sneezing, though silently grateful for the wonderful and solid Helen Orbeton, who had come with the Public Safety Office furniture.

For the past twenty-five years, Helen had stoically answered phones and typed forms, while weathering the good will and bad moods of Public Safety Officers along the way. A widow of many years, she embodied that certain matter-of-factness found in coastal Mainers. And her wardrobe stayed the course—dark knit pants and pastel knit tops, always with a simple piece of mundane jewelry. Even her short hair retained that steady look of middle-class and middle-age—never more than two months away from the next curly perm.

"It's one thing to kill someone. OK. You want someone dead. You plan it, or maybe you don't." Jane hiccupped, twice. "You do it. I get it. But this? Shove a lobster down someone's throat?...like to what?...finish off the job with an artful flourish? It's too insane and horrible." Jane gripped the mug of tea to her chest and scratched her neck with her other hand.

Helen also began to look uneasy. Zeke waited for Jane to catch her breath and then he tried to quell her stress. "Take it easy, Guv. The State detectives are on their way to help us get to the bottom of this. Jolly old police science over whatever bloody impulse drove the killer to do this. We'll find the culprit. You'll see."

As Jane was about to throttle Anglophile Zeke, the sound of heavy boots vibrated outside and then, with a sort of minor quaking fanfare, a magnificent Being, who looked like a Viking warrior stuffed into a worn-out suit, arrived at the door accompanied by one very dark, possibly Indian colleague, and another officer who looked like a uniformed Ken Doll. The Viking warrior forced half of his jumbo self, and then his other mighty half, through the office entry. Jane could have sworn the floor boards cracked as this Norseman in lapels gave them all a hearty greeting from the Maine State Homicide Unit and took her hot hand in his warm, bearish paw. "Jane Roberts, good to meet you. I'm Detective Storm Nosmot, at your service."

Jane looked on with fascination, as if Moses had just touched down in her office, possibly bringing her the Ten Commandments of Murder? Why was a sudden surge of carnal dizziness making her face very hot, and how come corny lyrics about "this magic moment" began drilling a hole in her head? Zeke and Helen observed their boss's awkward blushing, and grinned at one another knowingly. Perhaps Jane had just met her Tarzan, even if he was wearing a wedding band.

The islanders and the mainlanders made their introductions and seated themselves at the long-plank Public Safety Office table where Helen quickly set out homemade pumpkin bread and hot coffee. Jane was relieved to see that pumpkin bread. Pumpkin bread with raisins and walnuts and chocolate chunks was just what you needed when you and the Homicide Unit were about to bang your heads over the most horrifying murder ever to occur in the history of St. Frewin's.

Once she got some pumpkin bread in her stomach, Jane settled down considerably, despite sneezes exploding out of her sinuses, and her cheeks turning crimson. She casually aimed a sidelong glance at Rajiv Basrak, who had been introduced as one of the investigators from the State Crime Lab. He had such incredibly dark, smooth skin, far darker than brown. One brush stroke away from black. Jane was looking forward to working with someone so un-Maine.

Jane turned her head towards Finn Gallinen, the Ken Doll junior officer. Sergeant Gallinen looked exactly like he should, born for Homicide. His dull brown hair was like coarse turf; his pleasant American face gave away nothing. She marveled how everything about him was regulation size—his neck, his frame, his voice, his smile; not a subversive bone in his officer's body. Jane thought he couldn't possibly be a Democrat. Not her kind of man. She wondered if his uniform might be a bit too snug. His thighs and buttocks looked vacuum-packed inside those pants. It made her want to grab a pair of scissors and take a snip or two so he could breathe easier.

Storm Nosmot put down his coffee, leaned back, and looked at everyone around the table. "OK...let's focus on how we're going to tackle this job. Jane, first tell us how you came to find the body."

"Right. Yesterday, around 6 PM," Jane began, "ACHOO! Oh, excuse me. Maggie Banner—she's the manager of Grand Harbor Inn—called me to help her find a dog that took off with some guests' underwear."

Jane could see Finn Gallinen start to snicker, and he didn't suppress it soon enough. Was he going to turn out to be an annoying prick? Maybe he was too good to be a Dog Control Officer. She would see how hard he could blush.

"That dog stole the undies and the clothesline they were on...ACHOOOO. ACHOOOO! We're talking bras, girdles, bikini briefs, T-bags—you name it." Finn's cheeks were on fire. 'So, I picked up Maggie at the Inn, and we drove towards Herinton Point, where the dog was headed." ACHOOOPPPPKKHEEEE!

Jane squirmed uncomfortably as she supplied the details of her discovery of the murder victim. Zeke distributed photos of the crime scene around the table. The team looked down at the images of the desecrated, young, black-haired woman.

"What else do we know?" Storm asked next. But then he noticed Jane's growing discomfort. "Your face is so fiery and swollen, Jane. Are you all right?"

"Do' know," Jane gasped. "Feel so itchy! ACHOOOOFFFF! ACHOOOAAAGH!"

"Righto, let's carry on, shall we?" Zeke put on his dark, intellectual spectacles and began to read from his papers in hand. "Maggie Banner called this morning to report that their guest, Ruth Farrow, has not been seen by her colleagues nor the Inn staff since Thursday evening. We checked with the State Ferry and water shuttle service—no one recalls a youngish, black-haired woman by that name leaving the island. Our assumption is that Ruth Farrow is missing and may be our victim, but nothing is confirmed at this time."

"Uh...can't breathe so good," Jane gurgled, waving her hand in front of her face.

"Very well. Now then," Zeke continued, "Crime Scene Investigation arrived last night at approximately 10:30 PM to study the scene of the crime. Heavy rains from the previous night cleared any trace of foot and vehicular prints, except those of Officer Jane Roberts and Maggie Banner, who entered the scene by chance at approximately 6:30 PM last night. Samples of their clothing...."

As Jane torpedoed out of her seat like a burst of spontaneous combustion, her colleagues heard, "Gotta get out of THIS UNIFORM!" She ripped away at her blouse and stumbled towards her office, honking and snorting, buttons flying through the air. "Helen!" Jane yelled as she tore off her pants and disappeared behind her door, "I need clothes. NO POLYESTER!"

"Oh dear, I'm sorry everyone. Let me see if I can help Jane," Helen explained as she got up and walked quickly towards a supply closet and began rummaging around inside.

"So, let's see," Storm said, attempting to summarize amid the chaos. "First of all, I want to emphasize to all of you that we are keeping the details of this case confidential. More than confidential. The specifics in front of us are bizarre, and we're working in a relatively small community where word could travel fast and wild. So, everything stays with us. None of this dribbles out in a bar, at a party, talking to your family, nothing. We never know when a tight rein on case details may prove to be an important tool in finding our killer. And Helen, please call Maggie Banner at the Inn and pass these same instructions on to her."

"I do recall, Storm, that Jane said she emphasized the same to Maggie last night at the crime scene. So, we're all set there," Helen called out from the supply closet.

"OK. So, what do we have?" Storm continued. "We have an unidentified, clothed female, between say twenty and forty years old, found lying on the ground in the woods off Herinton Drive. Hands rope-bound behind her back, a significant head wound, and a raw lobster forced down her throat. Whether or not this woman was murdered on site or murdered elsewhere and brought to this site—the Chief Medical Officer is studying the question right now. How are we doing on notifying folks...interviewing possible witnesses?" Storm asked.

"Jane? Everything OK in there?" Helen walked over and called through Jane's office door. "All I could find was a tablecloth in the utility closet, and I've got something for your top, though I don't think you're going to like it."

Zeke continued. "Um, yes. Brilliant. OK. Maggie Banner already reported the missing guest to her boss, Inn owner

Kendall Billings. He's due back on the island later today. Maggie Banner reports the Inn currently has ten guests attending a—I'm quoting Maggie—'holistic seminar for female digital content moderators.' It's been in session for the past five days and today is their final day. We also alerted the Inn to have all the guests report to the Inn's Great Room today at 1:30 PM for interviews."

At this point, Jane stepped out of her office.

"Zeke, pardon my ignorance, but what the heck is a digital...whatever...was it...moderator?" Storm was asking. Until he looked at Jane. And Jane looked at Storm. "Jane, what the HELL?"

Jane began shuffling towards her colleagues in stilted steps, her upper body and arms buried in a straight jacket and a candy cane tablecloth wrapped around her waist for a sarong.

"Please don't anybody say anything. Let me catch my breath." She looked disheveled and sheepish. Returning to the table, she cautiously maneuvered her stiff upper body and candy canes into a chair.

"I can explain about the guests, Storm," Jane said. "Oh, sorry, just a minute here. Could you please fan my face a little? There...use some of those crime photos.

"Thanks. That's better," Jane said. "So according to Maggie Banner, digital content moderators are supposed to weed out the violence that an internet company doesn't want on its site. These moderators pull murder and torture off the web all day long. Can you imagine?" Jane had to bob from side to side for emphasis, due to her confinement.

"The employees must get fried by all the filth and nightmares they have to review," Jane continued. "Maggie says employee unrest about their stress is skyrocketing, so the company decided to send the moderators on seminars to boost their health. The employees get plunked down in a peaceful place like St. Frewin's at the company's expense. They get a week of great food, lots of fresh air, yoga, hikes, and a total blackout of cell phones, screens, and social media."

Finn was the next one to look puzzled. "Wait a minute. Are you saying the Inn blocks worldwide connectivity to its guests?"

Jane beamed beatifically at Storm. "Your buddies didn't know what you were getting them into?" She pivoted towards Finn. "Actually, St. Frewin's Island has no connectivity...period. Cell phones and the internet don't work out here. As we like to say, the only thing stored in our clouds is stormy weather."

Finn seemed incredulous. He pulled out his cellphone. "Impossible. No connectivity? And Jane's sitting here swaddled like a Yuletide mummy? How can this place function at all?" He glanced at his colleagues. No one seemed fazed by any of it.

"You'd be surprised, Finn," Jane said. "St. Frewin's has actually boomed since the citizens shut down the internet. I mean, I can try to convert you over lunch about the philosophy of life without smart phones. But in short, we're capitalizing on the lack of instant gratification. And thanks to embracing the slow lane, St. Frewin's is now a premier destination for all kinds of healthy retreats—it's lucrative. Yoga aficionados, corporate retreats, meditational groups, therapy conferences, medical meetings, back to nature and slow movement groups—they're all racing to reserve space. The island is swarming with human beings eager to be left alone without their own devices. You should try and live without your hello stick for a few days, Finn. You might love it."

"Absolutely quaint, but primitive. Nearly a Mennonite colony," he said.

"People, enough. Let's focus on our murder, OK? Thanks for this, Helen," Storm said as he began eyeing the potential witness list Helen passed around. "Finn, I want you to head over now to check on Ruth Farrow's room at the Inn. We don't have to collect her possessions yet. She may show up soon, for all we know. But take a look and see if there's anything strange or out of the ordinary. And see if she left any form of ID in her room—maybe a driver's license, cell phone, or wallet."

"Got it," Finn nodded.

"We'll lunch at the pub," Storm said. "Then we'll move to the Inn to interview the staff and guests. Stick to the basics. Names, contact information, where were they the past two days and nights, did they see or hear anything odd concerning Ruth Farrow, anything unusual. For now, we're not releasing the victim's photo—not to the public, not to the interviewees—not until we have official identification. And remember, no details whatsoever go out the door. We'll focus on what we always look for: MOM. Motive, Opportunity, Means."

"And Jane," Storm added, "Pardon me if I'm being forward, but right now you look like a geisha girl with hives who's headed for the county jail. Why don't you run home and change into something more comfortable, OK?"

6
My Diary
March 12, 2019

I don't know where this is all coming from. These bursts of light keep going off in my eyes when nothing's really happening. I'm sitting here at my desk like usual, in this pretty boring office space in the middle of some Iowa cornfield. I am a CCM watchdog. I wish the pay were better—who doesn't wish their pay was better? I wish I wasn't having my period today, and I wish the bursts of light would stop.

That guy at the other end of the room looks at me sometimes. I think he's cute! Maybe he likes how I look. I hope so. It's nice to feel men staring at me, maybe thinking all kinds of things about me...very sexy things. I really like that, and I'm probably thinking the same things, if you really want to know.

Gaaawwwwdddd...CCM. It all sounded so important and big-time when I was looking for a job. College graduate...Big Joke. Employment? Another Big Joke. So, this CCM stuff looked really great. CCM: Commercial Content Moderation. And I could handle the nightmare stuff. No problem. They put me through all these tests with pictures of the awfulest stuff on the planet. I scored strong on the scale for looking at blood and guts and tortured kittens. They told me I was going to keep the internet safe and less crazy for billions of people. I was going to sweep it clean of all this shit and horror. But what really happens? There's no end to what monsters people can be...to themselves, to their families, to strangers, to animals, to babies even. And God knows who's on the other end, all hungry to look at this stuff. What a bunch of losers.

My job is not cracked up to what I thought it would be. You think you're going to get into the fast and fancy high-tech world and keep climbing the ladder to the big bucks, but I'm so sick and tired of this

CCM shit. You say INTERNET? I say POTTYNET. I think it's maybe ruining my heart?

And who can I talk to? No one. They won't let us talk about our work. At first, that really sucked. I never saw it coming...how bad it would be to have to weed out blown up kids and human heads rolling down a road, eight hours a day, five days a week. Well, OK, there's a lunch break in there somewhere, but you try and eat your tuna fish sandwich and chips right after watching some guy in the desert sticking his sword through fourteen boys and even some goats.

It's not just bursts of light any more...I'm actually hearing in my head some kind of talking and in my head I'm seeing little kids lying on the ground. But I don't think they're the same shit I'm supposed to be vacuuming off the worldwide web. I don't get it. I don't know why this stuff is popping up inside me. Is it work? Or is it me? There's not only the kids, but I smell smoke and gasoline, too. Oh, somebody help me. It's all driving me kind of crazy. It won't stop, but then it does stop, and then it's all blank again in my brain. I've got to get away from this. I'll go out tonight to that bar on Stanger Avenue in town. The paneled walls are really cozy, and it'll be heaven to have about five drinks. Ha ha!! Just kidding. But alcohol sure helps. And guys.

Like I said, the pay really sucks. Some girls were talking after work about how to get a pay raise. In this corporate shithole, there is no such thing as a pay raise. But Jolene said if you wear a cross-your-heart bra, that'll get you a pay raise. Ha ha!! Pathetic aren't we? Who even owns a cross-your-heart bra anymore? We are all padded casabas, Honey, and those who are not padded are thinking about re-joining Weight Watchers. There is no middle ground, is there?

Today the flashes in my head just kept coming. There's even some screaming. I can't tell if things are in color or not, inside my eyes. But I think the visions are starting to show color. That's what I'm calling them now...Visions. Sounds kind of special, doesn't it? I am having Visions. Maybe I'll get nominated by the Pope and they'll put a rosary around my neck. Sick fuck that I am.

7

Saturday, May 25

Storm eyed Jane as he began to dig into his fish and chips...the crunch of the light beer batter on tender haddock gave him such satisfaction. Jane had recovered from her polyester attack in the morning, but she still seemed stressed. Even her long hair looked stressed. It was so wild, like horse tails sprouting out of her head.

Storm understood the violent death on her doorstep was not the usual territory for a Public Safety Officer. Which might explain why Jane seemed like she was on the warpath, or maybe just uptight. Like a gun, a small handgun, about to go off.

He knew from his superiors that Jane stood out at the Police Academy for her ability to analyze criminal details and patterns in all kinds of information. He'd also heard office chatter about her quirky personality...and that porcupine side of her—"Dressed to Quill." He was eager to see what she would bring to this case.

"So, Jane, are you enjoying the day to day in Public Safety?" he asked.

"More or less," Jane said. "Actually, I take that back. This really is a heaven-sent place and a heaven-sent job. But the whole Dog Control Officer bit...you know, maybe the owners need to control their dogs better.

"I spend hours each month chasing them down. And half the time, the dogs I catch up with act like they're tripping on marijuana or something poisonous to their system, like xylitol. People should really not throw roaches and xylitol gum on the road where some mutt will gobble it up like candy. That stuff can kill a dog. In fact, I'm going to get the vet to help me organize a public seminar on that topic down the road."

"Makes sense," Storm said. "Good for community outreach."

"And don't let anyone tell you being a Shellfish Warden is a cinch, Storm. It's a bizarre job. When I'm out there measuring some guy's juvenile clams he's harvesting and reminding him he's got to have longer clams, every once in a while some wise guy shoots back lascivious innuendoes to twist it all into a conversation about how looooong his clam is. Such bull. It can get tense, and it's demeaning, right?" Jane looked at Storm for his reaction.

"So just tell the guy you're afraid that he is personally in possession of an undersized clam," Storm suggested. Jane didn't think she knew Storm well enough, but she lightly punched him in the arm anyway.

"What about your netless world on St. Frewin's, Jane?" Finn said with an evil grin. "Rajiv and I don't buy it. Storm here may be on the fence. How can the general public accept the lack of digital civilization?"

Jane cherished her beloved lecture that she was about to launch at her colleagues. "Well, Gents," she began, "it boils down to choice. The people on St. Frewin's voted years ago to get rid of the web and live their lives truly 'Hands Free'— without the endless presence of a cell phone in their palms. Basically, we're talking about addiction. People are addicted to their cell phones and the internet. They are not interested in moderation or abstinence. This whole country lives and breathes for the right to make the worst choices. Over and over again, a billion times a day...junk food, alcohol, drugs, guns, lack of exercise, the internet, compulsive shopping, compulsive cell-phone monitoring. St. Frewin's took a stand to take back its life."

Storm nodded his head in Jane's favor. "At one of our town meetings, they talked about the impact of cellphones on parents and children. Digital devices are now the second or third parent. Everyone's fingering some kind of screen. When I was young, my mother played cards with us, helped us make stuff out of construction paper and cardboard, read to us. Kids hung out together, all kinds of outdoor games, playing in the woods. What's happening to that?"

"Exactly!" Jane applauded. "Practically speaking, Finn, we also benefit from any money the State and the utility companies save by not having to connect our island. That money is plowed back to the public in the form of free phone booths scattered throughout the island, and an internet café in the ferry terminal waiting room back on the mainland. That's where ferry passengers can chill out and get a shot of WiFi. On St. Frewin's, it's all about human beings being in control."

Rajiv almost looked like he wanted to be converted. "How about you, Zeke? How is your day-to-day life without an internet connection?"

"Not so bad, Mate," Zeke assured him as he grabbed a few more fries and took a bite out of his crab roll. "If I need to be online, I jump on the ferry and plug in at our internet café on shore. We've got landlines and fax machines on St. Frewin's. They work bloody well."

"But you sacrifice the convenience of immediate access," Finn insisted, drumming his fingers on the table with each phrase. "You're removing yourself from the daily current of modern life. And what about rapid response to safety issues? I can't see any gains; only losses."

Just then Samantha Lloyd, all spunk and dynamo, her throat bound in a beautiful turquoise necklace, rounded the bar and zeroed in on the homicidal luncheon. Samantha was Jane's half-Apache, half-Irish roommate from freshman year in college. If you walked past her, you would think she was a dancer, with lilting blue eyes, and skin the color of a pale cherry wood chopping board. Samantha and Jane had somehow migrated to St. Frewin's Island through entirely different channels—caterer versus cop—and it was a boon to both of them to be sharing their world again.

Close behind Samantha was Connor Mulroy, the pub manager. "Hi there," Samantha said with her inimitable cheer. "What a handsome trio we have here, Jane. Surely you're going to introduce me?" The pub manager squeezed past Samantha and leaned down to Jane's ear. "Sounds like the office needs you, Jane. Helen says you'd better come back ASAP."

"OK," Jane said, taking the last bite of her lobster taco. "Pardon me, men and Sam, but something's come up at work. I'd better go. Helen doesn't ask lightly or frivolously. Zeke, kindly make the introductions, and as soon as I can, I'll catch up with you guys at the Inn in the Great Room for the interviews. Thanks, and ciao!"

....

Dashing from the pub back to Public Safety, Jane found Helen precariously hosting a youngish woman, and when Helen could do so surreptitiously, she twitched her eyebrows in a seasoned warning to Jane. Jane mentally parsed the office visitor in a mega-second. Standing before her was a regal totem pole with hair the color of the inky void, a plateau of flawless make-up, and two blue stones for eyes. She was extending her hand to Jane, and all of her fashionista-self leaned towards Jane. Very straight and very stiff, like a mixing spoon stuffed up a jacquard sleeve.

"Hi, Officer Roberts. I'm Torrance Balankoff," the mixing spoon said in a voice cool as a river. "Thank you for meeting with me on such short notice. This may sound bizarre, but my family's summer cottage is located off

Tamadge Lane, and we've been smelling a lot of smoke coming from the property next to us." She cranked up the strain in her voice. "Especially at night...it usually begins at about 9 PM. It's becoming a nuisance and starting to feel invasive."

Jane guided the woman to take a seat at the Public Safety Office table. "Have you talked to this neighbor? Or to other people who live nearby? Does anyone have any idea what's going on?" Jane said.

Torrance Balankoff's jaws locked down for the next drumroll. "We moved in last fall and we don't have a clue. We know it's an older woman, but we've never met her...just her odors. The neighbors seem to look the other way. Do you want to know what I seriously think?" Leaning towards Jane, she wriggled her nose and scrunched her lips in a further sign of disgust. "I think the woman might be running an off-grid crematorium."

Jane tried to sit up taller to keep from bending over with laughter. She willed her face into a look of Public Safety concern.

Torrance raised her hands up, palms out in either direction. "Maybe burning pet bodies? Who knows? It certainly smells like it's illegal, but I'm just guessing. We definitely want it to stop."

Jane wriggled her own nose, too, and tried to look like she was scrunching her brow. She pondered the raven-haired cucumber's boots, which Jane suspected might be Ralph Lauren, or Gucci, or Versace maybe, all of which made her nervous. This meant money and she knew money with a big complaint could mean a long day ahead, which Jane could hardly afford, because she had the body to deal with, interviews to conduct, homicide investigations to pursue—a stew of work. Jane looked up at the ceiling, over at Helen, secretly sighed...when who should suddenly pop back into the office on his way to Grand Harbor Inn but Zeke...the Perfect Bloke (in Zeke speak)...solution found!

"Torrance Balankoff, let me introduce you to Zeke Pendleton, our Office Manager. Zeke has lived on the island all his life. He has a winning way with instigators and perpetrators. I'm going to have him assess your situation. You say the suspect crematorium gets fired up around 9 PM? OK. Zeke will go to your home tonight around 8:45 PM to scope out the scene. He will report back to me and we'll get to the bottom of this. Does that work for you?"

After making sure Torrance Balankoff would hold fast in the meantime and not go off the rails and shoot her neighbor, Jane sent her on her way, but not before admiring her attire. "I love your boots!"

"Ha. Thank you," Torrance called out as she exited the office. "They're from TJ Maxx."

Once the door had closed, Jane looked at Zeke. "You know, Zeke, the odd thing about TB is that she herself came in here at all. Maybe it's a sign of spunk and self-initiative? But why didn't TB do the rich routine and have Her People contact My People?"

"And who would 'My People' be?" Zeke queried.

"You!" Jane laughed, as she too headed for the door, this time to catch up with the interviews at the Inn.

8
Last Tuesday, May 21

"Anthony's got to have some cashews somewhere around here. Where does he keep his nuts?" Zara Billings was talking out loud to herself. She scrounged around in the cabinets of the main area of the Inn's kitchen without luck. It was Tuesday, and she was in a hurry to finish packing and get on the ferry to the mainland. She would catch up with her girlfriends for their annual trek to Moosehead Lake for the Moose Mania 10 K race. But she wanted to bring some trail mix with her and she was missing her last ingredient in her own home kitchen. The Inn kitchen came in handy now and then. What was the point of being the wife of the owner of the Grand Harbor Inn if you couldn't "borrow" supplies now and then from the Head Chef?

Zara was ecstatic to be getting off the island. And getting a break from Kendall. For the past year or so, she always felt this invisible cinch around her lungs and shoulders slowly unwind, one full turn around her at a time, as she drove away from the Inn grounds, down the road to the ferry. Her departure pattern had taken on a rhythm, become a chant in her mind: Drive onto the ferry, get out of the car, walk up to the open deck at the top, look out on the patchy ocean, look up at the sky and the mountains ahead, and know that soon she would be back in the real world.

It wasn't like she felt suffocated while she was on St. Frewin's...it was her home after all...had been for five years. But when she made plans to leave, that's when the relief slowly raised its head, and she knew she would feel "normal" again when she could return to so many of the things she had always taken for granted in her former life: Big grocery stores with fresh fruit, her Twitter account, her hair salon, roads that didn't just end up in the same place where you began twenty minutes earlier, her favorite wine store, lots of restaurants, Reny's, T J Maxx. And getting a break from Kendall.

There, she was being honest with herself. She felt like a queen when she first met the guy in the Bahamas. He owned all the goods from the start—he still had them in fact. Money obviously, bearing, a family background she would love bragging about later on, tall and lanky in a way that was boyish and manly at the same time, and he made her laugh. Of course she fell for him, and better than that, he fell for her! That good old mega bomb of love and sex exploded between their eager selves, and that's what got them into trouble. They ended up marrying. And then one day, or not even one day, but just like air itself, the fallout began. What went up, had to come down.

ANYWAY, Zara just wanted to get the cashews and get going. She went into the Inn's back pantry to look further, but she never found any cashews. She totally forgot about the cashews because she found something else that so intrigued her, and with only an hour to spare before her ferry, she did what any ordinary, nosey person would do: She grabbed the leather carryall she had just discovered on the pantry counter AND the tape recorder within (Whose was it?), exited the kitchen, and quickly walked down the path back to her house.

As she walked, she pushed the play button, but no sound. (Hadn't she seen Maggie with this bag?) She hit the rewind button; still no action. (What's with this tape recorder?) She went into her house, grabbed some AA batteries from the battery drawer, and finally brought the machine back to life. Zara knew she was being Little Miss Snoop, but why not? She would just listen quick and then put it back. No big deal.

CLICK: "Hello, my name is Margaret Simmons, and I'm eighty-nine years old. I was born and brought up on St. Frewin's and [coughing, hacking].... Oh, sorry, Maggie, can we start the machine over again?" ...then abruptly, like a sharp, stinging slap to the face, the tape recorder jerked into "Oh, oh, aaahhhhh," sounds of thrusting, knocking around, big sighs, bucking, laughing...desperate whisperings: "I want you, I want you so bad. Your cock, yes, yes, I know it's big. I knew it the minute you stared at me. Uh, uh, yes, kiss me harder."

Zara heard nothing but sexually-charged (what else could it be?) incoherent air-sucking, mouth-sucking, mashing and shoving and hands banging on the counter and groaning and then Kendall, KENDALL!, panting like a male walrus mounting his blubbery damsel, and making the exact same throaty, guttural sounds Zara had heard him excrete for the past five years of marital duties, three to eight times a week—in their car, on the sofa, on the floor, in their bed, in the shower, on the grass, ON THEIR KITCHEN COUNTER—so much for originality! FUCK HIM. FUCK HIM. FUCK HIM! WHAT WAS HE DOING ON THIS TAPE Goddamitalltoshitsdom????!*@#@&*#$@$*?!!!

Zara froze. She went into automatic pilot. She could not deal with this right now. This was not going to be her destiny. The Moosehead 10 K race was more important at this point. Getting off the island was more important. She was in control of her life. She was the boss. Automatic, automatic. OK, OK. She got some alcohol, wiped off the tape recorder, put it back in the carryall, walked back to the Inn casually, opened the kitchen door, no one could see her, no one was around, she put the bag right back in the pantry, exactly where she found it. She swore she could smell sex on all the cabinets and counter tops now, but it could just be she was losing her mind. She noticed, however, though not to her surprise, that she was not crying. Not at all.

9
Saturday, May 25
Afternoon

On any other Saturday, on any other island, the spirited flock of young women who were gathered in the Great Room of the Grand Harbor Inn might have been the ingredients for a wild and crazy summer bash, rather than this somber murder inquiry. Storm and his men observed nine human beings, some of them Towers of Pisa swaying unsteadily on wedge espadrille heels, some in leggings that couldn't have been thicker than a human cell, many with their faces buried in makeup, black-top on their lashes, and half of them wearing all kinds of boob-exploiting, spaghetti-strap tops in shocking orange, acid yellow, and hot pink.

Though they had certainly dressed inappropriately for an interview on death, the digital content moderators' emotions gave them away. You could almost scoop up the nervousness and titillation wafting through the scented air that emanated from their persons. Their curious eyes darted from Storm to Rajiv to Finn to Jane, and then over to the Inn staff, including Maggie, her new assistant India Barton, the chefs, the chambermaids, and the Inn owners. The Inn owners...Kendall and Zara Billings especially looked like they would give anything to get back to work like nothing had ever happened...like maybe one of their high-paying corporate female guests had stayed tucked tight in her bed this past Thursday, instead of maybe being sized up for her coffin this very moment.

Jane surveyed these Birds of Paradise and began tsk-tsking to herself about their immodesty. She wanted to rush them all to a nunnery. No Yankee restraint in this Iowa milk herd. What were these women thinking? A breast would always be a breast. Walloping someone over the head with generous dollops of exposed flesh and curves took all the steam out of forbidden fruit. Nothing remained forbidden. These women were trying so hard to reduce the space between impulse and action—to the point where there would be no mojo left for the action.

Well, Jane Roberts could forget it. She had failed there; her "for better or for worse" had run off with all the exposed flesh he could find. But Jane was standing her ground. Without a full kimono, how could anyone open the full kimono? Better to start each day sanely clothed, never knowing what unexpected encounter might occur. Say one hot afternoon you bring a glass of cold cider to a neighbor who's helping to clear a fallen tree, and as you give him the glass, in that moment your hands touch lightly and you will never forget the warmth of his hand, even as you hear him yelling with a loony grin, "Is it SPIKED?" And you can't for the life of you think of a funny comeback, so you say, "I forgot!" And the heat of his skin on your skin lingers and that moment of unexpected warmth, well, that moment will be with you forever.

Jane snuffed out her daydreaming but held on to her hatchet of judgment and started to walk over to Maggie Banner. She would be a good ally in this manhunt, or should Jane say simply "hunt"? It wasn't every day you bonded with someone over a corpse like they had. Was Maggie also a murderess? Jane surely hoped not. But Maggie had inadvertently led Jane to the victim's body, hadn't she?

"Maggie," Jane said in a lowered voice. "What's with these half-naked girls? One of their own may have been murdered and they're all out here spilling their body parts, like we're supposed to start bidding in some kind of a sex-slave raffle?"

"Jane—How can you say such things?" Maggie scolded. "You really tend to be very opinionated. Has it ever occurred to you that maybe people who are less endowed want everyone else to cover up, because they're jealous, or they unconsciously want to level the playing field? You have to face facts. People with movable assets learn very quickly they can get a lot of mileage out of those movable assets."

"Moveable assets?" Jane squeaked.

"Yes. There's no end to society's focus on the power of those assets. So why not...uhhh! Don't get me started. I'm crazy enough today as it is," Maggie said bluntly. "I feel like my whole world has gone through a blender. Are you feeling scared at all? Did you even sleep last night?"

"God, this is all new to me, too, Maggie. I don't know what I feel at the moment, except way too alert. Sounds like we both need to decompress," Jane said. "You know, Samantha Lloyd is coming for supper tonight so we can gab about normal stuff and get away from this tragedy for a while. Do you want to join us...say 7 PM?"

"That's a nice idea, Jane. Thanks. Count me in."

Finn Gallinen was also scanning the interviewees and made a mental note to keep track of Maggie's new assistant manager, India Barton. *"Definitely silky"* was his first impression. She was going into his "Possible Date Pile."

Three of the Inn chambermaids sat together on a nearby sofa, looking down at their laps, or smiling hesitantly when looking up, with some low conversation among themselves. Storm had noticed their names on the potential witness list—lots of Ks and Ls and Vs in the spelling. Maggie said they were part of the seasonal Eastern European migration who came and went through the revolving doors of international work-study programs in America. So strange that Serbs and Croatians and Bosnians made hotel beds and mixed bar drinks and explained menus all over Maine in the summer, when just a couple of decades ago, their elders had been busy butchering each other in the Balkans. What a difference a summer in Maine could make.

"Jane," Storm whispered when he caught up with her, "Are these the same chambermaids who worked this past week? They haven't changed over to a new crew already, have they?"

"I'm not sure, Storm. I'll check with Maggie or Kendall Billings. But are you really concerned? I mean, look at them. Do you think they even know enough English to commit murder?"

"That's ridiculous, Jane."

"Pfffft," she responded.

"All right. Let's do it," Storm muttered as he clapped his hands for everyone's attention.

10
Saturday, May 25
Afternoon

Storm found himself in a circle of chairs with three moderators—all of them nubile, warm-blooded, young women. He was waiting while the women each completed a form with her contact information. He was thinking about the sexual harassment seminars the Homicide Department had held the last three years to try and "sensitize" the force about respect for women. There were all kinds of topics covering fellow female officers, personal boundaries, caution about police intimacy with distressed women, especially women who were dealing with the death of a family member, respect for the bodies of murdered victims (both female or male), and lots of hot-button topics that no one ever use to pay much attention to.

In the "old days," if you were a man on the force, you just looked at what you wanted to look at and acted like who you were, but you didn't police yourself too much about sexual harassment. You just did what seemed normal, or natural for your job and yourself.

Storm's way of handling the brave new world was to think about his sister, Emma, when he was in close quarters with other women for work matters. He knew he should stop looking at these women below their necks. It should not be that difficult, but sometimes it was. He would look at what some women were wearing, and somehow it did not equate with what they expected from him. But he wanted to do the right thing, so he would do it for his sister. He would treat these guests he was interviewing like he would want his sister treated. He'd want that for his sister if she were sitting here now being questioned by Finn Gallinen.

....

While his trio of guests were filling out their forms, Finn sat with his note pad and acted like he was taking notes. But he was really just sitting there and internally stewing about the "war of the sexes." They didn't call it that anymore, but Finn did in his own mind.

These women were an example of liberated women, who wouldn't have dressed like this in public if they weren't liberated. They got all this freedom to show all kinds of cleavage and high thigh territory, but Finn and his fellow officers had to rein themselves in. At least that's what the police sensitivity training classes had been trying to pound into their thick Neanderthal skulls. Finn, however, could not see how that was fair. Men were for real, hormones and hot blood. Men were not androids.

....

"Ladies—let's move over to this area and we'll begin." Jane ushered her three moderators to a banquette along a broad window looking out on the Inn's grounds.

"As you know, we're interviewing you today in connection with the murder of a young woman who may have been one of your colleagues. I'm taping our conversation on this tape recorder. You are not under arrest, and you are free to terminate this interview at any time. Please tell me where you were this past Thursday and Friday."

The three interviewees nodded their assent and began their mundane accounts. Then Jane switched the topic to Ruth Farrow, and the conversation picked up.

"Can you tell me about your missing colleague? What she was like as a person, what did she do on the island while she was here?"

One of the women raised her hand slightly. "I think I can speak for most of us here. None of us knew Ruth very well. She didn't hang out with us too much after work. Kind of kept to herself. And I don't mean to put her down, but she seemed sort of immature, like she was still a teenager, even though she wasn't. And you hear stuff in the office...people sometimes saw Ruth out at local bars...with different guys, that is. I guess you'd say she was a partier, but not with us."

Jane thought about this last comment. "Do you know if Ruth met or visited with any men on this island?"

"Again, like I said, Ruth really was a loner. I don't think I saw her at every dinner at the Inn, but I can't remember for sure. I do know she decided not to go on the overnight sail with the rest of us. But I don't know why or anything else."

"She did tell me something odd a few weeks ago," another woman added. "Ruth said she started to get these flashbacks and headaches at work that were really bothering her. She didn't go into it much more than that, and I guess I didn't ask her for details. It was just something in passing."

The third colleague finally had her say. "Yah, well, many of us start to feel cross-eyed or headachy after a while. But we're not supposed to discuss our jobs in public, so I can't talk specifics. But I'm not surprised Ruth was affected by the job. I guess I can say that much."

11

Saturday, May 25
Afternoon

When Storm and Finn had finished their interviews, everyone in their two clusters relaxed a tiny fraction. "How did you like your stay out here on St. Frewin's?" Finn asked the women in general, which brought out a bunch of giggles and moans.

"We're nearly out of our minds without our cell phones working," one of the moderators exclaimed.

"Yah!" another woman agreed. "We're not used to all this down time, nothing to thumb through on our screens. It's such an empty feeling. I can't wait to get out of here, to be honest."

"The program instructors knew we'd be kind of strung out without our phones," the first moderator elaborated. "So, they tried to keep us busy. We actually talked with each other a lot, which was kind of different and fun. And we even wrote postcards to people back home. Some of us have *never* done that before."

Another moderator got up and started humming and dancing in place, and jerking her arms and legs to illustrate what she was telling them. "One instructor had us doing Zumba to music by this guy named Beethoven. I think I may have heard of him. But they should not let him anywhere near Zumba. The instructor kept saying how fantastic this Beethoven was, but you should have seen us. We looked like spazzed out puppets. It was so weird trying to do our dance workouts to this guy Beethoven. His music is kind of spastic, and then kind of wild. We're lucky one of us didn't break a leg or something."

Another woman chimed in, "We're more used to those hot, Latin jazz songs with lots of drums and a really strong beat. I don't know what got into the instructor's head."

Storm asked, "Not to point a guilty finger, or anything, but who was your Zumba instructor?"

"Oh, her name is Torrance Balankoff," the Zumba dancer said.

"We can't wait to be back home," one of the younger looking women sighed. "Back to our Iowa beef, WiFi, and junk food!" Lots more laughing and grabbing each other among the giggling, scantily clad moderators.

....

"Mr. Billings, I'm Storm Nosmot from the State Homicide Office, and this is Rajiv Basrak from the State Crime Lab." Storm went through the introductory blurb. Kendall Billings responded, "Sounds good." He seemed quite at ease, running his large hand through his thick head of hair, leaning way back in his chair, but then, he was practically at home.

He began: "I'm Kendall Billings, Owner of Grand Harbor Inn. On Thursday, I worked at the Inn all day and part of the evening. Then had dinner at my own home, which is on the grounds of the Inn, and stayed home all night. On Friday, I traveled to the mainland for Inn business, stayed overnight, and returned to St. Frewin's late this morning, following a call from Maggie Banner about the murder."

Storm asked, "Do you have witnesses who can confirm your report, Sir?"

"Well, let me think. From Thursday late morning through Friday morning, I was working on Inn business while many of the chamber staff and all of the kitchen staff were off from work. I don't recall crossing paths with any of the chamber staff that night. And the guests went on a sail to Deer Isle to camp overnight. So, no one can confirm that time for me. But my wife, Zara, did return to the island late on Thursday evening, so she can vouch that I was at home then.

"On Friday, the ferry staff saw me depart the island on their boat. And if you will give me a few minutes, I can write up a list of the various stores and businesses I went to for Inn matters on Friday. I stayed overnight at Young's B&B and, like I said, I came home when I got the news."

Rajiv remained quiet throughout. The words flowed from Kendall Billings' mouth like smooth caramel. Caramel one could almost taste. Rajiv shifted in his chair but said nothing.

"And what can you tell us about the guest Ruth Farrow, Mr. Billings?" was Storm's next question.

"You know, in this business, we have so many people coming and going, I tend to take care of the big picture and let Zara and Maggie handle the personal details. I don't think I met any of this last batch of guests. Like most of our holistic gatherings, people are running in and out of the Inn and gone most of the day for hikes, presentations, etc."

"How about at meals, Mr. Billings?"

"I can assure you, Detective Nosmot. You wouldn't want my cooking," Kendall warned in jest. "Zara and I don't usually eat with the guests. Our chef, Anthony Meade, and his sous chef, Joseph Sprague, prepare all the meals. Maggie and India help out much of the time, and the chambermaids double as servers at breakfast and at dinner. I stick to the admin side of the business—you know, the finances, keeping the Inn complex in good, working order; marketing, taking care of permits and legal stuff, that kind of thing."

....

"One more interview and I'll pass out," Jane mumbled under her breath to Rajiv, eighteen interviews later, as they were winding down and bidding the guests farewell in the Great Room of the Inn. Storm concluded the session, thanked everyone for his or her DNA sample, and advised them of the strict need for silence as far as the ongoing investigation. If anyone had anything new or relevant to report, they should call the Public Safety Office, day or night.

12
Saturday, May 25
Evening

"You two are in for a very special post-mortem dinner," Jane beamed as she greeted Samantha Lloyd and Maggie Banner at the door. Jane bent down to shove aside her hiking boots and brooms, a shovel and packages of 100% recycled toilet paper. Then straightened up and handed them each a piece of paper. "Here's our menu."

Arctic Char à la Abenaki
Mashed Potatoes à la Frewin
Roasted Carrots and Avocado
Salad of Clementine, Ricotta Salata & Pistachios

"Jane, you nutzel," Samantha said. "Do you think we'll have enough food?" she asked with a chuckle, looking around for a place to hang her jacket in all the clutter.

"It sounds delicious, Jane," Maggie added. "Thank you for having us over, especially after the crazy past few days."

"You two know each other, right? Sam, premier caterer; Maggie, runs the Grand Harbor Inn."

"Of course I know Sam. She's worked her culinary magic at many of our Inn events," Maggie said as Sam took an exaggerated bow.

"So tonight we're not going to talk about Mr. Wrong, right, Jane?" Sam asked, while Jane trooped them past unpacked boxes and paraphernalia—a rake, pitchfork, and weed whacker standing next to a bag of dehydrated cow manure and a hodge podge of sweaters and cookbooks; towels and bed linens stacked next to sacks of bone meal and blood meal. "I think it would be therapeutic for you to focus on the real men in your real life, here and now. Or we can talk about your work. How about that? Who would have thought you'd end the week with a cadaver on your desk?!"

"Sam...Cadaver? That's sacrilegious! And don't forget this is an ongoing investigation, meaning we have to drop the topic." They snaked around more of Jane's domestic heaps and headed to the kitchen to fill up their plates before settling in the living room.

Sam was pleased to see that Jane was keeping her neatly organized kitchen in decent shape. The bright white walls and weathered pale grey table and chairs brought an elegant serenity to the space. Sam had to subtract points, though, for the bicycle in the corner shrouded in spider webs, and the two old carpets rolled up on the floor next to a dusty dog crate jammed with cans of sugar-free peaches and bags of "Eye of the Goat" heirloom beans.

"Jeez, Jane. Can't you take some time to clean house and get your nest in order? What's the point of all these magazines about home perfection?" Sam grumbled as she moved stacks of *Country Home* and *Dwell* to the floor to clear a place for herself on the sofa. "Did you come across any articles about 'taming mayhem' by any chance?" Maggie was shifting piles of *House Beautiful, Maine Home & Design*, and *Architectural Digest* to create her seat.

Sam continued complaining. "After six months, Jane, you still have half your life boxed away and everything else looks ridiculous...jumbled and disorganized. It's going to take an exterminator to pull this place together!"

"Here, have some trail mix to calm you down," Jane offered.

Sam scrutinized the kibble up close. "Any mealy worms in there?"

"Hey, back off," Jane barked, shoveling clementine salad into her mouth. "I used to be the perfect homemaker and it didn't pay off, did it? So now I'm nearly 99% divorced, and I'm almost liberated. Comprendo? And my first three months here I slaved to transform that pit of a Public Safety Office into a livable space. Anyway, everything takes time."

"OK. Cool your jets. What do you think of Sonny Mannix, the divorced State Ferry captain who broke up with his latest girlfriend last year?" Sam asked, toasting her idea with a swig of diluted grapefruit juice. "She's moved away; he's got to be lonely."

"Oh God, no," Maggie rushed in. "Sonny's my ex-brother-in-law. I'll say no more. But what about the new owner of the water shuttle service? Have you guys noticed him at all? He's quite the specimen."

"Are you looking, Maggie?" Jane asked.

"Well...you know, who knows? I'm busy with the Inn all day and I have my son, Ned, who's three years old now. My mother lives next door to us, so that's a blessing...and a curse!" she added. "But sure, I'm divorced, so I guess I'm basically open to suggestions. It's certainly different compared to the first time out of the gate."

"Is your ex still in the picture? I remember right before we found the body, you said something about how it's eventually all behind you. Is that true?" Jane wondered.

"Ah, my story's kind of dull," Maggie said. "I married a Wasp, you'll be thrilled to hear, Jane. And we had little Ned. And then the tires went flat. It's as simple as that. Unfortunately, my ex remains a sensitive topic. He wasn't well, and he still isn't well."

"Sounds complicated," Jane concluded. Maggie nodded yes.

"So, have either of you met Hamidi Louca, that new organic farmer on the North Shore? I think he's Cypriot, or something like that. Tall, dark, and handsome." Sam registered her enthusiasm with a big mouthful of potatoes.

"How do you happen to have the goods on all these guys, Samantha?" Jane said.

"I cater to them. Ha ha!! But seriously, there really are a lot of fish in the sea, Jane. Don't you agree, Maggie?"

Jane feigned a bored look at Sam. She was such an optimist. Disgustingly positive. Glass not only totally full...gushing water tank standing nearby, too.

"Here? Right now?" Maggie asked. "I'm not so sure. There are men in every direction you look. But they're all a bunch of movable love units if you ask me. Going from one female to the next. I know a little more now, compared to when I was nineteen. And St. Frewin's is so loaded with male baggage, it's pathetic. Maybe someone off island would be a better bet."

"I tend to agree with Maggie," Jane said as she crumpled further into her arm chair. "The more I wonder, the more I feel I should not get involved with any local man whose safety is in my hands."

At that last comment, Sam cracked a devilish smile.

Jane frowned at her and stood up. "Would anyone like some frozen mango chunks in cranberry juice for dessert?" Then she added, almost as an aside, "What do you think of Storm Nosmot?"

"He's married, isn't he?" Maggie asked.

"You're right. You're absolutely right. I couldn't. But when I look at him...there's so much of him...all I can think is 'Warm' and 'Bulky.' Like the choices of laundry cycles on my washing machine. So cozy...Warm and Bulky."

"Oh, Lord," Samantha groaned. "Maybe we should switch to work after all, Jane. How's it going with Zeke? Is he still acting like he jumped out of the Thames River?"

Jane thought for a moment. Zeke, her Office Manager. Her cross to bear? Why did his oddities drive her crazy? What did she care if he was "Blimey" this, and "Righto" that? And his religious do-dahs? Did it really annoy her when he burned those flimsy incense sticks, producing such nauseous waves of gagging scent?

And what about the little altar he kept fidgeting with on the corner of his desk, with the ever-changing parade of buddha statues? And those ratty prayer beads? Enough already. She hadn't applied for this job to end up in some kind of phony, cheesy monastery with Monty Python begging to hang prayer flags across the restroom walls.

But then she remembered how Zeke hadn't complained an iota when she dumped Torrance Balankoff and the off-grid crematorium into his lap earlier today. And she and Zeke enjoyed the occasional hike in the State Park on the mainland—for office morale, he called it.

She also thought back to how he took charge when someone called in that corpse last February. No foul play, but poor old Warren Gould was frozen dead solid to the floor of his barn, like a glacial deposit. Jane was afraid they would turn him into a poached chicken if they poured boiling water on him to loosen up all those rigid body parts that were fused to the floor. So, Zeke ran out and came back with a hair dryer, plugged it in, and voilà. He blow-dried the old geezer long enough to pry him off the boards and move him along.

"You know, Sam, maybe I need to relax about Zeke. He's always talking about English crime shows he's watched. Maybe they've hijacked his brain. But he does a pretty good job at work, so I should leave it at that."

13
Saturday, May 25
At Night

Earlier in the evening, Zeke had begun to stake out the house located next to Torrance Balankoff's summer cottage. It was now 9:30 PM and Zeke could smell no noxious odors or smoke coming across the field from the house or the yard. The only smoke about to erupt might shoot out of his own ears. He hadn't grumbled a negative word when Jane gave him the task, but he was certainly not thrilled to be slinking around these properties, after hours, when he could be downing a pint to calm his nerves. Jane acted like she was the only one who was frazzled by the death of that woman from the Inn, but Zeke had feelings, too. Sure, he had kept his mouth shut, but he was as freaked out as anyone. And now, with this inane neighbor complaint, he kept asking himself what could Jane hope to accomplish by sending him over here on this fool's errand?

He knew and had confirmed with research at the Town Office that afternoon that Shirley Jensen still owned the property that triggered Torrance Balankoff's complaint. Zeke recalled he had not seen Shirley around lately, but that could be typical. Maine in the winter brought on a lot of "hunker in the bunker" behavior. Between awful weather and ice underfoot guaranteed to break your neck, many people opted to stay indoors and wait until May. Maybe Shirley Jensen was waiting a little longer this year.

From the road, the house, a modest traditional island cape half hidden by mature firs and dense stands of maples, looked like it had aged respectably over the years. Zeke got up from his lawn chair and started across the long open meadow towards Shirley Jensen's. The air had grown cooler and the drop in temperature seemed to bring out the loneliness of the place.

As he moved closer to the house, he began to see how dilapidated it actually was wherever he pointed his flashlight. He climbed the cracked, uneven steps to the screened-in porch, where he could see loose triangular patches of mesh hanging down limply, small flags of neglect, filmy green with mold. He peered past the space of the porch and saw the rotting edges of the front door—nailed shut against the world.

Zeke moved away from the front yard and strode along one of the sunken parallel grooves of the driveway, towards the rear of the house. As he rounded the corner, he immediately knew what he saw ahead of him in the yard. What would likely prove to be Torrance Balankoff's cremation culprits. Two rusty, lidded barrels set up on cinder blocks certainly looked like they were used for burning. Zeke hesitated to take a peek inside the barrels. He wasn't prepared to see the worst yet, but he didn't want to waste time either.

He walked over to one barrel. As he lifted the crusty, crumbling brown lid, sharp, scaly shards of rust came off on his fingertips. He aimed his flashlight downward and waited for his eyes to adjust. Looking closer, he finally focused on what he was afraid he would see. Mounds of powdery pale ash filled half the barrel. Scattered in the ash, white on gray, were clusters of thin ribs, countless little bones, and delicate bones in many tiny shapes. They looked so fragile and innocent. Zeke felt suddenly very lonely.

He exhaled some of that lonely feeling and turned towards the back door behind him. It rivaled the front door for wear and buckle, but this door's hook and eye were secured by a single baggie wire tie coiled round and round.

He shook his head at this naive system and unwound it in a second. So much for security.

The sagging entryway was scattered with rounded nests of straw clumped randomly on the porch floor. Some clumps were topped by drugged-looking old cats; other clumps were imprinted with the weight of a cat who had last slept there. The kitchen door was long gone, and ahead of him his flashlight caught dusty clouds of cat hair drifting through a hazy atmosphere.

The first wafts of odor, quickly followed by pure stench, forced him to breathe through his mouth. A frigging face mask would have been a good idea. He aimed his flashlight around the kitchen, a product of the 1940s, with a rippled white enamel drain area built into an old-fashioned sink, both yellowed with age. The location of the long-gone refrigerator was outlined in a smoky halo of accumulated grime, and the stove stood in its rightful place on a cracked, yellowed linoleum floor. This once homey setting for human cooking and daily meals was now the site of a massive feline feeding station.

Zeke fumed as he stood in the midst of the stinking, fetid piles.

Scattered layers of filthy, bent paper plates on the floor were smeared brown with days-old canned food, looking exactly like what would come out the other end—of the cats. Wobbly pillars of unopened cat food cans advertised their essence: Feast, Delight, Wellbeing, Natural, Petlove, Finest Fare, Cat Heaven. Zeke had no doubts that he was in a hoarder's paradise. To move forward into the rest of the house, he had to tip-toe around the food, and shimmy back and forth between waist-high shiny, black plastic garbage bags bulky with empty cans and other items he did not want to look at closely.

The cabinets, countertops, and walls were in close competition with the state of the floor. Rusty brown streaks poured down every vertical stretch. Crusty pyramids of near-empty cat cans toppled onto every horizontal surface. In between lay the territory for hair balls, used syringes (for the cats, he hoped, and nothing else), and bowls of water crisscrossed with lacy fibers and islands of cat hair.

What Zeke didn't see in front of him, he could smell, and it left him feeling dizzy. He narrowed it down to ammonia— due to years of floorboards saturated with cat urine. The heavy scent grew as he moved on to the hallway and into the front parlor.

No furniture to be seen. He tiptoed through the empty parlor towards steps leading to the second floor. He repeatedly swished blobs of cat hair that raced towards his shoes and ankles. Cat hoarders were clearly intent on salvation, but he was revolted by how woefully short they could fall on sanitation.

Once upstairs, he only saw a few pairs of eyes glowing into his flashlight, but he heard the pitter patter of numerous cat feet racing away from his presence. If even one cat dared to rush him, he was afraid me might drop kick the hell out of it. And he loved cats. But he kept telling himself to get a grip on his mounting disgust...just do the job. That's what this night was all about. Just do the job.

As he waved his flashlight around what appeared to be a decrepit bedroom filled with piles of clothing and trash on the floor, he saw some photographs on a filthy, cracked bureau. He crept closer for a better look. He was surprised to see himself in several photos of bunches of kids from his youth. The pictures depicted some old summer fairs where the young people on the island were lined up, gripping a thick rope for a tug-of-war, with Shirley Jensen as the referee. No point in this ancient history lying around. He took the pictures and exited the room.

He descended the stairs and started to return to the kitchen through a butler's pantry of sorts. Two huge old white freezer cases stood against the outer wall. Zeke tugged the first lid open for a quick look. Unfortunately, his imagination was not quick enough to convince his brain to slam the lid down. He stared inside and gasped at cats, a burial mound of frozen felines, cats stacked five cats deep, big and small, black, white, tabby, tortoise, ginger, gray; cats whose eyes were frozen open, looking up at him as if surprised to see him.

Zeke didn't know what to say or think, except that Jane was going to burst a gasket when she heard about this. He took a deep ammonia-laden breath. He should walk out right now and leave this godforsaken pit. Just go home and report to work the next day and let someone else get weirded out by this place. But he wanted to do the right thing. He was going to have to open the other freezer. To be honest, he dreaded seeing more small, stiff, furry bodies. But he needn't have worried. When he opened the second lid, the single body within (human) was not small and not furry, but it was definitely stiff, and it might be Shirley Jensen.

14

My Diary
March 27, 2019

You will not believe it! You will not believe what happened at work last week! I mean one out of a gazillion, gazillion chances! Sara Proctor in the Porn Unit just quit. She's out of here. She's had it. Moderator, Shmoderator. Adios! I don't really know Sara much at all, because her Porn Unit is a whole other unit from my Violence Unit, but what happened was so O.T.T., we ALL heard about it. So, like, two days ago, Sara's grubbing through the porn trash like she does every day, right? And some anonymous web surfer has reported some dog sex act shit as "inappropriate," and it pops up on Sara's cue to check out (though if you ask me, who are these little coppers out there typing in "dog sex act" on their computers, and just by chance? What kind of prudes are they if they watch the whole damn thing first AND THEN report it? FatsoHippocrits!)

So, Sara checks it out, right, like she's done ten thousand times before. Easy you would think. And then what happens? She sees on her screen these people all laughing and drinking beer and waiting for some show to begin. And out walks this bare-naked, big-tits broad, who starts to act like a sex maniac with a dog! But that's not the half of it! Sara should have cut the video that second and tossed it off the web. But she just watches it a few seconds too long, because something's clicking in the back of her mind and she stares and stares at the big tits broad trying to get the poor dog to do a 69 with her and Sara watches and watches and BAM! It hits her in her gut. The big tits broad is her computer science teacher from high school! In...fucking...credible!

I just don't know. This job rips the rose glasses off you quick. Some days it's so bad, some of the girls end up in the can having a puke-fest...one girl to a stall, each girl yelling out the grossest thing she saw today just as she's about to toss it. "Eyeballs getting dug out!" "Man chopping off breasts!" "Soldiers raping girls!" "Kids stomping on puppies!"

The stuff we have to look at CONSTANTLY. It knocks you down flat, you know. So far, I've been OK. No barfing at work for me. I'm strong. But that's probably not true about me and porn. I guess I must have tested lousy when the bosses screened me for porn. I told them I could look at anything and feel nothing. But they steered me to the Violence Unit. They must have secret ways to tell if you're getting horny in the porn tests, even though you're trying not to show it. And once they smell that on you, off you go to the Violence Unit. I have no idea on earth who ends up in the Porn Unit. Maybe failed nuns?

15
Sunday, May 26

"Well, that was a tiny bit fruitful," Jane reported as she slapped her interview notes on the Public Safety table on Sunday morning, along with a photograph of Ruth Farrow, age thirty-one, of Wheatshare, Iowa. The picture faxed in by the Iowa State Patrol caught everyone's breath. Here was a lovely young woman with so much promise in her eyes, who was the farthest, saddest cry from the death mask they had all carried in their minds since Zeke first handed out the crime scene photos. It was difficult to feel neutral any longer. And the photograph unquestionably matched the driver's license Finn had located in Ruth's room at the Inn.

"So, I trust everyone slept well last night at Penobscot Inn? No bed bugs nibbling on you, Finn? No nightmares?" Jane inquired.

Rajiv nodded happily. "Never raised an eyelid. And I loved their apricot cream cheese French toast and all the fresh air."

Finn gave Jane his regulation smile. "Actually, I did have a great night's sleep."

Jane grabbed the chance. "I bet that's because your weren't spending half of it flipping through your cellphone, Finn."

The Homicide mainlanders quickly settled themselves in at the Public Safety table so that everyone could begin sharing their findings. Zeke stood at attention with stickies and felt-tipped pens to track their evidence and analysis on the giant whiteboard in the main room.

"Maine State Police have notified Iowa about the case," Jane updated the crew. "Iowa's detectives are investigating

Ruth Farrow's background, and they'll be talking to her workplace on Monday. As for our corpse...if you ask me, those women we interviewed hardly knew our victim, unless they're keeping something from us. And did you notice how they all seemed kind of flat about what happened to Ruth Farrow? Not a tear shed."

"Maybe they're in shock right now and don't know it," Storm suggested. "Or maybe they're very stolid individuals to start with. That would go along with their job requirements, right? Anyway, we have the digital moderators' contact information and they know how to get hold of us if they remember something later. This process takes time, Jane. Try to keep your patience handy."

"Putting our interviews all together," Finn began, "it looks like the guests and most of the staff were absent during our time frame. Maggie also said there was no lawn crew at the Inn on Thursday and Friday. They do their landscape work on Mondays."

Finn looked down at his notes. "So, people present at the Inn boil down to Kendall and Zara Billings, the Chef, Maggie Banner, and one or two chambermaids. Kendall was at the Inn all day and night Thursday and Friday morning. Zara returned on Thursday night around midnight, after being away since Tuesday morning. Chef Anthony Meade and Maggie were absent all Thursday and both arrived at the Inn early Friday morning for the breakfast shift."

Zeke jumped from column to column on the whiteboard, tallying up who had the most points for murder.

"And none of them recalls seeing Ruth Farrow during the time frame," Storm said, looking at their faces and shaking his head. "Jane's interview with three of the women contains a line of inquiry we need to track down. One of the girls mentioned that Ruth hung out with men at bars back in Iowa. That she may not have attended all the group dinners at the Inn. So, we need to ask the pub owner and his staff if they remember seeing anyone resembling Ruth and anyone with her."

"I'll make a copy of Ruth's picture and head over to the pub and check on that right now," Finn offered. "Good to catch the staff before the lunch wave arrives."

Rajiv raised a question. "Does anyone think the responses of the Inn people were a bit slick, or maybe too rehearsed?"

"I don't know," Jane said. "Kendall and Zara are both business types and they have so much at stake here. I mean, even if they're somewhat wealthy, the Inn is their livelihood. It's their pride and joy from what I've heard. I'm not surprised if they prepared themselves for their interview.

"Just put yourself in their shoes. They must be fretting day and night as to whether the Grand Harbor Inn, even the whole goddamn St. Frewin's Island, will now get blacklisted as a Premier Destination. They hosted a holistic R&R retreat where one of the guests seeking peace and tranquility ended her last moments being nibbled on by maggots. I bet that won't go over well with the Maine State Tourism Bureau."

"OK, OK," Rajiv backed off. "I just sensed too much polish in the Billings interviews. That's all."

"And Jane, the rest of the world doesn't know the details about the maggots...at least not yet," Finn pointed out as he was leaving.

"Well," Storm reminded them, "the basic conflict in our search is that legally everyone is innocent until proven guilty, but our job is to consider everyone guilty, until we can eliminate those who are not. So, it's good, Rajiv, to question everyone and everything. For now, go with your gut if it feels right. OK, why don't we look at possible motives of Kendall, Zara, the Chef, and Maggie. What do you say, Jane?"

Jane stood up and walked to the whiteboard, pointing to the different columns. "Kendall does not recall meeting Ruth Farrow. Zara checked the moderators into the Inn when they arrived, but then she was out most of the week until late Thursday night when she returned. It doesn't look like there was much contact between these people and Ruth. So, we don't have any idea of a motive for either of them at this point."

"But wait a minute, Jane. Can we believe what we've been told?" Storm pointed out. "Without a solid alibi, who knows what Kendall Billings was up to during our time frame? We should check his telephone records, talk to the people on the mainland he referenced. And how do we know Zara didn't come home earlier than she's reported. You should get the names of Zara's friends to confirm her statement of her whereabouts and check the ferry and the shuttle as to how and when she returned to the island." Zeke scribbled away on the whiteboard.

Jane still wrestled with Storm's point. "OK. So, Kendall has no witnesses who can confirm his activities on Thursday and Friday. But I want to believe him, because I can't see why he would jeopardize his whole existence by killing Ruth Farrow. That makes no sense. As for Zara, think about it. She's the type who wears cashmere twin sets. She runs for charity in all the 10K races in the county. Does that sound like a murderess?"

"Jane, let's review your, uh, criteria for murder at our next break. We need to go over some fine points and analyze these assumptions you're making. As for the basics of murder, murder often makes little sense until we learn the unfortunate facts," said Storm. "Right now we don't know what was churning inside the murderer before he...or she...killed. Maybe anger or hatred? Maybe fear? Once we unearth that anger or hatred or fear, then we may understand why the murder occurred, or who did it. So please keep that in mind."

Storm continued. "What about the Chef and Maggie? They only returned to the Inn early Friday morning to do the breakfast shift for the guests. Otherwise, on Thursday, the Chef says he was at home with his wife and kids, and Maggie was at home with her son. Again, we don't have outside witnesses to confirm alibis for either of them, but we don't have any obvious motives either."

"So, we're missing a reason for anyone to kill Ruth Farrow," Jane said. "What about opportunity? Who had access to Ruth during our time frame?"

Storm elaborated. "All the people we're looking at could have easily caught up with Ruth. As for the means to kill her, we can't eliminate anyone on the island yet. Assuming it's household rope that the killer used, anyone could get their hands on the rope that was used to tie Ruth's hands. And lobsters are everywhere. In fact, everything the killer used can be found in your neighborhood grocery store."

"About the lobster," Zeke added, "Maggie reported the Inn bins were picked up as usual on Friday morning. And here on the island, twice a month on Fridays, including this past Friday, the bin contents go on a lorry to be transported to an out-of-state facility. So, we don't have any rubbish we can comb through for evidence from the Inn, or anywhere on the island for that matter." More info for the whiteboard.

Storm moved closer to Jane and said in a low voice, "I've been meaning to ask. What's with the Guv and the bins and lorries—and those prayer flags in the bathroom? Is Zeke a British Buddhist?"

"Huh—more on that later," Jane whispered back.

"So, who had the ability to get close enough to her to kill her?" asked Storm. "Maybe that's where we should focus. Who would have been able to get close enough to her at all?

Her colleagues told us she was a loner, but she liked to be with men in bars. Maybe Finn will bring back something useful after talking to the pub people." Storm stretched his thickset arms up to the ceiling and took a deep breath. "But right now, we're going around in circles. Let's take a short break."

16
Sunday, May 26
Early Afternoon

"Well, I think I've got something," Finn announced when he returned to the Public Safety table a half hour later. "The bartender says he distinctly remembers someone who looks like Ruth's picture coming into the pub both Wednesday and Thursday nights. She apparently met a Nathan Herinton on Wednesday and caught up with him again at the pub on Thursday."

"Hold on, Mate. Nathan Herinton?" Zeke looked slightly amazed. "I can't imagine him doing anything dodgy. His family's been summering on the island for centuries. I also think he's getting married this summer."

"Well, we don't know about 'dodgy' at this point, but the bartender remembers Ruth and Nathan knocking back a lot of drinks and then leaving as a twosome...both nights," Finn added. Zeke hesitated to add Nathan Herinton to the whiteboard, but then caved in, plastering him on the far side of the suspects' gallery.

Storm thanked Finn for the good work. "This is important, People. We now have a trail for Ruth on Thursday night, and we have the identity of someone who was able to get close to her. Jane, let's have Helen call Nathan Herinton and get him in here to talk with us. Monday, if possible."

"Now, before we lose the light," Storm continued, "let's drive over to the site where the body was found. The Augusta office sent someone over to the island this morning to deliver the rest of the investigators' photographs from the night Jane discovered the body. We can take a good look at the whole setting with those pictures in hand. Let's see if there is any logic or sense in why and where the body was dropped off along Herinton Drive. Let's look at it through the eyes of this Nathan Herinton."

17
My Diary
April 24, 2019

Wow, this will make your jaw drop! Our boss came out with a doozie today. None of us can believe it. But Baby, we are cutting out of here and fast! They're going to send us to an island in Maine for R&R...that's what they called it. R&R. And fresh air and Mother Nature to help our pickled brains. One of the guys said he overheard another boss saying it was part of a government grant...not really the company's money. But I don't care who's paying my way. I just wanna pack my bag and get on that plane.

Kind of wish Mom and Dad were still around. They'd get a kick out of me going to a Maine island on a "business trip." LA DEE DAH. But now, well, it's too late now. They're never going to know what I'm up to...ever. I guess I don't really feel super sad any more. It was really hard at first, Dad dropping dead just like that...Whammo. Then Mom falling apart and getting cancer. Left me with zero family. There's no one person around to call family.

But I can buck up. I'm tough. I'm a survivor. Had to be after whatever shit hit the fan when I was sixteen. Can't remember NOthing until I turned seventeen. And even after that, all those years in rehab. Moving my arms, moving my legs, all those nursey types walking me up and down the gym and driving me crazy with how to hold a fork, how to tie my shoes. Sheesh! They made me feel like a rag doll.

But, OK, I'll back off. They were trying to help me. They were trying to turn Ruth into Ruth again. A girl with nothing upstairs. Mom said not to worry...Dad said it didn't matter. The past is the past. They were just happy to see me up on my feet again. You know what I think? They sheltered me too much. They were protecting me way too much. God knows from what. I mean if you can't remember shit from your childhood, what's there to protect? Nothing's there, right?

I'm a nobody before sixteen years old. And a Raggedy Ann in rehab for ten years after that. So fucking weird. No memory, no past. Which is how I turned out. Which is probably how I got the CCM job...I'm just a pleasant zombie.

But I must have family somewhere. How can you not have family? Makes no sense, though that's what Mom always said. We're it, Ruth, she said. End of the line. No strings attached. Boy, maybe it's true. But maybe Mom just didn't know. She didn't look, that's for sure. Maybe she and Dad were hiding something. What about that? Maybe they were scared. This is getting interesting. I am really curious now. It killed the cat, but it's not going to get me. And there's all kinds of stuff on the TV about ancestry something or other. Finding your genes, something like that. I'll take a peek at work during my break and see what I can find on the web. They say you can track down your great, great, great grandfather. Shit. I don't need to go back that far. I just want to know if I have anybody in my tree, even a monkey. Ha ha!! It'd be my luck to find a pack of idiots or deadbeats for relatives.

It's strange, those bursts of light going off in my head. They don't seem like just flashes and bits and pieces. I mean they're getting clear...like kind of a movie...not just bursts anymore. I can see I'm in a car that's driving somewhere. I think the car may be going really fast...that's about all that's happened so far in my head video. I'm pretty sure it's not stuff about work. I used to think it was because of work, but driving in a car doesn't have a lot to do with the stuff I drag off the web. There are no people chopping up animals and pulling off toenails in my brainy pictures. Ha ha!! "brainy" pictures...MY brainy pictures. Turd brain, bird brain.

And what about Maine? None of us, me, Mom, or Dad, was ever in Maine. When you live in Iowa, why would you even wonder about Maine? But something's bugging me and I can't tell you what. Something about Maine...maybe I just heard the name along the way and that's all it is. Doesn't matter. Can't wait for Sunday to hit the road. Sure hope there will be some hot man pie waiting for me on that island. Really strong man pie, Baby...sexy man pie!

18
Sunday, May 26

Storm parked his car on the right side of Herinton Drive where the bright yellow crime scene tape was staked. He and his team got out. "You really do live in a fantastic place, Zeke," said Rajiv, breathing in the whiff of salt air that blew towards them. "Wish my relatives in Bangalore could see this place."

"I'd be daft to live elsewhere, Rajiv. My grandmother likes to quote a line from some poem—'Sunlight, trees, and fields...these are the pieces of heaven,' " Zeke recited.

"So, we've parked the car...logically on the right side of the road, which is the approach to the Herinton house," said Storm. He, Jane, and Finn walked forward a few yards and stepped into the woodsy area where the body had been found. "The Medical Examiner's report isn't done yet, but their initial findings suggest Ruth Farrow was attacked at one spot and then driven here and dumped. I'll pass these two sets of photos to you, Jane and Finn, to look at. Rajiv and Zeke can pace the surrounding area."

Finn studied the pictures Storm had handed him. "I'm looking at these photos of the approach from the road to the location of the body. I can't really distinguish a significant pattern of broken branches or disturbed ground that would suggest the murderer struggled with someone else as he or she entered the woods," said Finn.

"Do you know if the investigators found any fibers or torn fabric on any saplings or branches?" Jane asked next.

"I'm afraid there were no helpful traces of anything," Storm answered.

"Well, that makes me wonder if the murderer could have approached the body drop area from the other direction, from within the woods," Jane suggested. "I don't really recall that the investigators explored deeper into the woods, but we should check on that."

"That's definitely important," Finn said. "If the killer came from the woods, we should do a larger walkabout to look for evidence...signs of where the murderer came from and where the murder may have taken place."

"Then again," Jane countered, "however the killer may have caught up with Ruth that night, wouldn't it seem most likely that the killer had a car? And if so, I'm guessing the killer parked on Herinton Drive, walked into this site with the body, and dropped it here. But I'll look at a map and figure out where the woods lead to."

"OK...let's put that on our to-do list—check the map, and ask the investigators if they searched deeper into the woods," Storm said.

"What else do the photos tell us, Jane?"

"When I first saw the body, I remember thinking it looked like the woman might have jerked back and forth on the ground. As I look at these photos, I see there is evidence of some movement that the rain didn't wash away—some dirt and debris rubbed into the right side of her face and hair, and dirt stains and wrinkling on her clothing on the right side of her that was touching the ground. The skin on her right arm and right leg in these two shots looks dirty and chafed."

Jane moved from one picture to the next. "And these photos of the ground after the investigators removed her body show how the turf is sort of hollowed out where she may have bucked back and forth—you know, struggled—before she couldn't any longer. What do you think, Finn?"

"Seems to make sense. But there isn't all that much dirt or chafing, which suggests the victim was still alive when dropped, regained consciousness, but she wasn't moving around for long...wasn't conscious for long, I'm guessing."

"I sure hope not," Jane said with a shudder. "Can you imagine choking to death with a live lobster in your throat? And the lobster maybe thrashing around. I just can't stop thinking about how that would feel. How she must have felt. The back of your throat heaving repeatedly or worse yet, totally stuck, and you can't get enough wind in you to do anything. How horrible."

Finn attempted to lower the boiling point. "Jane, I try to keep my fantasies and emotions about death out of my work. We've got to concentrate on the facts and the science before us to solve the case. It saps your energy to get caught up in the victim's trauma. You need to stay neutral if you're going to be a good cop."

"Yes, but, Finn, you mean to say you haven't thought at all about her spasming and gasping in those final seconds or minutes? And the frenzy consuming her? And something else I don't understand...why wouldn't she keep breathing through her nose?" Finn looked blank.

Storm took back both sets of photos. "That's a good question, that last one, Jane. Maybe something was obstructing her nose? Or maybe the gagging from the lobster closed down her windpipe. When we view the body up in Augusta on Tuesday, the Medical Examiner will probably have answers for us."

....

Rajiv, meanwhile, was walking methodically up and down along one half of the crime perimeter furthest from the road, weaving among the trees and branches, a new row with each turn, back and forth, advancing slowly over the area, looking for anything that might have been missed. Zeke walked the half of the perimeter of the crime scene closest to the road, looking upwards and downwards for any other hidden clues.

The Medical Examiner's report due in on Tuesday would give the Homicide team a better picture of the manner in which Ruth had been killed. But Rajiv knew from speaking with his office colleagues that that there had been very little blood on the body and none on the damp dirt around the body. The Examiner's team told Rajiv that the signs of trauma suggested the sequence leading to death would have been a punch to the head to knock the girl out, hands bound behind her back, and then the lobster forced down her throat.

While Storm discussed the murder with Jane and Finn, Rajiv continued his pacing over the far end of the site. He stopped when he saw it...barely visible in a mess of broken branches...a bit of shininess. He stooped down and pulled out a small object wrapped in foil paper. He took one quick peek and closed the foil gently. Inside was a half-eaten chicken leg—chunks of meat bitten into and the rest still clinging to the bone. Mistakenly discarded? Or maybe it was just random garbage tossed out by a passing driver. He called out his find to the others, stashed the food in an evidence bag, and pocketed it, still deep in thought about the forensic details of Ruth's demise.

About those maggots in the corpse's mouth, Rajiv knew they were late to the party, though not to the banquet. First, flies would quickly find their way to the flesh of the lobster and to the body itself, and lay their eggs on site. Within twenty-four hours, the eggs would hatch into maggots. But all their feasting would likely occur post mortem, so no amount of maggots born in the lobster and the body itself could have devoured enough crustacean flesh or body tissue to create a breathing passage as the girl lay dying. Even IF the maggots had somehow *miraculously* tunneled sufficiently to allow oxygen into the girl's lungs, nevertheless, the girl would have choked to death because the larval excavation would have come too late.

....

"Zeke, let's say Herinton brought the girl back to his house to party," Rajiv hypothesized as he completed his search on the grid of the crime scene. "And let's say she ended up dead somehow, we don't know how. And if Herinton was crazed to get rid of the body afterward, why would he dump it so close to his property?"

"Go on. Keep talking," Zeke said.

"But let's say he lost it, and he did dump the body as he drove out of his driveway away from his house. Wouldn't he brake, get the body out of the car and dump it on the nearest side of the road, which would be his right side, in that case? And that dump spot would be across the road from where we're standing right now, where the body was actually left. But like I said, I don't buy it that Herinton would dump the body so close to his home."

"Under your reasoning, then," Zeke was formulating a possible conclusion, "it must have been some other bloke who delivered the package to Herinton Drive. Someone driving towards the house...not away from the house."

"Precisely," said Rajiv.

As the team gathered to head back to Storm's car, Storm gave them all an assignment. "I want you to think about the actual body drop. If we assume the killer came here to drop the victim, why here? Or was it just chance? Was it because of the remote spot on the road—no homes or intersections in sight? How does the location fit into whatever Nathan Herinton may tell us when we interview him? Let's focus on all of that."

19
My Diary
Wednesday, May 22

B.O.R.I.N.G. BORE *me to death. This island is the pits...one big schnooze. Such a drag! No internet, can't surf the web. Are they insane? Who really wants to tramp around in the woods all day and get all sweaty? My makeup is dripping off my face. Gross. And what's with the bug shit? They keep telling us to use the spray. Don't walk in the leafy stuff. Duck if you see a giant motherfucker zooming in to bite you. WTF! If I don't want to get Lyme disease in Iowa, I sure as hell don't want to get it in Maine. How dumb is that.*

And after all that flying and driving to get here, you'd think we had landed in Paradise. But guess what? NOT. This is NOT Paradise. And they're trying to poison us, I swear. The very first night they served us something they called fried clam bellies with something that looked like pus...tartar or something?? What is wrong with this place? Do I want squirmy gut marbles coated in greasy crumbs in my stomach? No way, José! And I'm cooped up with just girls from work. I thought it was supposed to be boys and girls. Why didn't I say no thanks? This is not vacationland. Prison camp stuck in the ocean is more like it.

At least the island guys aren't boring. I've scored two of them so far. Probably won't have time for another one. That slick dick that threw himself on me the other day thinks he's pretty hot. Well, he's right, but I can tell you, he's a serial dick...done it with lots of other girls. You can just tell. A real pussy tripper. And it all happened way too fast. But I like fast.

The other guy has a humongous bed! And a humongous you know what! Ha ha!! Really great to get all boozed up in a bar and let my face fall all over the guy's big, wide smile. Laughing, gushing, a little peck on his lips, then another...that's how you reel them in, Baby. And drinking. Guys love a gal who loves the booze. He finally asked me to go home with him. Bingo. A fucking house tour. Fun ride home. We must have parked five times to make out on the way. Hot, hot, hot! And super nice wheels this guy's got. But seriously, what's with all the dog hair? Disgusting! All that leather and jazzy dashboard, but so much crud all over the car, on the seats, on the floor, mucked up windows. Yuck! Get a vacuum, Dude!

Oh, don't let me forget...kind of weird. At the pub tonight, I saw this blond guy giving me a serious once over. Big thrill...ha ha...have no idea who he is....

Ohhhhhhhh, man, I am so tired right now. Got to sleep it all off. My mouth is parched. My lips are blown out. No saliva left. Saliva...ah, right, saliva. Glad I got that package off to the genes place before I left home. They'll probably tell me I'm one-part gin, one-part vodka. Ha ha!! You're a human cocktail, Honey, a diablo martini, they'll tell me. Your ancestors came out of a bottle. Shoot me already.

20

Monday, May 27

Jane and Zeke looked a bit apprehensive as Nathan Herinton, an eighth-generation descendant of Nathaniel Herinton, one of the original settlers of St. Frewin's, took his seat at the Public Safety table the next day. Helen had rung up Nathan, and while he was annoyed to be asked to come in, he didn't refuse.

As a total package, Nathan Herinton carried his family's heritage well...riveting blue eyes, perfect skin and nose, slightly wavy brown hair, and a Grand Canyon of a smile hosting a long white river of teeth...clearly a born winner these many generations later.

Storm and Finn took up the slack at the table. Rajiv was back on the mainland working with his team at the State Crime Lab.

"Thank you for coming to see us, Mr. Herinton," Storm began.

"Well, not the best Monday I've ever had, but I'm willing to help, if I can," Nathan assured them. "I hope this won't take too long. I've got to ship out on Thursday."

"Just some questions, Mr. Herinton, and you'll be on your way. As you may have heard, one of the Grand Harbor Inn guests has gone missing. We think it may be her body that was found last Friday. And we believe the dead woman is Ruth Farrow of Wheatshare, Iowa," Storm explained as he placed Ruth's photograph before Nathan. "Does she look familiar to you?"

"I wouldn't be here if she didn't, would I?" Nathan sat back abruptly in his chair. "Yes, I met Ruth Farrow...this past Wednesday night at the pub. And Thursday."

"Could you tell us what you and Ruth did both nights?"

"OK." Nathan Herinton was not pleased. He did not want to lose control of this grilling. "I'll cut to the chase here, to save your time and mine. I met her, we had drinks, I took her home. We partied, and yes, we ended up in bed. Consensually, I might add. Both nights. And then I drove her back to the Inn. Both nights."

"Mr. Herinton, just to get the full picture, was anyone else at your home while Ruth Farrow was there with you? Anyone who can support your statement?" Storm's calm gaze had not wavered. He was a sailboat gliding on a smooth lake.

"Unfortunately, no."

"Please tell us what Ruth talked about...anything different or peculiar that you remember?"

"Ah, well, she did say she was in some kind of high-tech work, I think. But she said she couldn't really talk about her work. She also mentioned something about flashbacks...something that didn't make sense. But she was short on details, and like I said, we were drinking and shooting the breeze generally."

"So, on Thursday night, you say you brought Ruth back to the Inn. What time was that?"

A deliberate sigh from Nathan Herinton..."I guess around 9:30 PM or so."

"Another question, Mr. Herinton. Did you purchase any lobsters last week?"

"Not that I recall, though I do love them," Nathan replied, the pull of his eyebrows showing his surprise at the change of course on the questions.

"Did anyone bring you lobsters?"

"Someone may have, Detective Nosmot. But you're losing me. What do lobsters have to do with any of this?"

"Just part of our inquiry, Sir," Storm said quietly.

"Look, Jane, Zeke, Detective Nosmot, and crew," Nathan addressed them in hard, clipped sentences. "I had nothing to do with Ruth after I dropped her off at the Inn on Thursday night. I didn't kill her. My lobsters didn't kill her. And none of this is making sense. I had nothing to do with Ruth Farrow's death, assuming she is the one who died."

"In that case, Mr. Herinton, may we count on your full cooperation when our crime scene investigators arrive at your home later today?"

"That doesn't sound like a question," Nathan said.

"No, sir. It isn't. We're under an obligation to search your personal property and your residence to support your statements completely. This will work in your favor," Storm assured him.

"Then, by all means, Detective Nosmot."

There really was nothing more to say. This man, whose forefathers were maybe one boat behind the Mayflower landing on the New World's shores, had had enough. After a few more wrap-up questions and the collection of a DNA sample, Storm accompanied Nathan to the door and told him Public Safety would get back in touch with him if anything came up before Thursday. "Where are you shipping off to, may I ask? You're not military, are you?" Storm said.

"No military, not that. I'm crewing in a yacht race off Nantucket," Nathan Herinton said with a smile, and a goodbye, but no thank you.

21
The Previous Week, May 24

When you drive North on Maine State Route 6, about ten miles outside the town of Shirley, you first look upon the vast and endless multi-branched beauty of water called Moosehead Lake, the blue miracle of "Earth's eye," as Henry David Thoreau wrote more than a century ago. It is impossible not to feel the wonder in this magical, shimmering expanse before you—118 square miles of glacial lake formed over 12,000 years ago—more than five times as large as Manhattan. For those last ten miles of nearly curveless highway running downhill, you find yourself plunging closer and closer into Earth's eye until you are back on the ground once more in the town of Greenville, Maine.

It was this stretch of highway flowing down into the blue yonder that saved Zara Billings from her own natural impulses on Tuesday. She had called her girlfriends and told them to drive up without her. She would follow in her own car; she had errands to run on the way back home on Thursday.

And now was Thursday. She patted herself on the back that she had survived the outing without spilling her soul in front of the gang. Though utterly exhausted and sorely tempted to spout off, for the past fifty-four hours Zara had maintained a façade of Cool, Calm, and Collected. The words were so stale, unlike Kendall's recent infidelity, still so hot to the touch.

Zara knew she would wait a very long time until she finally sat down and had tea with her heart to ask what had happened and how was her aorta doing after all? For now, she refused to pay attention to any of the many ways she would have reacted maybe one or two years ago. She would not imagine herself scribbling furiously to herself, writing about how her every molecule was clanging like a fire alarm.

Or how every fiber in her body had been stomped on, drowned, and hung back up to fry in the sun. How she was all alone, just her and the planet. All other people, all the stuff, all the buildings, all the places, nature, all the continents, all the oceans, what did they matter? How right now, it was all about holding her breath until things got better. She refused to consider how the fibers, strands, particles, and particulars of Kendall and she together had been smothered, smashed, dissolved, disappeared. And how Kendall didn't have a clue. How therapists would tell her to write her goodbye letter and then her hello letter...or maybe it was the reverse. Whatever.

Zara had nothing to say this time...nothing to get out of her system and down on paper. None of that. For as she had approached Moosehead Lake, the miraculous great pond pulled her soul down to its deepest waters and bathed her soul free of all misery and wounds. *So fold thyself, my dearest, thou, and slip into my bosom and be lost in me.* All the wounds (not just the latest rather spectacular wound that came packaged as last Tuesday's sex tape recording) but also all the other wounds caused by the little stink bombs and pipe bombs K had strewn in his wake whenever he welcomed a female guest a little too enthusiastically, or he put the occasional arm around a friend's wife, or the hasty body steps backing away, taken by K and another woman (pick a woman, any woman) as Zara walked into their presence.

Now she was Cool, Calm, and Collected. And one of her errands on the way home required a right turn onto State Route 16, and then a bit south to one of Central Maine's quiet towns that had lost its community sparkle and shopping plaza a long time ago. Zara took a few more turns and found the small package store she was looking for. It was time to buy an "insurance policy," pending any further surprises at home.

....

After a midnight water shuttle lift back to the island, Zara drove to the Inn and pulled up to the front parking area where the night lanterns lined the drive and entranceway. Kendall was standing on the lawn in the heavy rain, smiling at her in a daze and she could not figure out why he looked like a dark statue. "What are you doing out here at this time of the night?" she said.

"I know. I look kind of funny, don't I," Kendall laughed, and he turned and modeled his drenched, sleek physique sheathed tightly in black, like some summertime Zorro without his mask and cape. "How do you like my wetsuit, Babe? I bet it turns you on, Zara, doesn't it?" he teased her.

"That is appealing, Kendall. Come here," Zara said with open arms.

"I was just down in the ocean earlier tonight, stirring up the phosphorescence," Kendall went on. "The turbulence from this storm was really kicking up a glow."

"Come here, Kendall." Which he did. "Don't you think it's time we unzip this wetsuit and see what's inside? Maybe the storm has blown in a big piece of driftwood?" Zara started to whisper with her hand moving downward. She took a slippery hold of him quite firmly, too firmly, and she threw her pelvis against his, and swooped her arms behind him to rip open the wetsuit zipper. She was handling him rather hard, and that was exactly what she was in the mood to do. She wanted to jolt him enough to make herself feel better, enough to make him excited and make him think this was going to be rough sex and a wild ride.

She was fully capable of jumping on him next and tickling him such that they both collapsed onto the mushy wet grass.

She knew the guests were all away, and it wasn't like someone was going to show up unexpectedly in all this downpour to start weeding the creeping phlox on the ground right next to them. She hated him, and she wanted to use him. She wanted revenge, and she wanted to think about how much she hated his mother, too. She hated them both, mother and son. Zara was dominating Kendall with her tools of pleasure right now and she wanted to imagine the worst, to imagine he'd probably even done it with his mother, too, the Matriarchal Bitch Goddess. She hated them.

22
Tuesday, May 28

Storm drove past the law enforcement complex to the parking lot in front of the Chief Medical Examiner's office in Augusta. Jane noticed they had arrived at 30 Hospital Street. Hospital Street? Of all places, an optimistic address for the dead being sliced and diced on the Medical Examiner's cutting table.

Storm and his team entered the brick building and were escorted to the Medical Examiner's work room. Like anyone who grew up with television, Jane had seen her share of faux autopsy scenes where very grave faces were standing in an airy tiled space filled with harsh bright light, cold metallic tables and counters, people in green scrubs, and maybe the TV camera veered over to a wall of filing cabinets for cadavers, who were in the pipeline for inspection. Which posed the question—*Was it an oxymoron to use the word "who" for a corpse?* On TV, one of the law enforcement team was often turning away to avoid barfing, or the person did barf, or the person whipped out of the room to deal with the barfing. Jane had to admit she was about to flip into one of those three modes any second now. What an awful feeling. Her maiden voyage.

"So, Ms. Roberts. Storm tells me this is your first post-mortem review," the Medical Examiner commented to Jane as she, Finn, and Storm drew closer to the body on the table...Ruth Farrow, looking like a pale, sleeping saint.

Jane nodded at Dr. Andreas Kerner and smiled weakly. She didn't dare open her mouth.

"Ja, ja. Very well," Dr. Kerner responded. "So, let us travel together from head to toe to explore the physical trauma of this victim, our 'silent witness' as we say in the trade. First, we see these two distinct wounds at the back of the head...right there," he said as he gently parted the victim's hair and pointed with his pencil. "Very nicely fractured areas of the skull—one clean, open fracture with bone visible. And this depressed fracture....can you see where the skull has actually penetrated the brain cavity?

"No doubt both impacts caused profuse bleeding. The murderer likely used some sort of blunt instrument—maybe a sledge hammer or a 2 X 4?—to knock the victim unconscious. However, her lovely hair was thick enough to prevent evidence of the weapon being left on the skull. And the rain later on washed away any other sign."

Jane made sure to keep gulping. Finn and Storm stood stoic and silent.

Dr. Kerner pointed to the wrists of the corpse. "Here we see an excellent example of pressure imprints and reddened friction burn where rope was used to bind the victim's hands. This epidermal stress and abrasion on the wrists suggest she was conscious at some point and strained against the rope. Would you like to take a closer look, Storm...Finn or Jane?" All three heads shook no.

Dr. Kerner lifted the rope off the table and showed it to them. "The rope the murderer used is generic household rope found in grocery stores and hardware stores. The knots in the rope were ordinary knots—nothing significant."

Dr. Kerner moved closer to the body and gently manipulated the mouth so that Jane, Finn, and Storm had an improved view of the raw interior of the throat. They could see inside a short tunnel of shredded flesh. "There we go. Now you have what I call a 'Buena Vista'! " Dr. Kerner remarked with a big smile. Jane involuntarily grabbed Finn's arm and dug her nails in. He yelped. She let go.

"The murderer shoved the lobster body into the length of the victim's mouth with enough force and torsion to rip into her tongue and crush the back of her mouth and even her uvula. Look here...more closely...you can see the extensive damage. Very impressive. This, of course, caused significant bleeding and aggravated the choking. Due to the presence of the lobster interfering with her swallowing mechanism and putting intense pressure on her nasal passages, we can estimate death would have occurred in about ten minutes, caused by the loss of oxygen to the brain. Any questions so far?" Dr. Kerner asked his alert audience. All three heads shook no.

"So, what were the instruments of death? Well, we have an unknown weapon that produced the head wounds, ordinary rope, and a lobster. We would be looking for copious amounts of blood shed from the head wounds and from the mouth and throat trauma, but I understand the rains washed away all blood at the location where the body was found."

"Unfortunately, that's right, Dr. Kerner," Storm confirmed.

"You may, however," Dr. Kerner continued, "want to be on the lookout for a car seat or a blanket or plastic sheet covered in blood. Finally, most interesting of all is the pièce de résistance. I cannot recall that I have ever seen such a method in my career. I found two small pebbles, lodged snug and deep inside each of the victim's nostrils. The pebbles, coupled with the lobster stuffing the corpse's mouth...well, it's like something out of an ancient sacrificial ritual, don't you think? So simple, yet so effective." The doctor shook his head, a slight smile on his lips. "I am inclined to conclude the murderer wanted to make absolutely sure to block any means the victim might have to draw oxygen to her lungs."

Storm started to mention this must be the answer to the question Jane had posed at the crime scene, but Finn's upper body abruptly startled them by heaving forward. He turned to Jane with a twisted face of anguish. Then he yanked her large hobo bag half off her shoulder, jerked it wide open, and proceeded to retch inside.

"Oh no, Finn! Are you OK?" Jane yelled out, hopping away from the shower of vomit. "Oh god. What did you eat for breakfast?" Well, there. She had tried and failed to emanate more than an ounce of sympathy, when all she wanted was to dump this gallon of instant sour pudding in her bag all over his bowed head. He had beaten her to the stomach toss! And he had fouled her favorite suede tote. She couldn't wait to hear what came next.

"Uh...sorry, Jane. I lost it. Sorry," Finn gasped as he gained control. Dr. Kerner brought him some paper towels, and Finn's composure, a bit shaken, soon returned. That was it.

Storm gently patted Finn on the back. "Good aim, Finn. Ha ha!!" That was it.

That was it?, Jane thought. *That was it?* What about her bag full of Finn's stomach contents? Would she have to get on her knees and beg Harriet Buxton in Human Resources to cover the cost of a replacement hobo bag? They weren't cheap, you know. And her wallet? Her hairbrush? All the odds and ends she dragged around with her for no good reason? And why the hell didn't he spill his marbles straight on the floor? What was he anyway? A dog that had to hide its duty from sight? For crying out loud! But she would keep this all to herself. Curb her reactionary tendencies. She would behave.

"Finn, I'll get you a cup of water. That should help you feel better," Jane said, walking to the lab sink. Better to pull in Florence Nightingale than to berate the poor chump.

23
Wednesday, May 29

"Uh oh, Jane," Zeke was waving her over to the phone. "Kendall Billings is calling from the Inn. He says his housekeeping staff found a bag of jewelry tucked behind the TV equipment in the Inn's parlor. The bag looks like it's embroidered with Fern Herinton's name. I think that's Nathan's mother."

Jane gripped the Public Safety table in a show of mock distress, but that's exactly what she really was feeling. How her idyllic island occupation had accelerated in recent days into a tornado of illegal and occasionally fatal endgames was beyond her imagination. She was tearing up the century-old turf of wealthy, genteel Island life on the one hand, by hauling Nathan Herinton in before a verbal firing squad. She'd just lost a longtime, down-to-earth resident to death in an ice chest. And a call had come in a half hour ago about bellowing cows who lived on a small dairy farm located across the road from an enclave of semiconductor multi-millionaires who didn't like the sound of it. Not a typical Wednesday by any means.

"Zeke, please ask Kendall to bring in the jewelry right away and we'll take it from there," Jane advised.

She grabbed the other phone and dialed the Herinton residence. "Mr. Herinton, so sorry to bother you again, but could you please come down to Public Safety for just a few more questions? Twenty minutes or less, I promise."

Storm and his team were due back on the island on Thursday, and they hoped to return with all the findings from the State Lab and additional insights from the Medical Examiner. Anything biological or chemical, Jane hoped, to help them leap-frog out of the inconclusive swamp of disconnected facts they had been wallowing in since Saturday morning.

Helen set out some cinnamon raisin walnut rugelach, which Jane prayed would soften the blow for Mr. Herinton when he arrived for his second interview. She wasn't at all polished about handling caustic witnesses, and with Storm and Finn absent, Jane held her breath that Nathan's interview would proceed peacefully, if not smoothly.

While she waited for this Son of the American Revolution to take his time getting to the Public Safety Office, Jane telephoned the State Medical Examiner's office.

"Jane Roberts. It's you again." Sean Peters, her autopsy contact at the Medical Examiner's office, sounded delighted. "Looks like you're joining our frequent flyer club."

Ha ha...bet they're full of pithy lines. "Hey, Sean...thanks for all your help on the Ruth Farrow case. We couldn't figure things out without your input, that's for sure. So, I'm calling to check on the Shirley Jensen case. Has your office been able to determine the cause of death?" Jane was crossing her heart, legs, ankles, arms, eyes. Anything to have this be a suicide (as tragic as that would be), rather than another murder.

"Glad you called, Jane. If you could hold on a moment, I'll check on the status. Just give me a second." Jane sat at her desk suspended in time. *It'd be nice to be home baking whole wheat walnut bread right now,* she thought. *Maybe I need a break, or at least a yoga class. I have to stretch something—bread dough, my glutes, something—before I lose it.*

"OK, Jane, Storm is bringing you our official findings with him on Thursday, but I can tell you we've logged in Shirley Jensen as a self-inflicted death. She had an enormous amount of aspirin and Ambien in her system, plus an awful lot of Vitamin C."

"Vitamin C? What's with the Vitamin C?" Jane pressed.

"It may be Shirley Jensen wasn't totally sure of everything she was taking and she just gobbled everything in sight. The investigators found no evidence of other individuals in the house, except for your Office Manager, Zeke Pendleton, and no other outside DNA."

"So, you're suggesting Shirley Jensen took leave of this life by bending her drugged self over, plopping into the freezer case, pulling the lid down, and calling it a day. Are you serious, Sean?"

"Jane, I know it sounds bizarre and gruesome, and it's both of those things and sad. But that is essentially what our findings conclude."

"Actually, Sean, I'm relieved to hear this. It means no murder. Thank you!"

Jane took a moment to sit back and wonder about Shirley Jensen's world. Had Shirley had a lonely life? How fatal was loneliness? Jane doubted the word "Loneliness" ever appeared on a death certificate as a cause. And maybe Shirley Jensen had not led a lonely life, given the cat jungle she called home. She was a pure example of people who find a niche in life that clicks, and they never leave. They grow old in their niche, doing the same thing day after day, year after year, allowing the contents of that niche to pile up around them until, in the end, it consumes them. Like Shirley. Taking in stray cats and taking care of them for decades. First one cat, then two more, then ten, until the cats—all fifty-plus of them—the cats' needs, the Niche, all of it became Shirley's universe and her boss and her finale. Consumed by cat care. That was it. That's how she grew old and then died, without a parade of caregivers or mourners and heirs. But not alone. Not with all those cats.

....

Zeke had overheard the bulk of Jane's summary of Shirley's death and he looked at the small memorial he and Helen had created on a bookshelf near the reception desk. The statue of Buddha, plus daffodils and bleeding hearts from Helen's garden, were their way of acknowledging Ruth Farrow's fate, and now he guessed expansion plans would be in the works to include Shirley Jensen as well. Maybe they could add some fruit, even incense, if Jane would go along.

....

Nathan Herinton walked in and sat down at the Public Safety table without any ado. His imperious vibes were all it took to vanquish the staff's reveries about Life and Death.

He frowned at the jewelry and embroidered bag that Zeke had laid out. "Where did you get this?" Nathan asked.

Jane quickly joined Nathan and said, "Thank you for coming in again, Nathan. You do recognize this jewelry?"

"Well, yes, I do. It's my mother's. How did you get your hands on this?"

"Nathan, we're in a delicate position, so please forgive me if I'm overstepping any boundaries. But we're concerned that perhaps you realized, at some point between last Wednesday night and Thursday night, that some of your mother's jewelry was missing. Is that possible?"

"That is not possible."

"But if you had noticed the pieces were missing, might you have questioned Ruth Farrow, and if she denied the theft, might you have become angry about it?"

"Jane, this is pure speculation on your part. Pure fabrication. You're really out of bounds." What little remained of Nathan Herinton's superficial civility had just fallen off a cliff.

"You see, Nathan, we have to explore all avenues in this case, and you are really the only person we know of, who got close enough to Ruth Farrow...."

"To kill her?" interrupted Nathan. "Jane, like I told all of you last time, I had nothing to do with her death."

"But if you had discovered somehow that Ruth took the jewels, would you have lashed out at her? Would she have fought back? Could some unexpected accident have happened, leading to her death? What aren't you telling us, Nathan?"

"Look. I am this far," Nathan's thumb and index finger were fused together, "from filing an official report of police harassment, or whatever your two-bit operation is here, Jane. What I haven't told you is that no matter how you got hold of my mother's jewelry, they're actually totally fake...they're all reproductions so she can leave her costume stuff on the island all year long and not have a goddamn worry about whether thugs will break in to steal it. Do you get my drift? The real goods are safe and sound in a deposit box at JP Morgan in Boston...and out of your reach."

Jane was flabbergasted and confused. Hurt even. "Why didn't you tell me this in the first place, Nathan?"

"Because I am sick and tired of being summoned in here unnecessarily. I just wanted to see how hard you thought you could push me; how low you would go to bust my balls. This 'Fantasy Felon' game you're playing is pathetic, Jane. I repeat. I did not kill Ruth Farrow and if you want to book me, go ahead. I'll just buy my way out. I can certainly afford the tab for freedom."

Helen walked back into the main room from Jane's office, and caught Nathan's eye as he got up from the table. "Thank you for taking the time, Nathan," she spoke to him kindly. "It was good of you to come by and help us figure out what happened to that poor girl. You'll give my best to your mother, won't you?"

Thank Heavens for diplomatic receptionists, Jane thought with relief. Herinton was probably on the verge of calling the Governor to shut down the PSO office.

24
Thursday, May 30

"Rather an arrogant guy, that Nathan Herinton, don't you think?" Jane was updating Storm, Finn, and Rajiv on their return to St. Frewin's. "His behavior in yesterday's interview was hardly charming. He's on such a high horse—a narcissistic blot on the New England character."

"Narcissistic, Jane?" Finn said.

"Too big a word for you?" Jane asked as she raised her eyebrows. "Nathan Herinton needs to fulfill his life, look for a job, fill out a W-9 form, get some kind of meaningful existence. I'm not saying he should be neutered at dawn," Jane said with a counterfeit smile.

In the background, Zeke was carefully removing the old sheet that shielded their white board festooned by now with stickies and bulleted points, but most of all question marks. He flexed his arms, ready to take notes.

"If he isn't guilty of murder, Jane," Finn said, "then maybe he's just highly insulted that you keep dragging him back for questioning."

"Yah, yah, yah, stand by your man," Jane mumbled mostly to herself.

"OK, OK. All right people—listen up. This is a busy day. We have the final reports back from the Medical Examiner's office and the State Lab," Storm announced. "And the Iowa State Patrol sent us their additional findings on Ruth Farrow. Now's the time to piece together all the parts of the puzzle. Rajiv, please begin with the Medical Examiner's findings."

Rajiv straightened up. "Ruth Farrow, age 31, of Wheatshare, Ohio, died as a result of suffocation sometime between 9 PM, Thursday, May 23 and 5 AM, Friday, May

24. I understand the Medical Examiner already reviewed with you the sequence of events: victim knocked unconscious at the back of her head and hands tied behind her back in one location; victim then moved somehow to the spot where the body was found, with a lobster forced into her mouth and throat, and stones pushed up her nose.

"Photographs taken at the scene of the crime support this conclusion," said Rajiv, pointing to the white board. "There was very little sign of struggle or activity heading into the site of the body, nor at the site of the body—that is, not much evidence of broken branches or trampled areas."

"That's right," Finn said. "That's how the crime scene photographs looked to me."

Rajiv continued. "After the murderer forced the lobster into her mouth and placed the stones in her nostrils at the crime scene, within about ten minutes, she was dead. Photographs of the scene suggest that before those ten minutes were up, the victim somehow regained consciousness while lying on the ground. She struggled in place for a very short time before she lost consciousness and then died as a result of suffocation."

"No DNA evidence other than the victim's was detected on the ground where the body was found. Heavy rains late on Thursday night washed away all traces of external evidence—footprints, blood, fragments, fibers, etc. With the exception of the footprints of Jane Roberts and Maggie Banner and the dog from the following night."

"Can we please hold it there a moment?" Jane broke in. "Remember how Dr. Kerner said we should be looking for a bloody blanket or blood in a car? Due to the blow to the victim's head. We need to think about what happened to that mess, which ties into the killer's 'means.' Is there a bloody blanket or car out there? How do we find one or both?"

"Good point. Let's keep the question of the killer's means in front of us," Storm nodded. "Go ahead, Rajiv."

"Tests of the victim's internal bodily fluids identified semen from Nathan Herinton alone. And one final forensic finding. Ruth Farrow had dyed her hair black, but she was actually a natural blond." More succulent details for Zeke to add to the whiteboard.

"Also," Rajiv noted, "I collected one discarded piece of foiled-wrapped chicken near the crime site, which I'm in the process of analyzing for DNA. I'll get back to you on that shortly."

"So, we're left with the same question. Who was able to get close enough to Ruth Farrow to hit her and tie up her hands?" asked Storm.

"Let's assume Herinton didn't kill Ruth. Then what do we have?" Finn said.

Rajiv interrupted. "Excuse me, Finn. I tend to agree with your assumption. I don't think it was Herinton who left the body, because it's simply too close to his property."

Finn picked up the State Lab report. "The investigators found no blood, nothing at the Herinton property that would suggest violence on site. Ruth's fingerprints and DNA showed up in a variety of locations in the home—kitchen, living room, bathroom, bedroom, and in Herinton's car. But nothing else incriminating."

"So, let's assume Herinton is telling the truth," Storm said, "about dropping Ruth back at the Inn on Thursday night around 9:30 PM. Then what? Did she go out again? Is there anywhere to go on the island for social activity after 9:30 PM on a Thursday in May? Probably not, according to Jane and Zeke."

Jane and Zeke nodded in agreement. Finn kept going. "So, the shops are all closed in the evening. The pub people did not remember seeing Ruth again after she left with

Herinton. But even if she did meet up with an acquaintance or a stranger, maybe while taking a stroll, going down to the shore, then what? What brought on the attack? Her body shows head wounds, but no internal DNA except for Herinton's and the victim's own. So, it doesn't look like rape, or at least not a successful rape. Someone wanted to kill her, but did not violate her sexually."

Storm suggested, "Let's hold that thought for now. So, did Ruth stay at the Inn after Herinton dropped her off? If she remained at the Inn, the only people who admitted being present were Kendall Billings and a few of the foreign staff, and by around midnight, Zara Billings was also back at the Inn. So, either Ruth left the Inn and ran into trouble, but we have no leads there. Or she caught up with Kendall, Zara, or the staff and something went wrong."

"Why are we so quick to dismiss Nathan Herinton?" Jane asked. "Maybe he was driving Ruth around and stopped his car. Maybe they got out and he managed to knock her out and then tie her up. Then came the lobster and stones. And he just happened to leave the body where he did. So what?"

"What's his motive, Jane?" asked Storm. "If Herinton had the opportunity and the means, what was his motive?"

"I don't know," Jane sighed. "Maybe his story about his mother's fake jewelry is a lie. Or what if Ruth threatened to tell Nathan's fiancée? What if that freaked him out and they struggled and she somehow got clunked?"

"Doesn't make sense, Jane. Finn checked with the Boston bank about the Billings jewelry...it pans out. We didn't ask Herinton if Ruth knew he's engaged to be married. But that kind of motive—Nathan attacking Ruth because, what, she was going to blackmail him? That seems pretty thin to me." Storm shook his head. "Nevertheless, let's check with Herinton on that point."

"So back to Mr. and Mrs. Billings," Finn continued. "They both had the opportunity and the means at some point after 9:30 PM on Thursday night. What would their motive be?"

Jane frowned. "See, this is the point I made the other day. What possible motive could Kendall or Zara have? Why in the world would either one of them, or both of them, commit a murder at their own Inn, kill one of their guests? That is the most idiotic marketing plan I ever heard of."

"Look, for any of these people who seem to have no motive," Storm summed it up, "we lack some vital piece of information that would explain their motive. What don't we know about these people that led one or more of them to murder Ruth? That's what we need to find out. OK. Next, Finn has new findings from Iowa law enforcement, but let's take a quick break first."

25
Thursday, May 30

"OK, about the new findings from Iowa law enforcement," Finn announced when the team sat down again. "It turns out Ruth Farrow's original name was Anna Stedman. Her parents, Benjamin and Jean Stedman, went to court in Iowa to have Anna's entire name legally changed to Ruth Farrow at age eighteen. There's nothing in the records to document why the parents requested the name change." Zeke stepped back from the whiteboard and stared at Finn.

Finn kept speaking. "So that may be something we need to follow up. The parents died in the past few years, and there are no other known relatives in Iowa. Also, the local Wheatshare police are keeping an eye on Ruth's apartment and checking her mail. Nothing of interest so far."

Zeke threw out his hands in astonishment. "Bloody Hell!" He looked around at everyone present, his eyes full of incredulity. "I definitely remember Ruth, or, well, Anna Stedman. Everyone on the island does. Helen, you remember what happened, right?" Helen looked up from her typing at her receptionist desk, quite a startled look on her face.

"Yes, I do remember," she said slowly. "Such a tragedy, for the family that was killed, and for Anna...." Helen's voice petered out and she stared at them in shock.

"This is just too blooming barmy," Zeke left the whiteboard and took a seat at the table. "It's so strange that we've been talking about St. Frewin's not being connected to the web. It all has to do with Anna. I mean, the reason the islanders voted to get rid of WiFi and the internet so long ago was because of Anna Stedman. She was the teenager who was driving the car that killed a whole family...mother, father, five little kids. She was on her cellphone when it all happened. It was the most horrible car accident we'd ever had on the island. Everyone was so shocked. So they banned cellphones."

"Unbelievable," Jane said quietly, putting her head in her hands. "This is all so wild. Ruth...you know, I'm going to keep calling her Ruth, because that's what I'm used to. What you're saying is that Ruth is the person who was on her cellphone when she hit the family in the other car. How strange. I guess I never thought to ask. I didn't know her name. I just knew about the accident generally and that the family all died. But I never knew what happened to the girl, to Ruth, that is."

"I remember she was in really bad shape from the crash...lots of injuries," Zeke started to reminisce. "And she got amnesia that didn't go away. I think her family left the state soon after the tragedy. I don't know what happened after that. They lost touch with people, and I don't recall hearing much more about them. Is that about it, Helen?"

"Pretty much," Helen said, grief still gripping her face.

Storm looked at all of them and knew he had to reign in this flood so they could concentrate on pulling the facts together.

"OK, let's start fresh here. Based on what Zeke's just said, we now know Ruth Farrow was on St. Frewin's Island when she was a teenager. She has a car accident while on her cellphone and kills a family, she herself has serious injuries, she can't remember anything. Her family moves away, they change her legal name. Fast forward to now, and she's living in Iowa, she gets a job as a moderator, her company sends her to St. Frewin's on a health retreat. She meets Nathan Herinton and gets involved with him, he drops her off at the

Inn late on Thursday night, and then something happens that ends with her dead."

Storm pondered what he had just said, and from the looks of his colleagues, most everyone else had also reached the same conclusion. "Could the car accident somehow figure into her death? There are far too many coincidences here. We need to know more about what happened. We need confirmation of what Zeke just told us."

Storm looked across their faces and said, "Finn, I want you to return to the mainland and find out about the accident. We want the fatal collision report, newspaper reports, maybe hospital records on what happened to Ruth in the accident, what happened to the family that died. Did they have other family on the island? I guess what I'm driving at is this: Did whoever kill Ruth have an important connection to the accident? Was revenge involved? Some kind of payback?"

"Wait a minute," Jane said. "I think there's another angle that also links us to the old car crash. Let's look at the lobster for a minute. It's really the strangest part of this murder. We know the lobster...and the pebbles up her nose...were what actually killed Ruth by choking and suffocating her. But it's such a weird method, don't you think? I mean, a lobster? So freaky and assertive. Psycho in a way."

"You think the murderer was making a twisted, unconscious point in silencing Ruth with a lobster?" Storm suggested.

"Oh, sure. As in 'Shut your trap'?" Finn looked skeptical.

"Well, yes, actually," Jane said. "Something like that. So, the old accident just might help to explain the lobster. Maybe the killer was intensely obsessed with making sure Ruth wouldn't talk about the car crash. Like the killer's mental state was in a pressure cooker. Enormous fear that kept rising and rising could motivate the killer to shove that lobster down Ruth's mouth to shut her up permanently—and symbolically. But why?"

Jane began gesticulating. "What did Ruth know? What did she know that was connected to the car accident? Was it something the killer could never allow people to hear? Something the killer was insanely afraid to have revealed…afraid enough to murder Ruth Farrow? God, I feel like the killer's vibrations are coming through right now." She gripped herself tightly.

Finn sat there staring at Jane. She had taken on a strange energy that made her look like some gangly Wonder Woman trying to talk and use sign language at the same time.

Jane continued. "And maybe it's significant that the killer broke up his so-called tasks into two stages. First he knocks Ruth out and ties her hands. Then he stops, presumably transports her to the body drop location in the woods, and completes her murder with the lobster and pebbles. Why did he do that? Was he too out in the open wherever they were standing when he hit her and tied her up? Maybe he felt too exposed to do more at that point. Maybe that's why he then brought her to the woods. So, he'd have more privacy to finish the job."

"Well that raises the question," Storm said, taking up the analysis, "of where the murderer and Ruth were when he knocked her out. Where did the murderer first encounter Ruth? Was that location significant to the case?"

"If we think the old car accident has something to do with all of this, maybe we should look at where that accident occurred," Jane suggested.

"I can help with that. Hold on." Zeke got up and went over to the St. Frewin's map hanging on the office wall. "The accident happened a bit south of Herinton Point, over here on Partridge Lane. If Ruth Farrow and her murderer were anywhere near the old accident, Herinton Drive is right up the road from there. And it's secluded, off the main drag."

The Public Safety phone started ringing. Helen answered the call, and motioned for Jane to take it. She punched the call into Jane's office, and Jane left the main room for her desk.

Rajiv thought of something else. "In the interviews, didn't someone say Ruth had flashbacks recently? What were those about? Could they be important? What am I remembering?"

Storm quickly leafed through the interview transcriptions. "Yes. One of Ruth's co-workers mentions Ruth started to have flashbacks and headaches at work." He shuffled more pages. "And Nathan Herinton said Ruth talked about flashbacks, but he said it didn't make sense."

"Do you think we should ask him in again for another interview?" Finn quipped. "Jane would love that, wouldn't she? Ha ha!!"

"We could, but he said he was on his way to Nantucket, didn't he? Let's call him and press him for any other details about Ruth's flashbacks. And let's hang on to Jane's analysis of the car crash and the murderer's desire to shut Ruth up as we move forward," said Storm. He got up from his chair and twisted his generous torso left and right. "At this point, we should go hit the pub for some lunch. Afterwards, Finn can catch the ferry back to do more research. And Rajiv, you're already scheduled to return to your office this afternoon."

"That's right," Rajiv nodded.

"So, we're on hold until Finn gets back to us with more info. I also heard from our chief at Homicide Headquarters. He's due in today on the ferry to have a look at what we're working on." Storm lowered his voice to a whisper of feigned concern. "He wants to know why we're blowing his homicide budget on all these lobster rolls and B&Bs, without any murderer in cuffs yet."

As the group picked up and prepared to go to lunch, Jane emerged from her office looking distracted. "Naturally, in the midst of this major murder investigation, I get called away on cow duty," Jane moaned. "This job is such goulash...."

Storm waved her towards the door. "Jane, tell us the whole thing at lunch. We're off to the pub and I think some food in your stomach will make a whole lot of difference for you."

"Thanks, Storm," Jane said, putting on her jacket. "I'll catch up with you guys later. First I have to run out to deal with this meltdown on the other side of the island—we've got some semiconductor multimillionaires complaining about bellowing Holsteins. I'm sure I can handle it. I won't be cowed!"

26
Thursday, May 30
Early Afternoon

Jane turned her truck in towards Stan Helmstadt's dairy farm and sucked in her last deep breath free from cow farts, which would have to last her lungs for at least the next twenty minutes while she planned to discuss détente and strategy with Stan on his front porch. His bovine Wagnerian divas were allegedly interfering with the REM sleep cycle of his neighbors down the road each morning at 4 AM.

These neighbors were the Texan semiconductor multimillionaires getting an early jump on their summertime peace and tranquility at their summer cottages. Knowing a thing or two about cattle, they were itching for a brawl about their expectations of beauty rest. And if they couldn't have a good old brawl, they were determined to buy out this last working dairy farm on St. Frewin's, which Jane wasn't so sure would be the correct path to resolution.

Jane loved fat free milk and she loved Petit Basque cheese and Gjetost. But cow patties were the last thing she wanted on her boots (*Yes. She had remembered to change into her Muck Boots at the office. Good Girl, Jane!*) or her car wheels, so she drove very carefully up the farm driveway and parked in what looked like a narrow, manure-free zone off to the side. She peered exceedingly closely and downward as she stepped out of her car. So far, so good.

"Jane! Jane!" Rickety old Stan Helmstadt came bolting out of his farmhouse, still pulling on his hunting-orange flannel shirt over a somewhat dingy sleeveless undershirt, all hot to trot. Jane could not understand why he was so thrilled and ecstatic to see her. But suddenly he was hollering and motioning to her to come this way with him. "QUICKLY. NO TIME TO SPAYAH!"

Being the responsive kind of person she was, Jane raced after Stan, who was half hobbling, have galloping around the side of his house and barn towards the cow field, with Jane in tow, and together, brave dairy farmer and brave Public Safety Officer plowed knee-deep into the biggest sea of cow shit Jane had ever seen or smelled or sunk into in her life. *(Muck Boots, Ha ha!! I have on MUCK BOOTS!)*

"THERE'S A COW GONE AWOL, JANE!" Stan bellowed some more as he parted the biblical waves of dung before him, his boots sucking up (schlupp!) and squishing down (thwunk!) with each valiant plunge forward. "I'm gonna run at that cow, SHOO HER over your way, and you're gonna STAND THEYAH with your aahms spread REAL WIDE so she'll know you're the BOSS and she won't try to STAMPEDE YA, OK? And then you're gonna kind a POINT THAT COW back towards the open paddock gate ovah theyah. GOT THAT, JANE?"

"Sure, Stan. Got it!"

In an instant, Jane steadied herself, improvising as best she could, her yoga concentration and mindfulness radiating through her body. Stan began rushing towards his black and white Holstein, flapping his orange flannel clad arms in the wind, and bellowing like a shepherd scorched on meth, "YEEE HAW, LITTLE MOMMA!" All of which inspired the runaway cow to commence bawling, and in turn, several bulls in a nearby pen took to bellowing and rocketing up a frenzy. "GIDDYUP THEYAH, SHUGGAH!" Fugitive Cow tore off like a searing missile.

Jane, now completely engulfed in a Holstein emissions vapor cloud the size of New Hampshire, flew into her mighty yoga stance of Warrior Two—Virabhadrasana—all limbs extended tautly. "SPEAK SWEET TO HER, JANE," Stan shouted. "Tell her it's SUPPAH TIME!"

Jesus Christ. Is he joking? This little monster needs encouragement? Jane could only hope she would be upright when this was all OVAH.

Prodigal Cow came stampeding straight for Jane, hitting about Mach 1 speed, her mighty, spindly legs drumming the earth, nearly breaking the island sound barrier with perturbed bovine yowling. Ahead of Momma, Jane stood poised, looking something like a scarecrow in her black V-neck shirt, stick arms stretched wide, big hairy weeds jumping out of her head, and screeching **"HANG A RIGHT! SUPPER'S READY, HONEY!"** The darling-faced beast cocked her head; she knew what those moos meant. Little Momma pounded towards the turn, zeroed in on Jane with a blast of hot urine as thanks, and flew into the paddock.

Beast and man. Cow-existence.

....

"You don't smell too sweet, Jane," the semiconductor grievant commented, wrinkling his bronzed nose as he and Jane stood on his elegant lawn some five minutes after she left Stan's farm. "By the way, I'm Salem Pratt." Semiconductor's designer sunglasses hid the rest of his reactions from her sight.

"We've got it all squared away, Mr. Pratt," Jane assured him. "I'm hoping you won't be startled out of your sleep at 4 AM anymore." She and Stan had agreed that he would try a solution he had been considering ever since the Texans started calling Public Safety.

"What did you and the dairy farmer decide?" Semiconductor Pratt was curious and more relaxed now, having finally stopped holding his breath.

"Well, believe it or not, with these new Holsteins Mr. Helmstadt got last year, he noticed how unhappy they've been the past two months or so with the time change to Daylight Savings. So he's going to put their milking schedule back on Standard Time, and that, he thinks, should take care of the problem. But if it doesn't, you know who to call!" Jane assured him cheerily, even as Salem Pratt backed off gingerly, too hesitant to go nearer. Jane was so full of cross-species bonding in that moment, she overcame Salem's resistance for him, grabbed his hand, and gave him a shake.

....

"So, tell us how your farm duty went, Jane." Storm gave her one of his wicked smiles, once she had changed pants and joined them at the pub. "Did you settle everything with Bessie the Cow?"

"You had to have been there, Storm. The case is solved. The farmer's going to keep his cows on Standard Time, believe it or not. But please don't ask me for details. What you smell is all you need to know. Ha ha!!" said Jane, cracking up and leaning forward in laughter.

Pub owner Connor Mulroy brought over more drinks for their lunch. Real drinks, during the day. They weren't supposed to imbibe alcohol before 5 PM on duty, but Storm gave them all his dispensation this once, and Jane started slurping on her Margarita.

She was thankful Helen wasn't there to see Jane burying her face in the citrusy liquid. Before they left for lunch, Helen had asked Jane if it wouldn't be any trouble for Helen to have the rest of the day off. "My son Josiah's been back for a visit—he thought he'd surprise me. It'd be nice to get to the mainland to drive around with him a bit. And honestly, this Ruth Farrow case has left me a little shell-shocked, Jane," Helen had admitted right up front. "I'll be in tomorrow as usual...don't worry."

"Boy, I am starting to feel exhausted," Jane yawned.

"Hang on just a little longer," Storm reminded her. "Don't forget, the Chief is due in on the afternoon ferry, and he'd like you to take him for a quick tour of the island."

"Heifer Ready!" Jane called out from her head flopped down on the table.

27
Thursday, May 30

What the HELL was Kendall doing in his wetsuit that night? WHY was he standing around in the rainstorm? That was the night they think Ruth Farrow was murdered, wasn't it? Was the wet suit to protect him from something? LIKE BLOOD AND SPIT AND FINGERNAIL SCRATCHES? Was he letting the rain wash him clean of Ruth Farrow?

The questions were racing up and down the stairs in Zara's mind, and some little knot of trepidation that had begun rolling around in her head days ago now felt like the size of a grapefruit. That damn sex tape had been the trigger. Although Zara could never be sure, the woman on the tape must have been Ruth Farrow. *(Not that Zara was about to ask K.)* And now that Farrow was dead, Kendall had to be at least a slightly smoking gun, right?

Of course, she could be wrong. She prayed to God she was wrong. The idea that her husband would be capable of murdering someone was so foreign, Zara couldn't bear to think of it. But here she was, thinking exactly that. *And why in the world did she return the tape recorder with that fucking tape in it? Why didn't she think it through? What an idiot, idiot, idiot!*

It was all Zara could do not to thrash herself 24-7. It was certainly proof of how shocked she had been that day...not so much by the idea of infidelity, but the rawness of its delivery. Or maybe deep down she was in a "pity me" state and wanted to leave the wild evidence in place so that others, at least Maggie, would get a taste of the crap Zara had to take from Kendall lately.

But now that Kendall had snuffed out that woman...if he had, that is, well, that changed everything. What would happen when Maggie heard Kendall and Ruth in heat on the tape recording? Would she recognize the panting duo? Or at least recognize Kendall? *And what would that say about Maggie if she did recognize Kendall?* Then again, how would anyone recognize him? Why would anyone? But it didn't matter. Maggie would probably run straight to Public Safety. And then what? The whole world would be listening to that tape.

It could go viral, for all Zara knew. Everything went viral these days. And then those detectives would haul Kendall in for more questioning. And Kendall would probably admit he was the fucker on the tape. But would the cops know it was Ruth Farrow on the tape? Would Kendall admit to that? Who else could it be? So there you go. Kendall would be carted away for lying earlier to the cops about not knowing Ruth Farrow. But was Zara sure it was Ruth Farrow on the tape? If not Ruth, then who? What a fucking mess! What a fucking mess....

These mounting anxieties distracted her from the immediate disaster control she and Kendall were now tackling in the wake of the harrowing news coverage about the Farrow death. Zara almost wished they could hire a consultant to usher them through all the details of this post mortem world. Kendall with his brash smirkiness kept joking he would have to check off the "homicide box" on their lodging liability insurance renewal application this year. At least they had one thing in their favor, as far as the Inn's viability—no one seemed to think the murder had taken place on their grounds.

Assuming Kendall did not kill Ruth *(because really, Zara, WHY would he kill Ruth???)*, if he and Zara could fend off any media disaster and public inquiries with aplomb for long enough, then maybe they would be in the clear in a few months. Only they would deal with the public's inquiries, not the staff. Zara and Kendall would decline all questions from the press or curious parties as prudently as possible, citing the State's need "to withhold information pending further investigations." Yes, they would field questions from booked guests or potential guests. But if necessary, they would refer only to "Ruth Farrow's passing," or the "tragic events surrounding" Ruth Farrow, rather than "the murdered Ruth Farrow" or "the victim Ruth Farrow." Language was very powerful. Words could make or break you if you weren't careful.

God, it was just so freaking inconvenient to have a family member kill someone. Zara wished there was an app she could turn to for "When Your Husband Kills a Woman." If she had the app, it would probably start with "Call A Lawyer." She certainly was NOT going to call the police. That new Public Safety Officer Jane Roberts was well-meaning and enthusiastic, but Zara could not bring herself to walk in with a murder report. Besides, (1) if K didn't kill the Farrow woman, then what would be the point of going to the police?; and (2) if K did kill the Farrow woman, Zara's primary goal would be to save herself and the Inn. Self-preservation. Forget Kendall—his goose was nearly cooked. And that's where her "insurance policy" might still come in handy. Justice, Zara decided, would have to take a back seat for the time being.

But WHY would he do it? Zara's internal rudder kept steering her life raft towards the looming wreck on the rocks. It was so fundamentally jarring, this feeling so vulnerable and almost guilty day after day. How naïve she had been to think that Moosehead Lake mystically cured her woes. That great body of water was a fucking mud puddle now, compared to the salvation she was going to need to survive all of this.

28
Thursday, May 30
Afternoon

"Now, Jane, this is not a warning or a reprimand by any means," Jane's superior officer from Major Crimes Unit-Central assured her. "But I'd like to suggest that you, Storm and the others make sure you're not gobbling up MCU's entire budget over here—what with all your complete shore dinners and overnights at fancy inns. We don't want the Governor's fiscal heavies coming down on us now, do we?"

A little disheveled from her late morning escapade in the manure department, Jane had only had a chance to rake a brush through her hair and throw water on her face, before retrieving Lieutenant Joseph Adderley at the State Ferry Terminal.

In his cotton twill pants, field coat, and Boonie hat, Adderley showed up well-outfitted for his jaunt to St. Frewin's—like he had just gone on a shopping spree at "J.T. Karl's Wild Open" and hastily jumped into his new clothes in the ferry terminal restroom.

He was a solid, Central Maine, white-collar professional, probably in his 60s, not so fat as many of his colleagues, and well-known on the force as a kindly man with a zeal for administrative results. The source of his slight limp was a mystery to Jane, but she was guessing the bit of flushed cast to his face might be due to a hankering for Glenfiddich.

As they settled into Jane's truck, she instantly saw the messy chaos of the interior with new eyes—Lieutenant Adderley's eyes to be exact.

"If you can just wait a second here, Lieutenant Adderley, I want to spritz this window a bit and wipe off some of that schmutz." Jane aimed her homemade vinegar detergent mix at the interior windshield while attempting to shield her superior officer from the droplets of cleaning liquid. She rubbed the guilty windshield spic and span with a pair of old sweatpants.

"There we go." Throwing the sweatpants behind her seat, Jane started scooping up a meandering trail of receipts and crumpled tissues, half of which were piled up around Lieutenant Adderley's feet. He was alarmed to think she'd be bending down to grab for garbage on the floor of his passenger side next and he quickly interrupted her. "That's enough, Jane. Good enough. But it does smell a bit strange in here, something cow-like it seems? Well, never mind. Nothing we can't live with. Let's head out for this tour Storm promised you would conduct for me."

Jane didn't have the heart or the energy to launch into her dairy farm diplomacy to explain the unusually earthy ambience they were sitting in, so she concentrated on motoring Lieutenant Adderley past the colorful food trucks and gift shops near the ferry landing and out along the pastoral island roads. She pointed out the entrances to the mansions of retired American statesmen and Wall Street kings along the way.

"Storm brought me up to speed on how the murder investigation is going, Jane. It sounds like it's taken a twist of sorts. Might mean more of MCU's budget flooding into the island for a few more days, hmm? Is that your take on it, too?" Adderley asked.

"Well, yes, Sir. We do need more time and information. Detective Finn Gallinen's going to research the car accident involving Ruth Farrow. We hope we can pull that information into a better picture of who knew our victim, Ruth Farrow, seventeen years ago, and why that person might want to kill her now. We still have a lot of unknowns."

"OK. I'll keep my eye on your progress, but I hope you realize, Jane, that you may be dealing with the entire population of St. Frewin's, as far as who knew this Ruth Farrow. It's a needle in a haystack, and both the needle and most of that hay must have known Ruth back then. Just keep me posted on all of that, OK?"

Jane nodded agreeably, not quite sure she entirely followed Adderley's logic of straw and forage.

"So, how are you doing in your job, Jane? Can you handle everything to your satisfaction?" Adderley continued.

"I hope I'm carrying out my duties above and beyond, Lieutenant. Lately it seems like I'm turning into a Mexican jumping bean...Public Safety out here really runs the gamut...OUIs, murder, mad cows. Who knows what the tourist rush will bring? But maybe you could ask Storm and Finn about my work. They've had a chance to interact with me recently, whereas I'm usually on my own out here...with the help of Zeke and Helen, of course," Jane noted, a bit hesitantly.

"As a matter of fact, Jane, I've done just that. And this isn't a performance review per se, and you shouldn't take this as any kind of a dressing-down. But I thought it wouldn't hurt to go over a few things that have come to my attention."

Jane clutched her steering wheel and looked at Lieutenant Adderley with a nervous smile. "Yes, sir. I'm all ears."

"Not to be hard, Jane, but I think we're all concerned that you're a bit of a loose cannon. Everyone likes a little irreverence now and then, but perhaps you display a bit too much of it? And disdain towards officialdom? Not enough respect for the people in your midst? Maybe you're too ready to pounce on others, spouting off on your pet philosophies too much, kind of a harpy, perhaps? What do you say to that?"

Nuclear flatten me, why don't you? was Jane's first, silent reaction. She almost wished she was back in the manure pile pacifying bovines with yoga.

"My apologies if I'm about to ask a blunt question, Lieutenant, but are those their words, Storm and Finn, or are they yours, Sir?" Jane was so mortified; she felt cornered. This WAS a dressing-down! A Drive-By Performance Review. Did those guys really say those things about her? So much for her dreamy thoughts of WARM and BULKY where Storm was concerned. Finn she could see relishing his complaints about Jane. Mutt and Jeff. Grrrrr!

"Yes and no, Jane. Yes and no. I'm just trying to give you a laundry list of tendencies you might want to soften up on a bit. You're in a job with public exposure that can be highly stressful on a good day. You're answering to all the public safety needs of this island's wide spectrum of inhabitants, seasonal and year-round. And now you have a stubborn murder on your hands where it seems there are no easy answers. I think your goal should be a level head and a steady hand. You don't want to go shooting off in all directions like the Queen of the Vortex of Tangents, do you? No, no, no. That's not the demeanor we aspire to at MCU."

Jane could not believe her flaming ears. But he wasn't finished.

"I have an idea for you, Jane. Have you ever read *Civilization and Its Discontents*? Freud talks quite a bit in there about repressing one's impulses for the greater good of society. You might find it interesting if you pick up a copy. Might get a few ideas to help tamp down your natural tendency to blast off at people."

I am the innocent lamb driving the butcher to my own lamby slaughter, Jane thought. On the other hand, Jane reminded herself she had received similar criticism over the years. She turned to Adderley with a suggestion. "Maybe I should take a day or two off from the murder investigation. Clear my head."

"I'll tell you what, Jane. Finn is researching the collision report about the car accident, among other things, but he's only going to pull a summary from the digital collision database. Full reports for accidents that occurred before 2003 are still archived in paper form at the Traffic Division in Augusta. Why don't you take a day off and head up there? Get out of your office and see what you can find in the original files. It'll do you good, and it may move the case forward."

As they approached the ferry complex, Adderley had Jane take a slight detour. "Let's stop at this gift shop for a minute. You can think about Augusta while I pick up a few souvenirs."

....

"So what do you say, Jane? A day in Augusta to get off the island?" Adderley asked on his return.

"That's a refreshing idea, Lieutenant. I'll make plans right away," Jane assured him.

"I also have a little something for you to tame your demons," Adderley said. "Here you go," and he handed her a small gift.

"This is so sweet of you, Lieutenant Adderley. What is it?" Jane asked, tearing off the wrapping.

She opened the box and jerked up in her seat. "Wait a minute. I don't understand...."

Adderley looked at her. "It's meant to be helpful, Jane. Just my little thank-you for our island tour. Shall we hang it up on your truck mirror?"

"Lieutenant Adderley, is this a joke?" Jane waved the contents of the gift in the air. "Hang this up on my mirror? What kind of woman do you think I am? I am not going to advertise something like this through the front window of my truck!"

Adderley looked at the G-string Jane was dangling in front of his face...a G-string smothered with tiny red-hot lobsters jumping up and down on a minute few inches of silky white fabric.

"Let me guess, Sir. Is this supposed to be a preemie lobster bib?"

"Oh...give me that," Adderley said, yanking the erotic lingerie from her grasp. "My mistake. Just a mistake. Hang on."

Jane watched him stuff the lobsters into one pocket and pull the same size gift out of his other pocket.

"This is for you, Jane. No harm done. We can forget the other thing, if you know what's right."

Jane accepted gift number two, but tucked it unopened on the dashboard.

"Thank you, Lieutenant. No problem at all. Now, should I bring you to the ferry for your trip back to the mainland?"

"Yes. You can drop me off at the ferry terminal. But I'm not planning on leaving quite yet. Mrs. Adderley is arriving on the last boat to join me for an overnight at a lovely inn she's picked out."

"Strictly homicidal business? ...maybe a little lobster?"

"Unequivocally, Jane." Adderley grinned conspiratorially, not skipping a beat. "And don't forget to forget everything that just happened. That's an order."

"Aye, aye, Sir."

29
Friday, May 31

Samantha Lloyd swung into a Public Safety parking space on Friday to pick up various permits for the annual "Solstice Spree" on St. Frewin's. Everybody loved the Solstice Spree! Or at least Samantha hoped they did. The event raised funds for important island concerns like affordable housing, the Island Library, the Annual Baked Bean Supper, and a vigorous recycling program.

Over the past few years, however, Samantha had noticed attendance at Solstice Spree was slowly trickling away. She finally sat the Planning Committee down and told them *enough* with choosing their Master of Ceremonies from the likes of Maine Potato Queen or Wild Blueberry Queen or Abenaki Sea Urchin Queen. Dowdy was not going to cut it this year. Samantha herself would find the perfect Master of Ceremonies to jazz up the stage and give Solstice Spree the jolt it was craving.

She had sat with the phone and badgered everyone she knew who knew SOMEONE until she found The Perfect Master of Ceremonies. Then, last week, Perfect MC called to cancel! The scoundrel! But Samantha's emotional makeup didn't know the meaning of anxiety or panic, so she calmly kissed goodbye her prized choice of MC, who just happened to be the star of a beloved *Masterpiece Theater* period piece and the British cousin of one of Samantha's friends on the mainland. If that person couldn't pull in the crowds, Sam didn't know who could. And now? Now she had to yank yet another juicy rabbit out of the hat. And what to do about the glaring, nation-wide news focus on the recent Farrow death? Solstice Spree was heading for shaky ground, and

Samantha could only hope things would calm down and firm up in a few weeks, wishful thinking though that might be.

What she needed was a huge magnet to draw in the crowds. Someone really spicy. Sam knew how to pack flavor into a meal. Now she had to figure out how to do that for a civic event...yet again. And quickly. She waved to several vendors and food truck owners piling in to the Public Safety parking area as she walked into the office.

"Hey Diddle, Diddle," Samantha called out when she saw Jane coming out of her office. "Your cow jump over the moon?"

"That is not funny, Sam," Jane snapped. Half the island had probably already heard about her romp in Stan Helmstadt's cow paddy.

"Oh, Jane, you are one..." and Samantha grabbed her to skewer her verbally in her ear, "grumpy lady. Ha ha!!" Then straightening up, Samantha said, "You know what you need, Jane? You need to enter the Chef Competition in Solstice Spree. You're a decent cook. You love food. It's totally you!"

"If I ever feel like myself again," Jane said wistfully. "What goes on with this competition of yours anyway?"

"Well, last year's cooking theme was Applied Physics, or something like that."

"How could that possibly appeal to anyone, Sam?"

"Come on, Jane. But you'll forgive me if I can't remember a single winner's dish from last year. You're right—the concept didn't really fly. I guess people lost inspiration when they saw the word Physics."

"Oh, Lord, you are a nutcracker," Jane laughed. Maybe I'll think about it. What's this year's theme?"

"Historical Events and Figures," said Samantha, her eyes lighting up. "Lots of potential there—like 'World War Stew'—that kind of thing."

Jane had to admit. She was almost feeling better now. And it felt good. Good to be out of the rut Lieutenant Adderley's critique had put her in.

"You'll have fun, Jane...no matter whether you enter the Chef Competition or not," Samantha encouraged her. "There's going to be theater, artists selling their work, food booths, games and music. Like a traditional English fête."

"I could probably catch some of the fun," Jane mused.

"Well, you can't miss the 'Speedo Shakespeare.' You know, St. Frewin's boasts quite a few thespians. Dr. John Leckman over at the Public Health Clinic, Grace Cleveland from Homemade Apple π, Connor Mulroy, Zeke— especially Zeke, even Stan Helmstadt. They all have a talent for acting. Wait until you see them...they're great!"

"Speedo Shakespeare?" Jane asked.

"You heard me. At first we were going to use 'Pseudo Shakespeare'—you know, the plays are take-offs of actual works of the Bard...spoofs really. But then we came up with 'Speedo Shakespeare'...it's funnier, a little sexier. Besides, a double entendre never killed anyone, did it?"

"You know, it just occurred to me, Sam. You should ask Torrance Balankoff if she'd be interested in helping with your Solstice Spree. She's got initiative. Give her a call."

30
Friday, May 31
Afternoon

On Tuesday Rajiv had begun his DNA analysis of the foil-wrapped chicken leg he had bagged at the crime scene. He suited up in his protective clothing and gear and retrieved his chicken bone from the DNA storage freezer where the bone waited patiently for his testing, safely isolated in its evidence bag, relatively free from the effects of heat, moisture, or microbes that might have seized upon the flesh under more favorable conditions.

Rajiv unwrapped the sample and looked at it carefully under the constraints of the non-contaminating unit of the lab. He could see the bite marks on the chicken that he had noticed when he first opened the foil packet. Those bites were precisely where he would collect saliva samples from whoever sunk teeth into the meat. That saliva contained cells from inside the mouth of the person who had eaten the chicken, and those cells would be the source of the DNA.

The DNA processing techniques had been improved and standardized over the past decade, but Rajiv still held the profound science in awe. DNA was the magnificent key to all of life. It was often a powerful key in understanding a violent death. Rajiv took a deep breath and held it as he began stroking the swabs for saliva DNA at the bite marks on the chicken. Over the next two days, he extracted the DNA from the swabs to determine how much DNA he had to work with. With that information, using test tubes and an enzyme process, he amplified the DNA into many thousands of copies he needed for his work.

About 0.1 percent of human DNA contains areas of variation, unlike the other 99.9 percent of DNA that all humans have in common. In Rajiv's world, this 0.1 percent was the heart of forensics DNA testing—what made each person nearly unique. Now, four days later, he was about to compare his 0.1 percent findings from his chicken eater's DNA to the DNA from people on St. Frewin's that the team had collected earlier. If he found a match between the chicken bone and one of the St. Frewin's donor's, then Bingo. While there was no guaranty the chicken eater was at the scene of the crime on the day of the murder, that person would need a good explanation for tossing fried chicken garbage where a dead woman had been found.

31
Monday, June 3

Jane and Zeke approached the city of Augusta, where the roads fed into one another like a merry-go-round to nowhere. Jane was fuming. "I don't understand how the state capital can be hostage to such a hodge podge of traffic patterns."

She maneuvered her truck through the Monday rush and around a rotary in a cluttered, uninspiring part of the city and headed over to the Maine State Police Traffic Division.

"Well," Zeke said, "I'm awfully glad you have a new Pine Tree-scented air freshener hanging from your truck mirror. Helps to muffle the cow manure odor."

"Aren't you the funny one, Zeke. We have Lieutenant Adderley to thank for that little gift."

Before Jane reached the Traffic Division, she dropped Zeke off at the Alzheimer Unit of the Chickadee Living Center, where his grandmother had resided for the past two years. Zeke made a point of visiting her as often as he could, and bringing her fast food for a change of pace from her institutional diet. He knew his grandmother loved the company and the attention, even if she barely knew who Zeke was.

"I'll be back for you around 1 PM," Jane told Zeke. "I'll come in and find you so I can say hi to your grandmother."

"That's cracking, Jane. Cheerio!" Zeke strolled towards the huge faux cottage exterior that suggested a fairy-tale life within. Jane watched him hit numbers on the exterior security console so the staff could buzz him in through the locked front doors. She thought this institution was the last place on earth she'd want to spend her own golden years—

puckered, nearly deaf, totally arthritic. She would prefer a minimalist designed complex...simple lines, lots of white, kind of Scandinavian...not all this Hansel and Gretelonian kitsch. But what would she care? She'd have mush for brains by then anyway, and it's not like there would be any younger generation to come visit her and worry about the architecture. Not even a dog. Maybe she should think about getting a dog.

As she pulled into the Maine State Police Traffic Division, Jane was relieved to see that this complex was more to her liking—minimalist design, simple lines, and kind of Scandinavian. Chalk one up for State government. But the aesthetics of the smart glass entrance were unfortunately diminished by numerous loud signs alerting the general public to SECURITY CHECKPOINT, RESTRICTED ENTRANCE, NO WEAPONS ALLOWED ...*Yah, KINDLY LEAVE YOUR ROCKET GRENADE AT THE DOOR.* What had the world come to? The thought often crossed her mind when she left St. Frewin's and entered the main stream of American life.

In the central hall, Jane pushed the elevator button for the basement level to begin her search for the records about Anna Stedman's car collision. Jane headed over to the clerk's desk and spoke with the middle-aged civil servant about her research.

He had a face you could not simply walk away from. Head round like a great white onion, big glossy eyes behind circular glasses, round cheeks, thick pink rubber bands for lips, a white hem of thin hair. He seemed so pale and peaked, she wanted to tell him never mind, let's go walk outside instead, so he could pump something into his lungs other than manila file micro dust and archival malaise. Oh well...maybe another time.

The Onion typed a bunch of words into his computer and asked Jane to have a seat at one of the visitor tables while he retrieved her records from a different part of the basement. "You can use our computers to search generally in our digital database, if you like," he said.

Jane looked around her and noticed it wasn't a full house today. In fact, except for the clerk, she had the whole basement to herself.

She sat down, input her search terms, and started scrolling through the multi-tiered crash data that appeared on the computer screen in front of her. The Bureau of Highway Safety offered an organized overview and pointed her to a higher level of crash searching.

She clicked on that cue and up popped a surprisingly colorful screen with the Maine DOT message "Welcome to the Maine Crash Public Query Tool!" ...like streamers floating down on rainbow paper napkins...party time! It was a really friendly greeting, considering she was about to pore over "a wide variety of crash statistics including date/time, environment, driver, and much more!" She would be able to "easily view where crashes are occurring in your community." Wow.

The DOT was so upbeat about vehicular destruction and the loss of human lives. But in their defense, once everything landed on their desks, all that was left was data bleached clean of blood and guts by the force of time and bureaucracy. Maybe DOT's goal was simply to provide a user-friendly digital environment for the actuaries and statisticians who would be plodding through the State's crash info.

In fact, Crash Query Tool was amazing. It offered Jane Location, Year/Trend, and four flavors of crashes. She input St. Frewin's, 2003 (one year after Anna Stedman's crash), and "fatal crash" and then hit "Submit Query." A picture of a red-ringed speedometer came up with a blue needle on ZERO crashes. Phew. That sounded accurate. Jane was only aware of the island's fatal cellphone crash in 2002. Just to be safe, she repeated her cues for the years 2004 through 2018. All clear for fatalities.

Jane began to fathom the fascination of these neat and tidy statistics. Everything you would want to know, on a plate with a fork and knife, ready for you to consume and digest. Jane next clicked on her county, Abenaki, plus the year 2013 (unlucky number), and again, she clicked fatal crashes. Whoa! The blue needle zoomed over to 6 on the instrument dial.

Immediately below the instrument dial were more bar charts and graphics in the vibrant colors of a Monopoly game—red, pumpkin, mustard, green, purple, lavender, pink, bright blue. These choices tracked Month, Day of Week, Time of Day, Type of Crash, Road Surface Condition, Weather Condition, Light Condition, Posted Speed Limit, Driver Sex, Driver Age, Driver Action at Time of Crash, Driver Condition at Time of Crash, Driver Distracted By, Vehicle Type...OMG! So many choices. Jane needed oxygen. God help her...if that clerk didn't show up soon with Jane's paper files, she might never get out of this basement—the statistics were burying her alive.

What did make the stats so useful were the clusters Jane began to identify as she input and re-input year after year, randomly across the State, slowly compiling her findings. The clusters showed that most fatal collisions occurred *on a clear day* (depressing), a *dry* day (surprising), during Saturday afternoons, *males* (it figures) driving passenger cars in 45 mph zones, seatbelts used, driver not distracted (Yah, right), no contributing driver factor (Oh, sure), no driver condition, and then, bam, cars went off the road.

In other words, the message of the data, as far as Jane could tell, was that mostly men tended to kill themselves and others on perfectly pleasant Saturdays when they were simply driving around and then their cars went off the road...Period. It was almost as if Fate took the wheel every time. What else could it be? Jane noticed there were no schematics to show how many incidents may have involved operating at a speed *over* the posted limit...hmm, but then again, without witnesses, it wasn't like decedents would be in any shape to sheepishly admit having crashed at 80 mph in a 45-mph zone.

"Ma'am?" ...*Oh! Holy Shit.* He'd scared her! The clerk had arrived back at Jane's table with the paper file on Anna Stedman's accident.

Jane came back to earth and thanked him for his help. The file he handed her was thin; the typed collision report inside was all of one page and vanilla in content, a skin and bones document. It wasn't quite the eight-inch-thick redweld stuffed to the gills with detailed photographs and witness statements that Jane had been hoping for.

Jane went back to the clerk and asked him about the original evidence file in the matter. He checked his computer records a second time. His answer wasn't what Jane expected. "Interestingly, Officer Roberts, the original evidence file never left St. Frewin's. Before the digitizing program began in 2003, most material from rural communities, including most of the islands, stayed put where the collisions occurred." Well, there you go, Jane figured. Her coming all the way to Oz in Augusta was kind of like Dorothy and Kansas and all that.

<h1 style="text-align:center">32
Monday, June 3
At Night</h1>

Jane lay in bed, the neurons in her overloaded brain stuffed and crackling with the information she had digested from the Maine DOT website. What a relief to be horizontal at the end of the day. She finally had a chance to let all her muscles collapse and time to ponder in silence the details of her waking hours.

All those statistics about crashes...good grief! It occurred to her that the data was both a revelation and a confirmation of the fatal end results for people who drove like her own father. Dad never flinched when charging the wrong way down one-way roads in unfamiliar territory on narrow city streets. "Where'd you learn to drive? Sears Roebuck?!" yelled one horrified driver all those years ago; others would wildly wave their arms and honk, which only made Dad laugh.

Jane replayed her memory of their family vacation to Disneyland...her father repeatedly turning to talk to her mother while doing eighty miles an hour on the southern California freeway, his eyes and attention oblivious to the traffic flying all around their car. Jane had watched her parents from the back seat, and she knew bad driving when she saw it. She grabbed her sister Desdemona's hand and silently recited Hail Marys to ward off the worst.

When Dad took up flying, the opportunities for disaster multiplied. People would tell her years later about his belly landings when he failed to lower the landing gear. And she would never forget that sudden blank, prolonged silence one Christmas, suspended in the sky in a snow storm, when it was time for her father to switch out of the empty gas tank in his twin-engine aircraft. With staccato beads of sleet stinging the tin can skin of the plane, he hesitated long enough for Jane to sense Death peeking through their tiny airplane window, in case her father forgot to open the line to the full gas tank. Clearly her father was a spaz, lousy at operating anything that could be launched into motion.

In contrast, Jane's mother had to be the steadiest driver who ever set foot in a vehicle. Never erratic, never making turns out of control or negligently letting the car glide into the oncoming lane. Her mother always got you where you were going—without incident, without a ripple.

Man versus woman...in cars. Who drives carefully? Who does not? A gender component had to play a role in all this, didn't it? Look at the Maine DOT data. Look at Jane's own upbringing. If there's a problem, it's more likely due to a man driving. It was true in her family; it played out in the stats.

Jane was starting to fall asleep, but she grasped the point as it slipped out of her ear and sat on her pillow all night. The *car*...was one place...where...sexism...had...a hold. The point was there smiling at Jane when she awoke the next morning in the half light. She smiled back. It would probably be just another fat-free-milk sunrise, but it would be a good one.

33
Wednesday, June 5
Morning

"You're coming to visit?" Jane tried to stay calm. What had Lieutenant Adderley said about a level head and steady hand? That's what Jane needed right now. And it had nothing to do with crime and safety. Especially if she took up heavy drinking right after this call. Her sister, Desdemona, was on the phone (!) and giving Jane ample warning (one hour) that Desdemona would be arriving on the ferry later that Wednesday morning.

"It will be great to see you, Jane! My first time on your new island. Don't worry about me at all. *(Never,* Jane thought.) I'll have my car (Jane winced—*that loud, red Alfa Romeo)* so you don't have to come pick me up. And I've got my Chamber of Commerce map with your office depicted on it with a little gold star at the center of St. Frewin's, so I'm all set. I'll come by Public Safety shortly *(What?)* to say 'Hi,' and you can point me in the direction of your house. *(No way!)* How's that sound?"

"Wow, Desdemona. I had no idea you were in Maine. What brings you to Maine at all?" Jane wondered.

"Oh, we're just here to scout out some locations. Nothing too involved at this point. And I can want to come see my little sister, can't I?"

"Hey, nice surprise, really, Desdemona. OK. I'll see you when you get here." Jane's head went back momentarily in a gesture of supplication to the gods. Then she added, "And call me if you miss your ferry *(or fall off the boat...Ha ha!!),* take a wrong turn and get lost...anything. But please keep a lid on it while you're here."

With that Jane hung up and collapsed into her office chair. She wasn't prepared for this. She was never prepared for Desdemona to visit. The successful, *very* successful, older, taller, gorgeous, busty (Jane refused to say "sexier") sister, whom Mom always liked better. Well, maybe Jane was exaggerating on the sibling rivalry front, but still, Desdemona was the one to whom Mom had given most of her Spode china over the years. And now Desdemona was to descend on Jane's office in one hour, which would be exactly when Storm and Finn would be meeting with Jane to review Finn's research and pierce the mystery of Ruth Farrow, fka Anna Stedman. *For God's sakes, BUCK UP, Jane!*

34

Wednesday, June 5
Late Morning

"So here's what I found out about Ruth." Finn began to read from his notes, methodically cataloguing the dead woman's tragic youth for Storm and Jane, who were sitting with him at the Public Safety table. "Seventeen years ago, on July 27, 2002, St. Frewin's Public Safety Officer Randall Crunby responded to a call from a passerby, Larry Traymor, who came upon a double car crash on Partridge Lane. Anna Stedman, age 16, was found lying injured and semi-conscious inside her parents' 1994 Toyota Corolla, with a cellphone in the car.

"The Toyota had crashed into a 1998 Buick Station Wagon owned by Martin and Rhonda Webber of St. Frewin's. The Toyota sustained substantial damage. The station wagon was demolished due to the force of the impact and subsequently rolling down a steep, rocky embankment. The Webbers and their five young children were killed or critically injured in the accident, and all of them died within hours. There were no known witnesses to the accident."

Finn continued. "The Webbers had no relatives on the island or in the State of Maine. At the time, Anna was a resident of Shipman, Maine, and had her driver's permit. She was visiting the island for the weekend with her parents, who had lived on the island about 15 years earlier before moving to Shipman. Anna Stedman was taken to Abenaki County General Hospital and ultimately to a rehab center due to both the significant injuries she sustained and a severe case of amnesia."

"Was she charged with any crime?" Jane asked.

"Actually, no," Finn answered. "Given Anna's minor age and her extensive physical impairment, the Abenaki County district attorney decided not to prosecute Anna for vehicular manslaughter or any kind of felony or misdemeanor and no civil damages. Anna and her parents moved away from Shipman, Maine, just months after the accident and settled in Iowa later that same year...2003."

Jane and Storm were looking at Finn and looking at each other, shaking their heads. The history before them was excruciating.

"I also called Iowa law enforcement concerning Anna's recovery in Iowa," Finn added. "Apparently she was in rehab for many years and did not regain her full cognitive abilities until some ten years later in 2013.

"According to the rehab center records, Anna had no memory whatsoever of the accident. The Iowa police further learned from talking to rehab staff that Anna's parents chose to shut the door forever when they left Maine. They decided not to tell Anna anything about the accident. It sounds like she had no idea what had happened and for all she knew, Maine was just another state in America. Mr. and Mrs. Stedman both died several years ago. That's about it."

"Excellent summary, Finn. It confirms and explains what we've heard so far. So, where are we after Anna, now Ruth Farrow, is a working adult? We know she began to have flashbacks," Storm said. "When we called Nathan Herinton and asked for more details about those flashbacks, he did recall that Ruth Farrow had mentioned that she thought Maine had something to do with those flashbacks. So it sounds like Ruth's arrival in Maine was merely coincidental to her flashbacks, but she herself was beginning to wonder if Maine somehow fit into the picture, though she didn't understand how. Jane, what did you find at the Traffic Division?"

"The one-page archive report I unearthed contains the same collision information Finn just reported. Nothing more than that. But guess what? I asked the archives Clerk if he had an original evidence file...maybe some photographs, or more extensive police reports. Something we could work with. And he told me they're here. On St. Frewin's. So...wait a minute." Jane raised her voice. "Zeke, where is Helen?"

Zeke called out from his desk, "She went to bring the processed vendor permits for the Solstice Spree to the Town Office. She's due back soon."

"When Helen's back, please ask her if she remembers where Public Safety stores the old evidence files on the island. She was working here in 2002. She must know something."

Jane then switched topics to her serendipitous crash findings culled from the basement computer at the Traffic Division. "So, listen to this. There's this crash query site sponsored by the Traffic Division that I started surfing through at their office. It summarizes all kinds of critical aspects of every fatal and nonfatal car crash in Maine since 2003. If you look across the state, year after year, it turns out the most common scenario for a fatal collision is this: A man driving on a Saturday with decent weather in a 45 mile per hour zone where the car goes off the road. It seems strange, don't you think?"

Finn interrupted Jane. "What do you mean by strange? It is what it is."

"OK. Let me finish," Jane said. "What struck me was that the statistical norm, or something like that, shows the most fatal collisions happening on an ordinary day under ordinary circumstances. All the things you might associate with an accident, like stormy weather, winter weather, late night hours, high speed zones, and so on, do not play as big a role. In other words, apparently the worse the conditions people are driving in, perhaps the more carefully people tend to drive."

Jane noticed Finn was yawning. "So, like I said, fatal accidents are most likely to occur when a man is driving in nice weather on Saturday at medium speed. Then I started to think about this pattern and how it might relate to Anna Stedman. I mean, there was an accident. People concluded she was driving because she was the only person found in the car. But we don't know one hundred percent who was driving, do we? Anna had amnesia and was never told about the accident afterward. So she was never in a position to talk about the actual crash. And from what we know now, Anna, or Ruth, had no idea anything happened, despite her recently having confusing flashbacks."

"So what's your point?" Finn pressed again.

"Well, if we don't have absolute proof that Anna was driving, then let's think about the statistical norm. The statistical norm suggests a *man* was driving the car."

"That's interesting and creative thinking, Jane. Go on," Storm said.

"So, that *man*, let's call him 'Person X,' may be the person who wanted Anna dead, before she finally recalled the truth about the accident. Maybe what really happened is that Person X, not Anna, was the guilty driver. And from that hidden guilt, locked away for so long, came the impulse to shut Anna's mouth permanently...with the lobster."

"But there's nothing in the record about another driver, male or female," Finn insisted. "The passerby who reported the accident did not see anyone other than the accident victims. There were no witness reports. There was no evidence of another driver."

"Wait, Finn. Let's freeze it right there," Jane said. "There were no witness reports. That's part of my point. No outside person saw what happened. If there had been another person driving, and let's assume that person left the scene, who would know? No one. But it's possible, isn't it? Person X may have been driving the car and after the crash, Person X ran away from the scene. Seventeen years later, Person X's life would be ruined if Anna, now Ruth, finally remembered the accident. So I want to find that old evidence file. There might be something in it that for some reason didn't get enough attention back then. It was such a traumatic accident, with so much loss, maybe some details got buried in the drama."

Jane sat back weary and hungry.

But Finn stuck to his guns. "I just don't buy your reasoning. I think you're trying too hard to force some fantastic revelation that will blow this whole case wide open."

"Finn, you can't standardize crime. Isn't that what you're trying to do here? You need to give your brain some leeway...let it be a slinky...stretch it freely and, in this case, work with the data." Jane said.

"Yoo hoo? Jane?" Desdemona stuck her head inside the Public Safety Office door and gave everyone a glowing smile. Jane felt slightly shell-shocked. Her sister really was a magical presence when she and her golden-red head of flowing long hair sailed into a room. But as Desdemona came through the door, Jane also saw her sister's Pandora Box begin to swell and raise its lid ever so slightly. Happened every time.

"Hey, Desdemona," Jane said. "Storm and Finn...and Zeke. Zeke? OK. Looks like he's gone out. Anyway, I want to introduce you to my older sister, Desdemona. She's come all the way from the West Coast."

Finn sprang up from the Public Safety table and offered his hand to Desdemona. She took it firmly, with mesmerizing eyes. Storm seemed to hold back a bit, politely, calmer than Finn's froggy leap into the air, in Jane's neutral opinion. She gave Storm points for that. Desdemona continued with smooth greetings...to Storm and to Helen, who had returned now from the Town Office.

"So, Jane, if you can sketch out for me how to get to your house, I'll leave you with the Law here and meet up with you for dinner tonight, OK? I'll pick up the fixings to make you a warm scallop salad with sliced apple, hard-boiled egg, crispy bacon, and mesclun. How about that?" said Desdemona, which in truth, did melt Jane's heart a smidgeon. Like sister, like sister.

35

Wednesday, June 5

"Now where were we?" Jane commenced after Ginger-Headed Goddess Sister had departed the building. "As you were saying, Finn, you don't like my theory that another person, statistically a man, might have been driving the car. But I think we should consider it a possibility, especially if we find any evidence that could be checked for DNA."

Jane watched Finn acting like he was listening to her, but he seemed lost in thought. "What is it, Finn?" she asked.

"Nothing," he said. "I'm trying to reach back into my hard drive for a memory, but I can't quite get to it. It will come to me...you know how déjà vu locks in and won't let you go."

He set it aside and summarized his opinion for Storm and Jane. "As I look at the big picture, I still think Anna Stedman was probably guilty in the crash. And what we have to focus on is the present...and who killed her...not some big *maybe* from seventeen years ago. No offense to your earlier comments, Storm, about a link between the murder and the accident, or to your analysis, Jane. I just don't think we should waste our time on ancient history."

Jane was already grumpy from Desdemona's call, and then her actual physical presence in Jane's office, and now Finn was deflating her brilliant idea, and Jane also thought back to Lieutenant Adderley's disapproval of her style—the only style she had, the style she doubted she could change. Her "emotional" back hairs started to wriggle, then bristle.

"So Finn doesn't agree with me. Fine. I'll pursue my line of thinking on my own time. But there's something else I want to discuss with you guys." *Or should I say Sweet and Sour*

Pork? Mutt and Jeff? She stopped short at Laurel and Hardy...she didn't want to insult Storm with a weight reference, though he really did need to lose some pounds.

Jane threw all work etiquette to the wind and began dishing out her insecurities. "Lieutenant Adderley told me he asked you about my work performance. And he had some rather strong things to say to me about how I interact with people. But in case you've forgotten, I never asked to be thrown into this Boot Camp for Murder. I'm trying my best to solve this thing with you guys.

"And it doesn't help if you run to Daddy Adderley to tell him I'm all over the map and kind of unhinged. How else am I supposed to handle my job and this murder? You've seen the stuff that passes through the door here. I've got an off-grid crematorium complaint that morphed into a frozen body. I've got high-tech neighbors crying about mooing cows, and I end up in animal shit as part of my job. Come on. Give me a break. Just accept me for who I am."

"OK, OK," Storm rushed to calm the waters. "Jane, the longer we've been here, we now see how much you have to shift gears and juggle different matters all day long. When we spoke with Adderley, it was just first impressions, that's all. Now that we've spent more time with you, it's helped us to see how we can work together, even admire your efforts and gumption."

"So that's a vote of confidence, Storm?"

"Sure, Jane. And it would help us if you'd accept us for who we are. It's all a big circle of give and take, easing off sometimes when you feel like revving up. Can we all live with that?"

Jane felt better already. She was glad she had spouted off, and she appreciated Storm's peace-making at the war table. "Yah, don't worry. I just needed to blow off steam. Let's get back to work. I'm glad you guys are here...seriously," Jane admitted, as much to herself as to them.

36

Wednesday, June 5
Afternoon

"Jane, as far as I know, any retired police files are stored in the basement at the Yacht Club," Helen was reporting. "I don't think there's too much down there, but maybe you can find something that's related to the old car crash."

"OK. Thank you, Helen. Let's hope we find something helpful. And Zeke's gone out?"

"Yes. He said he was going to Shirley Jensen's house to help some animal rescue folks who came over today. They're crating the remaining cats at the house. Sounds like they have their hands full. And Zeke said if you know anyone who wants a cat, just let him know. He's taking three kittens home with him."

"Oh, dear. That's a big job. And sweet of Zeke. OK...I'll be back later, Helen."

"I'll be happy to go with you, Jane, if you'd like," Storm offered. "Finn's going to catch the next ferry to get back to the office. But I'll stay to help so you're not stuck down in the basement all afternoon."

They set off in Jane's truck for the Yacht Club, traditionally referred to by locals and members alike as the "YC." At this time of the year, outside clean up and summer preparations were well under way.

When they arrived, Storm and Jane walked past gardeners staking supports around the fattening bushes of peonies about to bloom. Gardeners were also lurking in the hydrangeas and rhododendrons, busy whisking away the last of winter debris. Other workers were setting up the

Adirondack chairs and teak benches to welcome the private members making their way back to summer in Maine.

Jane and Storm entered the YC's expansive lobby, which was framed in honey-colored timber clear to the cathedral ceiling and packed with seafaring memorabilia—all slightly intimidating to Jane. Jaunty nautical flags in checks and stripes and crosses and Xs colored red, white, blue, black and yellow were streaming from the rafters; and fancy, shiny parts of old ships adorned the walls.

It all belonged to the world of WASPS, in Jane's mind. She had no idea what the flags spelled, though maybe they simply stood for "St. Frewin's Yacht Club." She didn't dare ask for a translation—that would blow her cover.

Storm on the other hand seemed right at home and started chatting it up with several of the sporty men and women manning their posts, even saying hi to some of them he knew, which surprised Jane. She heaved a downward sigh. Yacht Clubs and country clubs brought that out in her.

It all had to do with those damn Venn Diagrams—those multiple circles from 9th grade geometry class that overlapped or did not. Your circle either had something in common with another circle or circles (an overlap or multi-overlaps) or you had nothing in common, leaving two non-overlapping, separate circles. It could go on and on...some circles having mobs of overlaps with other circles, mushrooming into a kaleidoscope of happy overlapping concentric circles. While lonely solo circles just stood off to the side, looking around and hoping some day for a chance to overlap.

That's how Jane's circle ran around the rosy. She never quite seemed to crash through the boundaries of the super overlappers. She repeatedly tried to observe quietly on the fringe, hoping to tiptoe gently up to the edge and then catapult into the core of some black-tie circle where everyone was well-to-do and wore dresses that fit perfectly.

But she could never quite manage to make her attempted overlap overlap. It was like the super overlappers had a secret trampoline or something. She'd hit squarely in the middle of some super circles and then the trampoline would boomerang and whack Jane out of the super circles as fast as she could say "Venn." So, essentially, these days Jane lived day to day in her own modest circle.

Storm returned to Jane's side after overlapping with his apparently well-known circles at the front desk of the YC. "They're telling me if we can be quiet, their grounds manager, Mr. Yates, will let us into the basement for our search. The YC is courting potential new members today, and they don't want any disturbances."

"How do you know these people?" Jane asked.

"Oh...we go way back...from my sailor days," Storm said, without further elaboration.

37
Wednesday, June 5
Late Afternoon

The YC basement wasn't half as bad as Jane had anticipated, once Mr. Yates switched on the bank of lights hanging from the ceiling. At least the thick granite-block walls were dry, and no rats were scurrying around to hide from the invaders.

As she walked down the stairs to the tiled basement floor, Jane could see across the room to rows of bankers' boxes sitting on wire shelves against the far wall. She and Storm would have to wind their way through meticulously stacked shelves of life jackets, oars, coiled ropes, boat fenders, bumpers, paddles, seat cushions, inflatable rafts, folding chairs, and whatever other paraphernalia the YC had accumulated since it was first founded in 1840. But once they reached those bankers' boxes, therein might be Jane's mother lode of evidence.

As Jane turned to look around the rest of the basement, her jaw dropped when her eyes focused on the labels of cartons stored along the three other walls—*Johnnie Walker, Dewar's, Cutty Sark, Tanqueray, Gordon's, Smirnoff, Seagram's, Guinness, Maker's Mark, Remy Martin, Courvoisier, Bacardi, Mount Gay, Hendricks, Beefeater, Pouilly-Fuissé this, Pinot Noir that, JESUS CHRIST!* Seeing Jane's teetotaler shock and awe, Mr. Yates quipped, "I'll leave the two of you down here to do your work, but don't go getting thirsty on me."

"Storm," Jane whispered, as the grounds manager left the basement, "can you believe this?" she said to him, moving her arms in a big circle to take in the generous bulwark of alcohol. "There's enough of this stuff to marinate the entire county!" Jane was having second thoughts about trying to overlap with a YC circle any too soon, due to her realization that maybe it was a good thing her Venn circle hadn't overlapped a YC circle, because Jane's Venn circle probably wouldn't have survived all that booze sloshing around in her overlap region.

"Shh, Jane. Leave it. People need a buzz now and then," Storm said.

"You call this a 'buzz'? What distillery were you born in?"

They walked to the far wall and started in on the unlabeled banker boxes, boxes highest up first. Flipping through redwelds and manila files, it quickly became obvious the files from the year 2002 would likely be on one of the wire shelves towards the bottom.

Jane stooped down to the lowest boxes to pick through each box's various redwelds and files until she found a redweld labeled "Stedman Car Crash." She felt a slight brush of something go past her cheek and down into the files, and then she felt her ear and realized her earring had dropped down into the box. "Damn....I just lost my earring," she grumbled. "But I've found the Stedman file!"

Storm moved over to Jane's banker's box to assist. As Jane stuck her hand down into the box to feel around for the earring, she saw the file marked "Crash Report" in the Stedman redweld. A thin stack of handwritten pages appeared to contain the basic notes on the Stedman car collision that made up the official reports she and Finn had found at the State offices. Jane quickly scanned the notes and concluded there was no new information.

Meanwhile, Storm was down on his knees and swishing his hand around in the banker's box, feeling for Jane's fallen earring. He found a crumpled piece of paper way on the bottom of the box, partially buried under other redwelds. When he smoothed out the paper, he could see "Stedman Evidence 2002" written at the top. It contained the words

"cell phone—returned to Stedman" and "head sweatband."
A head sweatband? *What sweatband?*

"Jane, was there anything in the collision report about a head sweatband?" Storm asked.

"Not that I remember," Jane said and she looked over Storm's shoulder at the evidence list.

Storm, with Jane joining him on her knees, both started thumbing through all the redwelds and all the files in the box, looking for anything that looked like a head sweatband, but they had no luck. They found nothing they very much wanted to find. Except for Storm's one small victory.

"Jane, look at me a second." She turned towards Storm's face. They were quite close together, and she could feel the heat of his breathing. She could also see a deep peacefulness in his eyes. It was something she hadn't had time, or hadn't taken the time to notice during all their hours together at the Public Safety Office table. And then she felt how very gently he reached for her ear with his broad hand and hooked the wire stem of her earring tenderly back into place. His eyes returned to hers and Jane could not have told you how long they both knelt there, concentric circles suspended in time.

....

Something finally broke the spell. Jane thought it was her stomach growling for new input, but then she and Storm realized the grounds manager, Mr. Yates, had returned when he called down to them. "Detective Nosmot, a call's come in for you from the Homicide Office. Can you take it?"

"Let me see what this is, Jane. I'll be right back," Storm said as he rose from her side and headed for the stairs.

Jane was determined to find that head sweatband if it was the last thing she did before Lieutenant Adderley fired her for whatever odd reason he might come up with. Storm reappeared at the top of the stairs and called down to her.

"Jane—They need me back on the mainland. I've got to go Down East for a few days to help on another case. So, I'm going to have to leave you here. If it's OK with you, I'll take your truck back to your office, and then Zeke or Helen can come back for you when you're done. How's that?"

"Sure—fine. I'll keep digging," Jane answered while she sat there feeling crabby and at sea. She was positively steamy from that intimate moment with Storm, and she was negatively steamy now that he had to leave her awash in all these files. It was her feeling a bit plain old steamy about the missing sweatband that kicked Jane into high gear. But first she decided she needed a reward for her perseverance. *A sip, or two, or three, of Mt. Gay—who would ever notice ONE bottle gone? Give me a break.*

She began clawing her way through each banker box on the lowest shelves with a vengeance...redweld by redweld, file by file, each banker box a coffin for accumulated years of St. Frewin's Public Safety records. When she finally found that sweatband, she was going to make Finn Gallinen eat his words...or better yet, make him eat the sweatband. *Ha ha!!*

And Helen had it so wrong. There was a lot of stuff down here. Jane rummaged on briskly and methodically, on to the next shelf and then the next shelf of banker box coffins, waiting for her Eureka moment, any moment now. How could the head sweatband not be here, she kept saying out loud. How could it not be? Here she was on high alert for some narrow stretchy terry cloth miracle, but it was all getting boring. She started belting out a show tune in the spirit of her evidential quest:

Head Sweat Band, Head Sweat Band,
Am I going to find you?
Old and frayed,
Stinky gray,
Where the hell did they put you?

Head Sweat Band, did you disappear...?

Keep pawing around for that sweatband, Jane, keep pawing. You're now back in the files for 1992, and there's the "Statler Car Crash" file, and OH MY GOD...THERE IT IS. HALLELUJAH! MOTHER OF GOD, IT'S THE HEAD SWEATBAND IN ITS OWN SEALED EVIDENCE PACKAGE LABELED "STEDMAN EVIDENCE." HOW THE HELL DID IT GET MISFILED UNDER "STATLER"? MORON PEOPLE WHO CANNOT READ TO SAVE THEIR LIVES! BUT WE'VE GOT IT! WE'VE GOT IT!

...BLACK...TOTALLY BLACK...just like that. Everything was BLACK. Someone had turned off the lights. Jane's pulse blew a hole through her wrist, and she acted quickly to protect her precious sweatband booty.

"Hey, is that you, Mr. Yates? Storm? Are you there?" Jane called out. No answer. Jane stood still for a moment...didn't budge an inch. Didn't make a sound. If neither the grounds manager nor Storm had returned, then whose sly footsteps and breathing were approaching? Maybe it was just her imagination. Maybe a simple power outage? Maybe a Commodore of YC's ancient past was rising up to haunt the whole place.... Jane stopped breathing.

The other breathing did not cease. Jane had no clue where to duck, could not see to fend off a blow. The path of the oar slamming downward was infallible. The wood cracked sharply against her head. She did not see herself crash to the floor with droplets of her blood leading the way. And obviously she was not aware of the figure turning on a flashlight, looking frantically for something, not finding it, and silently departing as silently as the figure had come.

38
Wednesday, June 5
Evening

"Jane, Jane," shaking...someone was shaking her. "Officer Roberts...I'm here to help you." Mr. Yates was trying to raise Jane a few inches to place a towel wrapped around ice cubes under her bloody head. "Jane, can you hear me?"

Jane moved her neck slightly and was finally able to will her eyelids apart so she could see what was going on. Why was she on the YC basement floor and what was the sticky stuff all over her back? Not very pleasant, and the floor was cold!

"What, what...what saying?" Jane whispered back at Mr. Yates.

"Jane, you've somehow been knocked out by an oar and you're lying on the yacht club basement floor. I called Dr. Leckman and he's coming right over to check on you. Just hold tight. Don't try to move. And stay down...that's what he said...to have you stay still until he arrives. OK?"

....

"At least we have Desdemona's dinner to look forward to, instead of my having to cook after getting bashed in the skull," Jane remarked happily to Dr. Leckman, who was driving her back to her house. Fortunately, Jane was now in his excellent hands, instead of the clutches of her fleeting attacker.

Dr. John Leckman had been the General Practitioner on St. Frewin's for years. It was said he visited back in the 1980s and never really left the island again, except to pack up wherever he had lived and move it all to St. Frewin's permanently.

Given the island's remote location and the forces of Nature, over the decades, Dr. Leckman's practice had evolved far beyond routine GP care of his island flock. "Cradle to grave"—he covered it all, even now in his late 60s.

Another side of Dr. Leckman that everyone cherished dearly was his second set of professional credentials, completely laid out on the sign at his office, "JOHN LECKMAN, Medical Doctor and Doctor of Veterinary Medicine." Such a talented individual, was the majority opinion on the island, so long as he didn't use the same thermometer on both beast and man.

"I'd say you're quite fortunate, Jane. You're not showing any significant signs of concussion or internal damage that I can see. And those stitches we put in you should keep your brains where they belong. But to be sure, I want you to go to Abenaki County General Hospital for an X-ray tomorrow without fail. Don't let your work get in the way of taking care of that."

Jane nodded to assure Dr. Leckman, but she was flooded with questions that occurred to her once she awoke from the oar-induced slumber. She couldn't wait to go over everything with Storm and Finn. Had someone tried to steal the long missing sweatband? Could it be Jane's Person X? But how would Person X know where to find the sweatband? Or maybe it was no secret that old police files were in the YC basement? Jane would have to ask Helen about that.

39
Wednesday, June 5
Later in the Evening

"Whoa, everybody. Look at all of you," Jane said in surprise when she and Dr. Leckman walked into the kitchen. She had convinced him to join her and Desdemona for dinner. "A full house, Desdemona? Good to see you again so soon, Finn...and Sam, too. Glad you're all joining us. And just look at this place. So wonderfully pulled together!" Jane edged over towards Desdemona and quietly motioned towards the newly tidied rooms and the two additional dinner guests, question marks in her widened eyes. Jane also quietly whispered to her sister, "Keep a lid on it, OK?"

"Of course." Desdemona stepped up to the plate and drew everyone in with her smile. "I ran into Finn and Sam earlier today when I stopped off at the island grocery store, and I asked them both to join us. Five makes an excellent number, don't you think? And we can talk about putting the finishing touches on the Solstice Spree. But seriously, Jane...what happened to your head? There's blood caked all over your hair and gobs of it on your face."

"Oh...something just fell on my head during work...more on that later, Desdemona. I need to ask Sam a question first."

Jane then excused herself momentarily and maneuvered Sam into the living room and grilled her in a low voice. "How does Desdemona know about the Solstice Spree?" Jane demanded. "She just got here on the 11:00 AM ferry and she's already helping to plan community events? Is this your idea of funny, Sam?"

"Jane, you look like hell. Don't you think you should sit down?" Jane waved her hand at Sam to keep on talking. Sam continued, "Look, I know our lips are sealed about Desdemona. And I know how sensitive you are about the older sister burden. But I swear a lightning bolt went off in my head when I saw Desdemona at the store. She's the perfect solution for Solstice Spree, Jane! She's the perfect magnet to pull in the crowds. Just think about it and let go of your anxieties this one time. Desdemona would make a fantastic Master of Ceremonies! She has the perfect charm and esprit. So I asked her if she had time to return to St. Frewin's to present the opening ceremony speech and also announce the winners of the Chef Competition. Now that would shake things up, don't you think?"

"Sam, this is crazy. Desdemona is *too* good at this kind of thing. We're liable to be mobbed. And for all the wrong reasons. Have you thought of that?"

"I'm counting on it, Jane!" Sam declared triumphantly.

"Well now I've heard everything," Jane huffed and walked shakily towards her bathroom, which was unbelievably tidy and glistening, thanks to Desdemona. Jane spent a grooming moment on herself and spruced up her appearance, which took all of two minutes.

When she pulled her pants down to use the toilet, a small bag popped out of her underwear and slipped to the floor, nearly giving Jane a massive heart attack, on top of the clobbering her head had undergone just hours ago. She really wanted this day to be over. *But, Look! Surprise!* It was her beloved evidence. She had forgotten all about it. When the lights had gone out at the YC, Jane had no idea what might happen, so she had shoved the sweatband evidence bag inside her pants. That's how to foil a villain!

Jane returned to the kitchen and made a place for herself next to Finn while everyone began dishing out their warm scallop salad. "Let's talk a few minutes in private before you go. I need you to deliver a package to Rajiv when you get to your office tomorrow. Don't let me forget, OK?" Finn agreed and went back to splitting his conversation between Desdemona and Sam.

As they dined on the crunchy, sweet, and savory of the scallop salad and the soothing smoothness of the Albert Seltz "Sylvaner de Mittelbergheim" wine Desdemona had picked up (Jane abstained after a frown from Dr. Leckman), the disparate quintet enjoyed the simple pleasures of a civilized dinner...good food and good company...one Ginger-Headed Goddess Sister; one bandaged, hotheaded Public Safety Officer; one half-Apache, half-Irish island caterer; one regulation-mode, conservative, soon to be choking on a sweatband Sergeant; and one MD/DVM.

They ended their meal with a homemade strawberry rhubarb pie Desdemona had discovered at Grace Cleveland's roadside pie stand on her way to Jane's house. Dr. Leckman wrote down some instructions for Jane to tend to the swollen egg on her head and told her to call him in the morning to be sure she was OK. That brought everyone right up to the threshold of Paradise, and Jane wasn't asking for more.

....

In the peaceful time of unwinding after a dinner party, when the dishes were getting washed and dried, Jane and Desdemona finally got caught up at the kitchen sink.

"You know, Desdemona, you really didn't have to go to all this trouble," Jane remarked as she turned her eyes towards the rest of the kitchen and the hallway and living room. "I can't believe you found time to clean my house."

"Jane, how can you have people over to eat on top of bags of garden manure and bottles of bleach? Of course I felt inspired to clean up. Compelled even. And I'm happy to pitch in and help make your life a little more comfortable. You haven't said much to me lately about Nick, but Sam filled me on in all the divorce crap. It sounds awful."

"Yah, sorry I haven't kept you up to speed on Nick. I'm so livid about the whole thing, and I feel like such a failure. And you—you've always been very good at what you do, even if I don't like what you do. You know what I mean."

"Jane, you don't realize the half of it from my end. Sure—I fell into something weird. But work is work, and the money is great for now. Plus, I'm being careful, so thanks for your patience. Let's try not to judge the job."

"I guess that's one of my short comings—forever judging and assessing people and situations—and getting all huffy."

"Yah, you do," Desdemona nodded her head.

"But it's strange—I don't seem able to focus that same magnifying glass on myself...to judge my behavior effectively...to understand what makes me tick. I mean, here I am, supposedly pulling myself back together again on this island sanctuary. I don't understand why I continue to walk around like the living dead. There are so many parts to Jane Roberts I cannot figure out."

"Look, don't try to fathom your entire existence right now, Jane. Think of your divorce like a major medical operation. You still need to...well, to clot, emotionally. Give yourself enough time to heal. Don't expect to bounce back for six months—even a year."

"OK. But here's something else, Desdemona...and be honest with me. Do you think I've lost my tenderness...or my sweetness, in all this chaos?" Jane looked her sister in the eye.

"What? Lost your sweetness? Come on, Jane. Don't get loopy on me. There is definitely a soft side to you. You can be an endearing person. But that part of you may be kind of shattered right now. The pieces will all come back together again. You just have to be patient."

"I know. But this whole divorce business has made me so insecure. Nearly a zero." Jane made a poof sound with her lips.

"Well, if you don't mind more of my opinion, I think people need time for the world, time for themselves, and time for their loved ones," Desdemona said with assuredness. "Nick mostly wanted time for the world, or at least that's how it seemed to me living way out in L.A. during your married years. As for tenderness, Jane, for your own warmth and kindness to bloom, you also need it directed at you. In a healthy relationship, you would feel tenderness flowing towards you from the other person too. I'm not sure Nick has that in his makeup. But maybe I'm wrong."

Jane knew she should take Desdemona's advice, but divorce or no divorce, it struck Jane as odd that her inner sense of her "sweet" self was not in synch lately with how she behaved around others—like all the opinions and nagging that had flown out of her fat head in recent months. What had Lieutenant Adderley called her? A HARPY!

Could it be Jane was incapable of reaching her inner self? All she was aware of was often saying and doing things she later regretted. And really...why didn't she know herself? Why couldn't she connect with her own psyche? There were no issues in her upbringing that might raise barriers or put her on edge. It wasn't like she had been mentally abused, or raped, or beaten as she was growing up. She didn't have sexual identity issues, she didn't have a drug addiction, she had no disabilities. None of that. No psychic pain. No excuses.

Which meant she continued to chew on whether she had made the best choice when she dove into law enforcement and plotted her move to St. Frewin's Island. Her mother had been aghast. "Where did I go wrong with you girls? And Jane, if you hear Smith & Wesson, you'll reach for the vegetable oil. Are you really sure you're cut out for this kind of work?"

Well, why couldn't Jane of the middle class dive into the jungle? Why shouldn't she plunge into this career shift? What Jane yearned for was the mythical clean slate, a fresh start. And Jane wanted back her DIGNITY. Even if Normality was beyond her, she was always ready to try...to keep duking it out with Fate until the fit might be right someday. That was what drove her.

40

Friday, June 7

"Hey, Rajiv. Did Finn deliver my evidence package to you?" Jane asked when she called the State Crime Lab two days later.

"All set, Jane. I'm preparing to test the old sweatband as we speak. I feel pretty optimistic that we'll find something. Whether or not the specimen has been contaminated, I can't say for sure. But we'll see. As for the oar, I'm afraid nothing came up, except for your blood."

"That's OK, Rajiv. I'm not surprised to hear about the oar. If you can isolate DNA on the sweatband, please check it against Ruth Farrow's DNA and whatever DNA samples we've collected so far from island residents. I guess that would be Kendall and Zara Billings, Maggie Banner, the rest of the Inn staff, and Nathan Herinton. I'll call you next week to see what you've got. And before I forget, did you get anywhere with that chicken bone?"

"I've got a DNA panel from the chicken, but no matches with the DNA we've gathered to date. We'll just have to sit tight to see if there's a match out there," Rajiv said. "We're getting swamped by a bunch of new cases that have arrived, and I could get sidetracked. So please check back with me about the sweatband."

"Will do, Rajiv. Thanks! Ciao!" Jane hung up the phone and joined Zeke in the main office at Helen's receptionist desk. "OK—We have to have a pow wow about the old police files and about Anna Stedman. First off, do either of you have any idea who might know the old police files are stored in the Yacht Club basement?"

Zeke and Helen looked at each other with searching glances and looked back at Jane. She had told them all about getting konked on the head at the YC, so they understood the point of her question. Helen said, "It's probably been common knowledge for past Public Safety Officers and the Yacht Club staff. It's no big secret, but it's probably not general public knowledge."

"Blimey, Jane, it was news to me, and I've worked here for three years," Zeke added.

"OK. Now about Anna Stedman. Which men on St. Frewin's knew her and hung out with her before the accident? Can you narrow it down to a particular group of people?"

"I would say Anna and her family knew lots of islanders," Zeke recalled. "Her parents lived and worked here before she was born. They moved off the island when Anna was very young, but they came back every summer to visit their old mates."

"So which men in particular did she know as a teen, Zeke...or Helen?" Jane asked.

"Who did Anna know?" Helen looked back in time. "Well, she knew my son, Josiah, for one. And she knew Zeke, Kendall Billings, Nathan Herinton, Connor Mulroy at the pub, Maggie's ex-brother-in-law, Sonny Mannix, who's the ferry captain; and several other boys who have lived off the island for several years now. Can you think of anyone else, Zeke?"

"That's a good start. I guess if we have to find the blokes who have moved away, it wouldn't be too difficult," Zeke said.

"OK, well thanks for that." Jane chose her next words carefully. "I haven't cleared it yet with Storm, but I'm thinking we should collect DNA from these various islanders who knew Anna Stedman—it will help us put together a baseline for whatever Rajiv finds from his analysis of the old evidence. Rajiv left several DNA kits with us, so Zeke, let's collect your DNA for starters. We'll catch up with the other people after we hear from Rajiv about his results."

"Righto, Jane. No problem."

Jane walked back to her office and decided to put her head down for a few minutes. Dr. Leckman had said if she felt tired, to take a break...let her body have some down time over the next few days to keep healing. But the phone in the main room rang, and Helen put the call through to Jane's office, "It's Finn Gallinen, Jane."

Oh really? Jane thought to herself. "Hey, Finn. Thanks for delivering that package to Rajiv. Are you curious what was in it?" Jane teased him.

"Gee, Jane. Let me have ten guesses."

"So Storm must have told you I think I've found some evidence from the Stedman accident that was never analyzed."

"You know, Jane, I'm all for finding answers. If you've unearthed the golden egg, let's solve this case and wrap it up. But I'm actually calling you about something else. Do you have a minute?"

"Sure, Finn. What's up?" Jane had a suspicion, but she let Finn run with it.

"It's about your sister, Desdemona. I think I've finally figured out how I know her," Finn began slowly.

"Huh. I wonder how that could be. But you can stop right there. I've been through this before, Finn, and I'm going to tell you how we're going to handle this, OK? You are not going to say anything specific during this phone call. You are not going to tape this phone call. I'm willing to discuss this in an extremely circuitous fashion. But neither of us is going to say anything detailed or succinct to give anything whatsoever away to anyone who happens to work near you, walk by your desk, or listen in on your phone.

"And if you even think of piping this call throughout your floor in Homicide, or if Lieutenant Adderley gets wind of any of this conversation, or if you tell anyone about any of this, I am going to have to get my own kind of revenge, and it won't be pretty, Finn. Do you understand me, Finn? This is strictly confidential."

"For fuck's sake, Jane. Cool your jets. I just want to know...."

"Finn...don't say it. Talk around it if you want me to cooperate. Do you know the meaning of "circumspect"? That's all you've got to do...just be circumspect. Use euphemisms, OK?"

"OK, OK. I'm willing to play your little hide-and-seek game here because I want to have a civil conversation with you, OK? OK. So like, is your sister's official work name Desdemona Spode?"

"Why, yes, it is, Finn. Is that enough? Are we done here?"

"Hold on. Hold on, Jane. Just a few more questions. Humor me a little."

"You'll be lucky if I don't kill you the minute you set foot on St. Frewin's again. Ha ha!!" Jane sniggered.

"Is she in the movie entertainment business, Jane?"

"That's correct."

"Does it involve men?"

"That's correct."

"Would there be actual activity between those men and Desdemona?" Finn paused. "God dammit, Jane, this is ridiculous. Can't you just accept reality and talk straight with me?"

"Easy for you to say, Finn. Stick to the program. Do not step outside my guidelines or I will hang up. And as to your words 'actual activity,' let me tell you that there is no 'actual'...there is NEVER any 'actual'...there are 5000 layers of micro-thin, sperm-proof Kevlar between Desdemona Spode and her knights in no armor."

"Well, hell, Jane. You just about gave it away right there. How come you can be so blunt and not me? I mean your sister's a major fucking porn star. That's great. What's wrong with that? I'm a big fan."

CLICK. And Jane was gone.

41

Monday, June 10

"Well, Folks, here's what we know so far. Fortunately, the sweatband DNA remained stable enough in its evidence envelope all these years." Rajiv was on a conference call with Jane, Storm, and Finn to update them on his lab findings. "I guess we can thank the cool, dry basement at your yacht club for that. However, the sweatband does not contain Ruth Farrow's DNA profile. I did find what appear to be several different sets of DNA on the sweat band. And most interesting is that one set stands out as being a partial match to Ruth Farrow's DNA."

"By a partial match, you mean possibly a relative of Ruth Farrow?" Storm asked.

"That's right. But who that is at this point, I don't know which relative. Find me the person, and we'll be closer to knowing the relationship. Also, like I said, the sweat band was apparently used by several people, or touched by different people before or after the accident. So as circumstantial evidence, the sweatband may suggest someone else was in the car with Ruth, aka Anna Stedman, at the time of the accident. But it would be difficult to confirm."

"Well, can the door remain open for conjecture?" Storm asked.

"Sure...conjecture is possible. Also, I should add it appears the sweatband DNA does not match any of the DNA samples we've collected so far," Rajiv added.

"So all the Inn people and Nathan Herinton...it's unlikely any of them fits the DNA on the sweatband, is that right, Rajiv?" Finn asked.

"It looks that way."

"Couldn't we still try to collect DNA samples from a wider sampling of island residents...those people who knew Anna Stedman seventeen years ago?" Jane suggested. "Helen and Zeke came up with a few more names of people who are accessible right now. Maybe we could continue with that?"

"We can try, Jane," said Rajiv. "Send me your samples, and I'll see what I can do. Maybe we'll even find the partial match."

"Don't you think this is starting to sound like a wild goose chase?" Finn wondered aloud. "How are multiple DNA findings going to narrow our search or stand up to scrutiny after all this time? A defense attorney would likely try to rip Rajiv's work to shreds."

"Well, you make a valid point, Finn," Jane conceded. "But someone on the island on the night of May 23rd or early the morning of May 24th killed Ruth Farrow. And we assume that person had to have a reason. Early on, we had no idea where to look. Now that we know Anna Stedman was involved in the old car crash on St. Frewin's, why don't we work off of my hypothesis about the accident, and the idea that someone wanted to keep Anna from talking."

"So what's your plan?" said Finn.

"How about we pursue two avenues. We can gather swabs of DNA from men who knew Anna Stedman as a teenager, AND we can start to look for a bloody blanket or car...something with the victim's blood on it. Any helpful DNA findings, or some bloody instrument, could point us toward the murderer. Otherwise, do you have any better ideas, Finn or Storm, about how to close in on the answer, even if Rajiv can't be 100% sure about the sweatband DNA?"

Storm responded next. "OK, let's step back a minute here. It looks like we're stymied on the DNA for now. So let's change course, take another look at what else we have, and talk about the blood. Which means, I guess we'll sign off with you, Rajiv. Thanks again...we'll keep you posted."

"Jane, Finn, let's review our other information. Jane, can you get the statements from the public about possible leads in the murder? I recall you said they were hopeless, but let's read through them again in light of three things we know. First, we have Ruth Farrow's early history on St. Frewin's. Second, there's Jane's idea of the possibility of a male driver in the old car crash. Third is the fact that last week someone attacked Jane in the Yacht Club basement.

"And we've been staring this latest incident in the face and not seeing its significance. If we assume whoever clobbered Jane is the killer, then that points to someone who lives on the island. Or is often on the island, or at least has some familiarity with St. Frewin's. And who knew we were at the YC for a reason. So we can eliminate the random day tripper-cum-murderer theory."

"Hang on while I get the public statements," Jane said. After a few minutes she picked up the phone again but she hesitated because she could hear Finn talking to Storm. "I know this may sound harsh, but what if Jane manufactured that assault by herself, Storm? ...You know...hit herself on the head with the oar?" Finn said.

"I'M BACK," Jane yelled into the phone. God, what she wouldn't give to shove a stun gun up Finn's ass at peak voltage. Ha ha! But no. Take it back, Jane. Bite your tongue. "I have reports from four people. But before I begin, I want to point out, Storm, that the YC was packed with people the day you and I went to search the records. Lots of people knew we were there."

"Jane, after we hang up, be sure to call over to YC and ask the staff if they recall seeing anyone go down to the basement when you were there, or enter the basement through any basement doors that open to the outside. If need be, maybe we can get a list of the people who visited the YC or attended YC events that day and interview them," Storm said.

"Right. I'll talk to the YC staff," Jane said. She looked down at the public reports with a frown. "OK. Most of these struck me as crazy or not enough info when they came into the office. This first one is from Mr. Duncan Batchelder over at Diamond Cove. He told me he heard a woman screaming violently the night of May 23 as follows: 'No! No! God, no! Not a knife!' "

Finn perked up. "That's it?"

"Yup," Jane answered.

"What can that possibly have to do with Ruth Farrow's murder?" Finn asked. "I say discount it."

"But should we be concerned about that knife?" Storm wondered.

"As far as I know, Storm, there weren't any calls to the PSO about a knife attack," Jane said. "OK—Here's one of the Bulgarian chambermaids, a woman named Rada Markov. She called our office after Ruth Farrow was identified and her photo published. Rada said the photo 'made my memory jump.' She stated that she was tidying up the main parlor of the Inn around 10:00 PM the night of May 23rd, and she thinks she saw Ruth leave the Inn through the front door. But that's all she noticed."

"Well, that's helpful to show us Ruth left the building at that time. But, again, there's nothing more we can work with," Storm pointed out. "What's the next report?"

"This couple called in and spoke to Zeke, but they wouldn't give their names. They said, 'We were out on our porch late at night on May 23rd and we thought we saw two shifty characters carrying a really large sack along the beach. The shifty characters stumbled and fell, and one of them said to the other, 'Hey! Watch out for the crown jewels.' "

Finn snorted. "Are you kidding me? Another dud!"

"For the last one," Jane said, "we have Mrs. Cora Sprague of Whitcomb Road, who reported, 'Way past midnight on Thursday, May 23, I couldn't sleep. I walked around my house half the night and took a sip of bourbon to calm my nerves. When I stuck my head out the door for some air, I distinctly heard someone singing "I've Been Flushed From the Bathroom of Your Heart." I also saw the lights of a car parked on Herinton Drive.' "

"What? You know, Jane...augh, forget it. I'm not even going to waste my breath. A car on Herinton Drive is important, but did Mrs. Sprague have any description of the car?" Storm asked with an exasperated huff.

"No. I asked her for details, but she said she was too far to see anything but the lights of a car. So, that's it."

"You're right...hopeless," Storm sighed.

"In the meantime, my office is going to call the guys on the island who knew Anna Stedman and ask them for a DNA sample. I can't imagine anyone balking. And to keep the ball moving, I already sent Zeke's sample to Rajiv earlier today. We'll ship the other samples off to Augusta later this week. How's that sound, Storm?" Jane asked.

"Well, go ahead, but don't expect miracles. Now, about a blood-stained car. What are your thoughts on that?" Storm asked.

"OK. Like I was saying, let's assume the killer is some male friend Anna Stedman knew as a teenager," Jane suggested. "Why don't we have forensics inspect the cars of all those old male friends who were known to be on the island around the time of her death? And presumably this group would include whoever banged me on the head with the oar. So, we're looking at Zeke, Sonny Mannix, Connor Mulroy, and Josiah Oberton for additional DNA. And we want to check their cars and Kendall Billings' car. I guess we've exhausted our search of Nathan Herinton. In Josiah Oberton's case, it would be Helen's car, I imagine," Jane said.

"Well," Storm hesitated for a second. "It might seem to be overreaching, but we should be able to get people's voluntary cooperation unless they have something to hide. We'll worry about search warrants later, if need be. I'll get hold of forensics right away and schedule them to come over to the island...say this Wednesday?"

Finn interrupted. "Storm, look at who we're going to investigate. This is an awfully close-knit group. Zeke actually works with Jane, and Helen is Josiah's mother. I don't think we can simply assume people will go along with these searches. If any of them could possibly be guilty, then we've lost our element of surprise."

"I see what you're saying, Finn," Storm granted, "but that is the nature of this whole case...far too close for comfort. I'm weighing a surprise visit with a warrant against my gut thinking that anyone who is hiding something has already tried to get rid of any evidence. It's been a week and a half since the murder...more than enough time for the murderer to clean up. But maybe somebody slipped up.

"Anyway, I'll leave it with Jane to coordinate the car inspections with Anna's old friends," Storm said. "You never know but that forensics might find some small drop of guilt somewhere. Jane, be sure to downplay the car search aspect and the DNA samples as much as possible, as silly as that may sound. Act like it's just a routine review. And let me know if you run into blockades or anyone acts strange about this. OK, you two. That's it for now. I'm going to end our conference call, but Jane, can you hang on for a moment?"

"Sure."

Finn signed off.

"Jane, how are you feeling? You're going to be OK, right? I can't believe what happened. And I'm ashamed it happened when I should have been there to help you," Storm said.

"It's all OK, Storm. I survived...honestly," Jane assured him, while touching her earring. "I am a bit wary, now that I know someone would be willing to get violent like that. I'll just have to be careful until we solve this insane case."

"Well, I discussed the attack with Lieutenant Adderley and he wants you to team up with someone on all off-site work duty, for the time being. You can coordinate with Zeke, Helen, or if you get short-handed, I'll come over or send Finn over. Just don't go it alone when you're working out of the office. Promise me that."

"Aye, aye, Storm. And thank you again for finding my lost earring. That was very sweet of you."

"Look, Jane. I've been thinking...."

"Oh, Storm, Helen's flagging me down here...I'll catch up with you soon. Got to go. And I hear you on not working alone. Thanks! Ciao!" Jane hung up, dying to know, but also uneasy about whatever Storm had been on the verge of saying.

Jane walked out to the main office and turned to her next to-do. "OK, Helen, like we discussed earlier, Storm wants us to collect DNA samples from the island men who hung out with Anna Stedman when she was a teenager, and who were here the week she was killed. It's just routine. I think that would be Connor Mulroy, Sonny Mannix, Zeke—well, his is all done...and you reminded us your son Josiah was on St. Frewin's recently. So we need his DNA, too, all right?"

"That's fine," Helen said. "In fact, this reminds me that he had his profile done last year with two different companies."

"Well, that's helpful, Helen. Could you ask your son to fax us a copy of those reports as soon as possible? And I'll have Zeke contact the police where Josiah lives to arrange for one additional DNA test, for our own independent records. And Storm will give your son a call fairly soon— just a simple interview to cover all the bases. Storm's doing the same with the other guys, too, so we can log their alibis for the murder time frame. Let me know when Connor and Sonny can stop by. I hope they don't object." Jane started to walk into her office, and then she looked back at Helen.

"One more thing. Storm's going to have forensics over on Wednesday to look at the cars of all these men—and Kendall Billings' car, too. Again, just a routine inspection to cover our bases. We'd like to include your car to clear Josiah on any questions about using the car while he was here. All OK with you?"

"I'll take care of calling the men about all of this right away, Jane. And no, I don't think anyone will make a fuss. People all over the country are sending in their DNA samples for analysis these days. I know Josiah was happy to find out he is who he thinks he is." Helen shook her head. "I tell you, it's such a different world from when I was growing up."

Jane smiled at Helen. "Every generation says the same thing, don't they?"

42

Thursday, June 13

"We deserve this, Jane," Maggie was yelling to Jane as they left St. Frewin's behind them and bombed along, windows wide open and hair flying. They were heading south on Route One on the mainland to the city of Graniteville for their 10:30 AM appointment at "Nail It! Salon."

Jane shouted back, "You better believe it. Nice to get a chance to decompress from work! And you're going to laugh, but I have never, ever been to a nail parlor in my life. I think I'm probably constitutionally against them, but now I'll find out for sure."

"Jane, you're always looking for something or someone to trounce...just relax when you get there and you'll come out looking very posh...or at least cleaned up. Trust me."

Today was Maggie and Jane's "Ladies Day Off" to indulge in manicures and pedicures before the grand party being hosted on Friday night by Mr. and Mrs. Kenmore Billings, Kendall's parents, who were social big wigs from Boston. Generations of the Billings Family had summered on St. Frewin's for at least the past eighty years, so they had more than enough standing to welcome the Solstice Spree festivities with this first "soft opening" for major donors, organizers, Spree participants, and assisting Town staff. And St. Frewin's was turning 250 years old this summer, so invitations had also gone out to year-round residents of the island.

Maggie opened the door to "Nail It! Salon" and let Jane walk in first. Maggie could see Jane's head bobbing left and right and she knew this visit would trigger a stream of observations from Jane any second now.

"Maggie, this is unbelievable!" Jane exclaimed. "These client chairs look like mini thrones...and look at those square, white porcelain foot tubs at the base of every chair. They've thought of everything. All the manicurists each have a little padded stool and table at each foot tub. I guess that's the pedicure part, right? And I see they put up those long white curtains between each chair to give at least the suggestion of privacy. Not bad at all."

"Well, this is one of the nicer spas around the Midcoast area, Jane. So you're getting the princess treatment today. Once in your life is not going to kill you."

"You better hope I don't get addicted to this kind of pampering," Jane warned. She stopped her babbling and grabbed Maggie's arm to turn her away from the door. "Maggie," Jane whispered sotto voce. "Isn't that Mrs. Billings with some buddy, who just walked in? Holy shit. They're going to get snipped and painted, too. Now we have to behave ourselves," Jane lamented.

"Jane—just go with the flow. It's no big deal. We're all human; we all have nails," Maggie whispered back. To Jane's relief, however, Mrs. Billings and her friend walked down the main section of the room and turned the corner to a back alcove where there were additional manicure stations available to them.

Two petite women with hair pulled tightly back in glistening black buns came over and showed Maggie and Jane to their thrones in a row of fifteen plush, mauve, high-backed chairs. Everything was spaced closely together, without much room for anything more than one person to a throne, one handbag under the throne, and one's feet in the wash bowl. Maggie hesitated a moment and then asked the two manicurists if she could put her tape recorder on an empty manicurist table across the aisle from their pedicure stations. Would it be OK to have the volume up enough so that she could hear the recordings across the room in her throne?

Maggie explained she didn't want to have the machine in her lap, and she didn't want the machine to get wet, but she did want to listen to the historical memoirs she had been collecting on tape for the island's 250th anniversary. It had been more than a week since she had gotten back to this project—in fact, she hadn't had a chance to listen to her recordings since before the death of Ruth Farrow.

"OK—are we all set?" Maggie asked the manicurists, who shook their heads yes with bright smiles. "All right, I'll start the tape recorder now and rush back to my throne."

Meanwhile, Jane was positioning herself in her softly padded, lavender-colored cockpit seat. She considered this her personal grooming space mission where she was about to shoot off in her own solo rocket to the moon. The pedicures began liftoff. Astronaut Jane's stinky, scaly feet with toe jam gummed between each of her little piggies were gently washed clean by the pedicurist's experienced hands. Then the toe toweling. Next up would be the cuticle removal, nail clipping, and flight check for oxygen, ascent speed, and preferred color of toe nail polish—Rocket Red? Galaxy Blue? Cosmos Green?

Houston Space Center's tape-recorded greeting to the Astronauts came through the loudspeakers loud and clear, actually a bit blaring, given the narrow dimensions of the "Nail It! Salon":

"Hello, my name is Margaret Simmons, and I'm eighty-nine years old. I was born and brought up on St. Frewin's and [coughing, hacking].... Oh, sorry, Maggie, can we start the machine over again"...then abruptly, like a sharp, stinging slap to the face, the tape recorder jerked into "Oh, oh, aaahhhhh," sounds of thrusting, knocking around, big sighs, bucking, laughing, desperate whisperings: "I want you,

I want you so bad. Your cock, Your cock, Your cock, Your cock, Your cock, Your cock...."

Jane flinched, plummeted back to Earth, hit the brake on the space mission, and looked at Maggie. "HOUSTON—WE'VE GOT A PROBLEM. What the hell, Maggie?" Jane yelped as the tape recorder kept wailing, "Your cock, your cock, your cock...." The two pedicurists had jumped up and run for cover by this time.

"The tape must be stuck!" Maggie blanched. She looked up and saw the salon door opening to three delivery men who quickly began pushing handcarts sky-high full of supplies down the narrow aisle. They moved their awkward, top-heavy loads forward and then halted, blocking both Maggie and Jane in their seats.

"What do you mean STUCK?" Jane yelled. "Why on earth would your interviews with St. Frewin's retirees be stuck on 'Your cock, your cock?' "

Astronaut Jane sprang to take command to do what she had to do: the immediate launch of a RESCUE MOON WALK. She leaped up into her porcelain foot bowl, but not anticipating slipping on the damp bowl interior, she catapulted her airborne self and the manicurist's tray of supplies onto the terrorized head and ankles of the last delivery man, now fused to his handcart in a death grip. Jane and the delivery man crashed towards the narrow aisle floor. Jane was penned in and had to act fast, especially since the tape recorder suddenly coughed and cleared its throat and began anew:

"YES, YES! I know it's big. I knew it the minute you stared at me. Uh, uh, yes, kiss me harder." Lots of sexually-charged, incoherent air-sucking, mouth-sucking, mashing and shoving and hands banging on a counter and groaning.

The first two delivery men, intrigued by the highly-charged entertainment, stood with their handcarts in place, transfixed and straining to catch every last grunt on the tape.

Astronaut Jane reversed her engine thrust and high-speed jetted back to her throne. Maggie was nearly on her knees, begging the delivery men to turn off the tape recorder, which she could not reach due to their parked handcarts blocking her entire access to the wailing machine. But either they didn't understand English sufficiently, or they liked what they were hearing too much to turn off the machine.

Jane pulled aside her spaceship curtain and began hopping from throne to throne, thrusting aside their spaceship curtains as well, and apologizing to two white-haired patron-Astronauts who had stood up out of their own thrones and were also listening to the tape intently. "So sorry, Ma'am. I just have to try...and squish...past you here. Oh, oops. I'm really sorry," Jane kept begging their pardon. "Didn't mean to step in your frozen yogurt. I have to turn off that horrible tape recorder."

"Oh, don't do it on our account, Sugar." One of the white-haired ladies made a show of flexing her wizened fingers into racy claws. "We used to be wild cats too, you know. A little fornication is a nice change."

Did I hear what that old dame just said to me? Jane asked herself. *What is happening to the over-70 crowd?*

Jane maneuvered past the sex-tape enthusiasts and was calculating her final payload needed to swoop around the delivery men glued to the tape recorder. As she precariously swished her way out of the last porcelain foot bowl in her flight path, all the pandemonium came to a halt. Mrs. Kenmore Billings reached for the tape recorder with her bejeweled, tidy pink fingernail and definitively stabbed the STOP button.

43
Thursday, June 13
Afternoon

"I can't believe we got out of there alive, Jane!" Maggie was gasping for air and choking with laughter as they both settled into her car.

"Yah, well, I still haven't had my manicure or pedicure. So where does that leave us?" Jane said.

"What I don't understand is what the hell happened to my tape recorder?" Maggie was thunderstruck. "I remember getting my leather bag and the tape recorder from the pantry at the Inn a week or two ago...some time right after the whole Ruth Farrow thing blew up. And this is the first time I've had a chance to listen to my interviews."

"Well, OBVIOUSLY, something happened to those interviews, Maggie." Jane looked at the Inn manager in absurd wonder.

"We've got to listen again, without all the distraction of you, Jane, trying to do the high jump over the pedicure thrones and all those poor delivery men and supplies. Let's listen carefully this time. I want to figure this out." Maggie hit the ON button for the second time that day. And they listened, repressing their urges to react out loud.

When the sex tape reached its end, Maggie gasped and threw her head back against the head rest. "Do you know who the man is on that tape, Jane?"

"If you do, what does that say about you, Maggie?" Jane challenged her.

"I think that's Kendall Billings. I'm not sure about the woman. But I don't think it's Zara."

"How would you know it's Kendall Billings? All the man on that tape is doing is moaning and groaning and having sex. How can you recognize him, Maggie?"

"Don't be naïve, Jane. I've worked with Kendall for eight years. We're only human, if you know what I mean."

"Maggie, all day long you've been saying 'we're human,' or 'we're only human.' What kind of excuse is that?" Jane blurted out.

"You don't make sense, sometimes, Jane. What I mean is Kendall and I have slept together. OK? Just a few times. So I know what he sounds like. Is that so unfathomable?"

Jane was floored. "Oh My God. Let's put an end to all of this. I need to take command of that tape, Maggie. It might turn out to be important in the murder case. And we should probably drop the topic for now. Let's stop at the Abenaki County Sheriff's Office before we get to the ferry. I need to call Storm Nosmot and update him about all of this."

They drove in silence to the County Sheriff's Office. Jane called Storm and he told her to keep the tape safe and act like nothing had occurred...status quo. He would drive down to catch a ferry to the Billings party tomorrow night and retrieve the tape then. "I'll be the one in the elegant black suit, Jane. Keep an eye out for me."

44

Thursday, June 13
Late Afternoon

Back on the island, Jane drove her truck to the Public Safety Office to check on the day's events. Zeke and Helen had held down the fort most of the day, with nothing earth-shattering to report. Details about the upcoming federal census and several tourist issues about lost possessions more or less filled their plates.

Helen transferred a call to Jane around 4 PM. It was Iowa Law Enforcement calling with an update. "We've periodically checked Ruth Farrow's mail and her apartment, and nothing of interest has cropped up yet, Jane. We'll check back with you if we have anything new. And by the way, the local probate court has appointed someone to administer Ruth's very modest estate. So we'll probably coordinate with the Administrator from now on about Ruth's mail and so forth."

"Helen—any update on Connor and Sonny coming in for their DNA sample?" Jane asked after she hung up with Iowa.

"They both dropped by earlier today, Jane, and then I shipped the samples out to Rajiv," Helen said.

Jane's next call was to Rajiv at his lab. "You are not going to believe this, Rajiv. I was with Maggie Banner, the manager of Grand Harbor Inn. We were listening to her taped interviews with old timers who live on the island. It's part of Maggie's research for the 250th island anniversary coming up. Anyway, the tape suddenly turned into this recording of two people having sex, if you can believe it."

"Jane—I was just going to call you. What is going on out there? Your island is a hopping place," Rajiv said. "I have some information for you, too. But you go first."

"I can't totally explain it to you. Maggie remembers she left her tape recorder in her bag on the counter of the pantry at the Inn. It was there for several days, and all we can think is that two people were in the pantry at some point and leaned on Maggie's bag and somehow—with their body movements or something?—they started the machine running without realizing it. The exchange on the tape is pretty heavy duty, if you know what I mean. So they were probably quite caught up in what they were doing and didn't pay any attention to the bag. God, I can't believe I'm having to tell you this."

"So why are you telling me this, Jane?"

"Well, I'm wondering if it's Kendall Billings and Ruth Farrow having sex on that tape. Maggie thinks it's Kendall...she's worked with him for years and knows his voice...." Jane decided to spare Rajiv the details on that. "So, if it is Kendall and Ruth, the tape might help to show a motive for murder on Kendall's part...or maybe Zara Billings' part, for that matter."

"OK. I'm following you now. Did you want to bring the tape recorder in for fingerprint analysis?"

"I hadn't thought about that. Maybe we should send you the tape recorder...that's a good point. But the reason I'm calling you is to ask you to check the sweatband DNA against Kendall Billings' DNA one more time. Just to be sure. Do you mind?"

"That's fine, Jane. I can double-check, but the odds are slim. I'll let you and Storm know what I find. Not a problem."

"Thanks so much, Rajiv. And please be on the lookout for DNA from other male islanders that we've sent you. Just keep a library of your findings until we get a bigger picture, OK? You're the best!" Jane was about to hang up, but Rajiv caught her in time.

"Jane, hold on a minute. Are you sitting down?" Rajiv asked, "because I finished analyzing Zeke's DNA this afternoon, and I may have found a match to something."

"You're kidding. What?" Jane said.

The irrefutable truth of Rajiv's research was simply the frankness of science, but a shock to him all the same at times. He had to deliver his latest news to Jane, but he was reluctant to shatter the peace. "Remember that fried chicken I bagged as evidence at the crime scene? To my surprise, the DNA from the chicken is a match with Zeke's DNA."

"No..." Jane gulped, while standing up to close her office door.

"Which means Zeke ate some of the chicken I found discarded at the edge of our crime scene. What that says about the murder, I can't be sure. But it does not look good for Zeke. You should let Storm know as soon as possible, so you two can decide how to approach Zeke about this."

"Oh, Lord, Rajiv. Like we need this. You're saying you found evidence at the crime scene of a piece of chicken that Zeke ate and may have left behind. You're not saying that pins the murder on him, but we need more information from him. Right?"

"That's right, Jane," Rajiv said. "Keep me posted and let me know how I can help."

....

"Jane—one more call just came in," Helen alerted Jane. It's Lieutenant Adderley. Sounds like he needs to talk to you."

Now what? Jane could feel herself crumpling. She didn't want to face any more facts. She didn't want to have to grill Zeke about his greasy fried food and littering...at the scene of the murder, no less! She just wanted minimal stress for the rest of the day and night. She wanted to go home and figure out which of her poorly fitting dresses and pinchy low-pump heels would make her look halfway decent for tomorrow night's gala, where Storm would undoubtedly be looking utterly dashing in his black suit, and all the island's high society would be showing off their glitter. Was that unprofessional and self-absorbed of her? Probably.

"Well, well, 'Miss Hap.' I'm glad I caught you before you flew the coop today." Lieutenant Adderley sounded his usual commanding self. "I'll make this quick for both of us. It's come to my attention that you created quite a scene of public indecency today in Graniteville. Are you following me?"

" 'Miss Hap'? Oh, Lieutenant Adderley, I get it. Funny. But I can explain everything, really," Jane said, wincing at what was about to hit the fan. "Remember how you wanted us to be aware of the needle and all the hay in this investigation? That's what we were doing today—well, inadvertently. Kind of winnowing through some extra chaff...and I can see how I owe you an explanation...."

"An explanation is exactly what I'd like, Jane. And Mrs. Kenmore Billings will likely want an explanation as well. She was present at the, let me see here, at the 'Nail It! Salon' this morning when you and Maggie Banner were supposedly there for pedicures. According to Mrs. Billings, and I think we can both agree she's an upstanding citizen who would have no need to fabricate this incident...are you with me, Jane?"

Jane managed to emit a strangled "Yes, Sir" from her slowly constricting trachea.

"Mrs. Billings reports that you deliberately played aloud in front of various salon clients and employees a tape recording of an extremely pornographic sexual encounter, while demonstrating flagrant disregard for hygiene at the salon by running wet and barefoot all over the furniture and foot tubs of the establishment, including actually stepping into other people's snacks, and finally assaulting innocent delivery men who happened to be there. Did I get all that correct, Jane?"

"Sir, if we can bring this down a few notches, I can fill you in on what really happened, if I may."

"You know, Jane, no matter what justification you produce for today's escapade, I don't know if I should discipline you, fire you, or pack you off to a mental institution, if they'd be willing to take the risk."

"Lieutenant Adderley, maybe the best thing would be for you to call Storm Nosmot. I filled him in on what happened at the nail salon today. You might get a better picture if it comes from him."

"Just hold it right there, Jane. Whatever version you spin, you need to know I have complete and independent verification of the events as reported by Mrs. Billings. You obviously have no idea who accompanied Mrs. Billings to the salon today, have you?"

"That's true, Lieutenant. I have no idea."

"Well, Jane, be aware that I am the only one standing between you and utter banishment from the Maine State Police for eternity. The person who would authorize your disappearance immediately, but for my good graces, is Mrs. Harriet Buxton, the head of our Human Resources Department. Mrs. Buxton and Mrs. Billings have known each other for decades, and yes, Jane, the head of Human Resources was the star witness to your messy, messy debacle today."

Jane could not resist the defensive temptation. "Isn't Harriet that constipated tightwad who keeps clamping down on my expenses, Lieutenant? And by the way, has anyone seen my reimbursement form for my hobo bag and general personal items that Finn buried in upchuck during the Farrow post-mortem review?" Jane tried to inquire as demurely as those two questions would linguistically allow. But she instantly asked herself why she had blurted it all out. To what end? Would she ever know when to keep her mouth shut?

"We won't have any more of that, Jane. It's high time for you to consider some intense self-examination. And given the fact that you and I both have to run now, I'll speak with Storm later about your version of this shameful incident and follow up with you on Monday, if I have any further questions. But do try and behave yourself at the Billings event, will you? And don't be half surprised if they refuse you entrance. After all, Mrs. Billings recognized her son Kendall's voice in flagrante delicto on that tape recording. We can only imagine, Jane, how high emotions will be running tomorrow night!"

Adderley hung up before Jane could break the news about Zeke's fried chicken. Well, Adderley could wait. Jane dialed Storm Nosmot next. He needed to know tonight, and she needed to know what to do.

45
Friday, June 14
Morning

Jane's office was a tight space even on a good day, but she figured that would work to her advantage this morning. All the better to look straight and deep into the eyes of her what— questionee?, interrogatee?, grillee? Storm had authorized Jane to interview Zeke, and she wished she had a technically flashy label for him, now that he was sitting across the desk from her. He wasn't looking sheepish; he wasn't squirming uncomfortably. He didn't know why he was there. Jane imagined this could be his feigned innocence before impending doom.

"I have to record our conversation, Zeke, so please bear with me on the formalities," Jane said as she clicked on the tape recorder and spoke the basic interview information into the machine, including informing Zeke of his Miranda rights. Then she switched it off.

"So, Zeke, Rajiv called me with additional DNA findings late yesterday. I have a few questions for you about his findings, but before we even get to that, could I ask you something that's been bugging me since Day One?" Jane looked at Zeke quizzically.

"Sure, Jane. Fire away," Zeke said.

"What is it about your Anglophilia? I just don't get it," she asked. "Where does it come from? Why do you talk like that constantly?"

"Anglophilia? Anglo... you mean the British stuff?"

"Yes, of course."

Zeke paused to look around the small walls and then back at Jane. "You know, it's just how I am. I've watched

British dramas and detective shows since before I could talk. All thanks to my grandmother, I guess. She basically raised me and tuned in to whatever she could find from England. She loved to borrow videos from the library, and then she got sucked into Netflix and we lived in those cop shows day and night, especially during the winter. I'm kind of a UK TV clone, you might say."

"Hmm. If your grandmother took care of you, do you mind my asking what happened to your parents?"

"I don't really know, Jane. I've heard bits and pieces over the years, but I'm not sure about any of it...like my mother and father had me, then maybe he died in a tragic work accident on a freighter in Hong Kong, and she felt trapped by me as a baby, so she dropped me off at her mum's on St. Frewin's Island...forever, as it turned out. About sums it up."

"Oh, Zeke. That's a sad history. You could sort of be St. Frewin's own David Copperfield." Zeke frowned slightly. Jane quickly added, "I'm not trying to be flip...though you probably don't see it like that. Anyway, I'm very sorry to hear all this. And I'm sorry I've been so short with you about the Brit talk and...well, your junk food, and all that. You don't need me jumping down your throat. But as far as your mother...are you in touch with her at all?"

"I say the less, the better. She probably hates me to this day, because I was the needy bundle left in her arms by a husband who ruined her life by dying on her so young...you know, no money, an uncertain future, who wants a kid on top of that?" Zeke rolled his shoulders and took a deep breath. "I try not to hold a grudge against her. In fact, I try not to think about her period."

"Well, thank you for filling me in, Zeke. What you've described certainly doesn't sound comfortable, so I apologize for asking you to drag it all up. And that makes it all the more difficult to turn to our next topic. But I really have to talk to you about Ruth Farrow's murder scene. Wait a second while I turn the recorder back on."

Zeke spoke his consent to questioning into the machine.

"OK, thanks, Zeke. So...." Jane looked at Zeke and plunged in. "Rajiv bagged as evidence a partially eaten piece of fried chicken he found at the edge of the crime scene. That was the day we all did the site walk with Storm and Finn. Rajiv ran a DNA analysis of the chicken and filed the data as part of our case. When he processed your DNA sample the other day, he found that it matches the DNA on the chicken found at the crime scene. So, I have to ask you if you threw out your half-eaten chicken leg during late May near Herinton Drive."

"At least that's easy, Jane. Yes, on Thursday, I think it was May 23rd?—we can check our work calendar if you want—I took a half day off to visit my grandmother at her elder home in Augusta, Maine. You know how she loves it when I bring her take-out, like Kentucky Fried Chicken...all that hot, salty, crunchy meat. You can see who I take after, right?" Zeke chuckled.

"Sure," Jane said.

"I must have had leftovers in my car when I got back to the island, and at some point, I tossed that chicken out the window. Probably shouldn't have littered. Sorry."

"But if you live at the north end of the island, why were you driving on the south end of the island on Herinton Drive, when you threw out the chicken?" Jane sat back and waited for Zeke's reply.

"Oh, that. Hah—good detective work, Jane. But I have an innocent explanation. We had an animal shelter meeting that night at Corinne Parker's house...she's a board member and she has a house on Herinton Point. You can check with her, if you want. I stayed until nearly 10:00 PM, and then I left to head home to feed my kittens."

"Are there any witnesses who can back you up on what time you arrived home and what time you went to bed that night?"

"Not really, Jane. You know I live alone, so I have no alibi after I left Corinne Parker's house."

"So, you're telling me that was it. You weren't involved, even peripherally, with Ruth Farrow's body being left near your fried chicken," Jane summarized. She felt a rush of relief in her chest, whether or not it was warranted. No one wants to think they're working in the same office as a cold-blooded murderer.

"That's right. I'm telling it like it is, Jane," Zeke said.

"OK, well I guess we're all done for now, Zeke, and you can go about your work as usual today. I will give Corinne Parker a call just to check what you've told me, and I'll report everything to Storm Nosmot. We'll let you know if we have any more questions."

46
Friday, June 14

Bulbous, gigantic, metallic gumballs and puffballs in swirling patterns of crimson, blue, and gold crowned the main residence of the Billings Estate, creating a multi-onion-domed horizon, and making it look, to Jane's mind, like a place where an old Russian Orthodox Church gang might want to hang out if they couldn't gain admittance to the Yacht Club. At the moment, Jane was trying her hardest and mightiest to pry open the humongous outer front door, but the stiff wind bearing down was cancelling out her efforts.

She had arrived late, of course, and alone, and no butler or footman was there to greet her. She managed to haul the massive slab of giant redwood—others might call it a "Sequoia Portal"—an inch or so towards her, but not enough to wedge her wobbly high-heel in far enough to hold open that door, so she could wiggle in to reach the handle of the next giant redwood making up the second door. *Who makes these kinds of doors?,* Jane wondered in frustrating silence. *Mom and Dad had one of those junky plywood numbers with three cascading little square windows and a puff of insulation inside it.* It must have weighed all of ten pounds, compared to this Pharaoh's tombstone she was trying to heave out of her way.

A rustling sound alerted Jane to someone rounding the massive hydrangeas near her to her left. A very tall man in very clean livery bounded up the stairs to tend to Jane's struggle. "May I assist, Ma'am? You look a bit like Stuart Little trying to open that door." She could smell the cigarette break he had apparently taken in the bushes. It delivered an unexpected, sour welcome to this swish soiree. *And what was with the mighty mouse quip?* Jane wondered whether she should allow this breach of etiquette to go unaddressed.

"Ma'am, one more thing. There are no portable recording devices or microphones allowed into the party tonight. So I'll need to check your evening bag, if you don't mind?"

"That's the most absurd thing I've ever heard, Sir. Who would bring any of that gear to this party, for one thing. And who cares if anyone did?"

"Apologies, Ma'am, but Mrs. Billings specifically told me to be on the lookout for you and to make sure you didn't enter with any electronic equipment."

"How could you know who I am, Sir? I don't believe we've ever met," Jane said in astonishment.

"If you really want the truth, Ma'am, Mrs. Billings said I should be on the lookout for you with your big hair, like maybe you stuck your finger in a socket."

47
Friday, June 14
Evening Party

Jane was still searching for her self-esteem after she managed to escape from that jarring encounter. Now standing in the Billings' arched foyer, she tossed her head backward to get a good look at the ornately painted ceiling. Above her whirled some kind of baroque take on a celestial day-care center full of flying babies with horrid little faces, romping about in blue bunting. Jane even thought she could discern baby Kendall Billings prancing among his putti pals with his nappies drooping below his knees.

Far beyond her, acre-size rooms forked off in every direction. In the upper reaches of the main hall, Jane could make out an enormous web of plaster cornices, swirling scallops, acanthus leaves, more freaky babies, ribbons and bows, mythic fruits, lions' heads, and florets. The prodigious pastiche looked like someone had gone berserk with thousands of cans of whipped cream and gold foil. *God help whoever had to dust all this stuff!*

As Jane tiptoed into the main hall and began wading through carpet pile that elevated her three inches above planet earth, she found herself swallowed up in a scintillating wave of summer residents. The billowing mass of tuxedos and summer gowns coiled around dowdier clumps of islanders and local oldsters decked out in their modest best. The democracy of the evening was quite impressive...high-browed society dons and matrons were mixing it up, sort of, with the rural and artistic folks, the administrative functionaries, and retirees from throughout the island.

Where was Maggie? Jane was starting to worry. They had planned to meet in front of the portrait of General Horace Billings, which Maggie had described as being located in the main hall. Jane had no idea who Horace Billings was, so she began scanning the massive walls around her, looking for someone Horace-like in jodhpurs, possibly with mutton chop sideburns.

In her ongoing guise as island historian, Maggie was going to talk to the old timers at the party about Anna Stedman and try to sniff out any helpful gossip about the devastating car accident. Jane wasn't so sure if drafting Maggie to quiz the elderly was by the books, but with a skeleton crew, Jane decided she simply had to improvise and keep going.

Jane also intended to collar Kendall Billings and ease him into talking about Anna Stedman as well. In her gut, she could not let go of the sex tape and the possibility that Kendall was more involved in Ruth Farrow's murder than he had admitted thus far. Zeke would team up with Storm to keep an eye on people in general and provide back-up if Jane ran into trouble with Kendall.

Zara Billings suddenly swept into Jane's sight, with several male companions close at her side. Her stunning dress in mango-colored silk and her ring—one of those big, fat, juicy watermelon tourmalines gripped in a gold bowl the size of an eye socket—made Jane want to run quickly for her little Venn circle hovering off to the side. There was no way Zara was going to let Jane puncture Zara's perfect orb.

But at least introductions could be made. "Jane Roberts, I'm so glad you could join us tonight. May I introduce you to my brother, Kazimir Ivanov? And this fine gentleman is Konstantin Balankoff, Torrance Balankoff's brother."

Jane needed one micro-minute to compose herself in the face of these three handsome race horses. By the time she had arrived home from work, all of thirty minutes remained for her to get ready for the Solstice Spree party. Shower; shave her shaggy legs; yank slinky, shirred black cocktail dress over her broad shoulders; suck in tummy; dump baby powder into ill-fitting black heels inherited from Desdemona; brush her long tumbleweed of hair; and carefully, carefully apply Lancôme's "L'Absolou Rouge" to her crinkly mouth. Jane hated how imperfect the human body could be when she tried to look her best. What to do about the hairy planks that were her eyebrows? The bumps and crevices where she should have had succulent, hormone-infused lips? Ach! Enough.

Fortified by her self-composing moment, Jane flashed her happiest smile at Zara and her retinue. Konstantin Balankoff intrigued Jane immediately and intensely. So what if he was obviously cut from wealthy yard goods? She forgave him. She could see he was a man of the finest tapestry, as perfect as a 1910 Steinway, as superior as a jar of malossol caviar. *God, she could be so corny when she waxed on like this!*

"I understand from Torrance that you recently investigated an unpleasant neighborhood issue for her." Konstantin was talking directly to Jane. "She's quite thankful and told me to be sure and try to meet you tonight. She's in the main parlor, so you may have a chance to see her."

He leaned in to shake Jane's hand and smoothly drew her towards his gorgeous mouth. Jane could feel the nearness of his Stoli-tipped breath when he whispered, "Perhaps we can get together later this summer. I'll be back and forth, so I'll give you a call. And, Jane, you have a piece of TP stuck on the side of your lovely dress." She swooped around to confirm and detach the culprit paper pulp. When she turned back, Konstantin was gone.

48
Friday, June 14
Evening Party

"Jane—There you are. Who would have thought this place would be so mobbed?" Maggie said with relief when she caught up with Jane in the midst of the glittering party crowd. "I've been trying to hunt down my old folks network ever since I arrived. See those two elderly ladies over there? One of them was the Town Clerk for years. I'm going to see what she has to say about Anna Stedman."

"Be casual when you start asking questions, Maggie. Don't go into the murder for now. Just try some off-the-cuff cocktail talk to help excavate buried facts."

"Well come with me at least to say hi to these women," Maggie suggested. "The Town Clerk's name is Trudy Moody." Jane agreed, and they wove in and out of various groups to reach a small seating area off to the side.

....

"Well, girls, I was Town Clerk on St. Frewin's for some thirty years, up until 2005. After all that time keeping the Town books, I would have to say no one is who they think they are." Trudy Moody still retained that slightly steely edge and knowing look that she probably projected all those years to make the Town records behave themselves.

"Why do you say that, Mrs. Moody?" Maggie asked.

"People were always asking me to fix the records. A change of date here; a correction on the name of a parent. A change of a baby's name. And you know what they say about the birth of a couple's first child. That one can come any time. The rest all take nine months." The two older ladies looked at one another and winked.

Mrs. Moody's husband walked over and took a seat next to his wife of nearly fifty years. He even gave her a peck on the cheek.

"Officer Roberts, I hear you're real big on peonies," Mr. Moody started in.

"Why you're exactly right, Mr. Moody," Jane said, thinking maybe she should be a little less overt about her passion for all things peony.

"I bring it up, Jane, may I call you Jane? I bring it up because I have all kinds of lo-am if you need it to start yourself a peony garden."

"Lo-am, Mr. Moody? What is lo-am?" Jane asked politely.

"That's the stuff you get in them big bags at the garden center. You know, lo-am, like dirt, soil. Lo-am."

"Oh, I get it. I get it now," Jane laughed. "You mean *loam*, don't you Mr. Moody. It's one syllable...loam."

"Ayuh—that's right. That'd be the same as lo-am."

49
Friday, June 14
Evening Party

Jane noticed from afar that Nathan Herinton was looking like a million dollars this evening and was no doubt eager to spend it all, since he hadn't had to earn any of it. Such was Jane's ruthless assessment of the man. She was still sore about his haughty demeanor when they had called him in for questioning in the Farrow case, but Nathan might know where Kendall Billings was in the crowd. And while she was at it, Jane would ask him if he remembered Anna Stedman and the accident.

Jane politely nudged her way past a drove of the Texan semiconductors in order to reach Herinton. Was it Jane's imagination, or were the semiconductors jokingly giving Jane the sniff test as she glided past them? The nerve of some people....

"Nathan, lovely to see you tonight," Jane glowed as she extended him her hand. "Are you on your own for the party?"

"Jane Roberts, fancy seeing you here. I hope you're not going to handcuff me to the punch bowl and interrogate me a third time," Nathan said as he took a sip of his drink.

"Not to worry, Nathan. I'm nearly off duty. But I do have two easy questions that couldn't possibly trigger your Miranda warning. Do you have any idea where I can find Kendall Billings? And secondly, do you have any memories of that tragic car accident about seventeen years ago where Anna Stedman's car hit another car and killed an entire family?"

Nathan scanned the sea of guests around him and pointed Kendall out to Jane. Kendall was surrounded by several women laughing at the drop of his jokes, and they seemed anchored in that spot for the moment. "Anna Stedman—Wow. I haven't heard her name in years. What a horrible accident. Horrible for everyone involved. Why do you ask?"

Jane threw out a non-committal answer. "Oh, just wondering in general. Some of us were talking recently about how St. Frewin's voted to shut down the web connectivity years ago."

"Oh, right," Nathan nodded. "I heard about the accident, like most people on the island, but I wasn't personally around that day. I did know Anna back then. We were all kids, teenagers hanging out in the summer. She was a lovely girl, blond, sweet, open, friendly in general. We only saw her when her family would visit on the island in the summer. But it was always fun to catch up. I think they lived in Shipman. After the accident, which by the way pretty much ruined Anna's life, or so I heard, I don't think we ever saw her or her family again. They moved away. People lost touch. You know how it is."

"Well, thanks for that, Nathan. It's a very sad history." Jane made a note in her head that Nathan had made no connection between the Anna Stedman of his youth, and the Ruth Farrow of his recent romps. Best to keep it that way while the investigation was ongoing.

"And Jane, before you pounce on Kendall, how's your friend Samantha Lloyd doing? It looks like she's catering this party, and I have to say, her food is to die for. Have you tried the shrimp spring rolls yet?"

"Isn't she fantastic?" Jane bubbled. "She not only has killer hors d'oeuvres, she can whip up the whole shebang for hundreds of people in one setting without giving them an iota of food poisoning."

"I should certainly hope not on the food poisoning, Jane. I'm thinking I'll give her a call one of these days. Maybe take her out sailing...have lunch on Sheep Island. She's a very appealing woman."

"But Nathan, I thought you were getting mar..."

"Zip it, Jane. You and I never had this conversation."

50
Friday, June 14
Evening Party

When Jane looked again for Kendall, he was heading for one of the bar stations, where Zara and her brother were refreshing their glasses. Jane swam over to them and put her hand on Kendall's arm.

"Hi Kendall! Thank you for this splendid party your family is hosting. You've done a great job." Jane praised him. "I was wondering if I could talk to you alone, somewhere less noisy?" Jane gave Zara a quick smile, as if to secure her silent permission.

"Sure, Jane. Why don't we move to the library, which is the second room on the left. You can head over there, and I'll meet you in a minute. I just have to talk to Zara about something."

Jane slithered her way across the main hall, nodding greetings to acquaintances here and there, and pausing once to look back towards Kendall and Zara. She could see Zara handing something to Kendall, and then he asked the bartender a question. Jane did not, however, catch any glimpse of Storm, and she wondered where he might be. Zeke she had seen somewhere along the way this evening, happily engaged in conversation with summer residents he had known all his life.

Stepping through the doorway, Jane felt right at home in the Billings library and its long rows of books, floor to ceiling, books big and small, leather, hardcover, softcover...the human mind on a shelf.

Libraries had been a sanctuary for Jane all her life. She loved how they were quiet and orderly. Quiet, because most people would rather be elsewhere, which meant you often had the place to yourself, and if anyone showed up, they kept their volume down because it was a library. Orderly, because shelved books bore the stamp of learnedness and stability, in contrast to the ongoing messiness and distraction of real life on the outside.

On two of the round mahogany, claw-footed tables in the center of the room, Jane saw a lifetime of Billings photos framed in sterling. She poked around for the teen years and found a picture taken at a soccer game, which looked like everyone in her mental mugshots for the Farrow case: Kendall, Nathan, Zeke, Connor Mulroy, Sonny Mannix, and several other boys, one of whom might be Josiah Orbeton. The girls in the picture Jane did not recognize, except she thought she could identify young Anna Stedman as one of them. Jane felt somewhat deflated to see that many of the boys wore head sweatbands, and so did some of the girls.

"Are you enjoying yourself, Jane?" came a question in a soothing voice from the window seat at the far, darkened end of the library.

"Oh my god! You scared me. Who is that anyway?" Jane asked, rather startled to be caught off guard like that. The distant figure rose from his seat and walked towards Jane, while putting away a book before he reached her.

"No need for alarm. It's Konstantin Balankoff, Torrance's brother. I see you're also seeking refuge in a peaceful part of the house."

"I'm sorry if I invaded your space, Konstantin. I'm just waiting for Kendall Billings. I need to talk to him about a work-related matter."

"Well, in that case, I'll make a dash for the door before the grand inquisition begins...but please don't forget my offer to see you again. I'd like that."

Oh Please, God. Help me to deal with this man. He's way too handsome for me to say the right thing. Jane swallowed hard.

"I'd like that, too, Konstantin. May I ask what book you were reading?"

"Do you enjoy poetry, Jane? I've left a book of verse not quite tucked in with the rest. There's a cocktail napkin beneath some lines that I saved for you."

With that, Konstantin took Jane's hand, gently deposited a kiss on the back of it, and left her alone with all the learnedness and stability in the room.

Before Jane had the chance to thank him, or to run and look at the book, Kendall swaggered in with a frosty, dripping, cut glass pitcher full of a golden beverage stuffed with mint leaves and ice.

"Now I've got you in my clutches, *Janie Eyre*," Kendall whistled to the astonished Jane Roberts. "And you can call me Mr. Rochester, if you please. Come on over here and let me pour you a big mint julep, my sweet."

Were it not for the murder of Ruth Farrow, Jane would have bolted from the temple of books right there and then, like Stan Helmstadt's incensed, runaway cow. Instead, she stood her ground and willed her professional standards into a shield. She was going to stay put and see this through. If she had to drink a half bucket of mint juleps, so be it. It was imperative to take a good, long peek under Kendall's pedigree and his family's wealth and determine once and for all if he had killed the Farrow woman. That was all Jane wanted tonight. And she wasn't going to let go until she got it.

"Well now, Mr. Rochester...pour me a stiff one, why don't you?" Jane cooed as she waltzed over to her Victorian buck. *If he wanted to play this silly game, two could play the game. Wasn't that the saying?*

Kendall demonstrated quite the serving technique as he boldly thrust Janie's glass out from his body, then yanked the glass back to his chest, and hoisted the minty brew up and tipped it slightly to top off a twelve-ounce tumbler for his willing governess.

It was a fact that Jane was quite thirsty at this point, not having had a chance to touch a drop of anything all night, what with all the dots she had been trying to connect so far. So it was a quenching joy to drain the whole damn drink down her throat without a thought to alcoholic content or carcinogenic impact on brain cells.

"Just what I needed, Mr. Rochester," Jane assured her enthusiastic dandy. In truth, Jane had to wonder what the hell had gotten into Kendall Billings. He had never had the time of day for her since she arrived on the island. A few dull hi's here and there, maybe an empty smile once or twice, but that was it. And now? She chalked it up to liquor. But seriously? She had never seen the man so grandiose and uninhibited...verily open to the universe and eager to live *big*. That was the strange thing. He was so eager.

"Here, let me pour you another one, my dear," Kendall was prompting Jane with his icy pitcher. She gave in. She needed the intoxicating boost to keep up with his bizarre behavior, and she also finally felt like breaking out of "Who" Public Safety Officer Jane Roberts represented. It had been too long that she had tried so hard to do the right thing. What was the point? Another drink wasn't going to ruin her life. It would limber her up for the interrogation she was about to bring down on Kendall.

"Sure thing, Mr. R. And why don't you come join me on this settee so we can go over a few things?" Jane eased herself down into the deep green cushions and made sure to show a little thigh.

Kendall enthusiastically plunked himself down next to Jane and she began the interview. "Tell me about that wonderful woman Ruth Farrow, who was a guest at your Inn. Do you remember meeting her?" Jane knew full well Kendall had stated he hadn't met any of the digital moderators, but after the sex tape, she highly doubted his prior statement.

"She was an IT GIRL, if I ever saw one," Kendall roared at Jane. "I'm not going to be a cad and divulge any personal details, but take it from me. She was one hot Iowa ticket."

I knew it! Jane's inner voice was crackling. *I knew it.*

"Did you see much of her that week she was here, besides, shall we say, punching her hot ticket that one time, Kendall?"

"Sadly, Janie, we only had one fantastic rendezvous. I never got a second chance. Then, poof, she was gone."

"What do you mean 'gone,' Kendall?" Jane asked.

"Well, that's what you and your crew reported to us, right? That Ruth Farrow was killed. That's all I know." Kendall poured himself another drink. Jane thought *Who cares? Do I care? I don't care,* and agreed to a third highball for herself.

"One more question, Kendall. Do you remember the car accident when you were a teenager where Anna Stedman hit another car and killed a whole family?"

"You betcha, Jane. That was one huge mess, all right."

"Do you know any personal details about the collision?"

"Hell no! I mean if it would make you happy, I could try and make something up...or, Ha ha!!...'fabricate' something, like you cops like to say. But I was away at a tri-state soccer match in New Hampshire when it happened. Once I got home, I heard all about it, but there's nothing special I can tell you."

Oh Lord. This was going nowhere and Jane realized she could now hardly see straight to save her life, and she was so tired of peering into the past to try and solve everything. She just wanted to give up and lie down.

"Look, Jane—I mean, I do know it's really you, Jane...why don't we cut out of here and head outshide for some fresh air. Have you ever sheen the phosphorescence in the ocean at night? It is the most incredible thing you can imagine!"

Jane tossed back the last of her third drink like a kid downing lemonade at a picnic. It was that easy. "I'm all for phosphorescence, Kendall. Show me the way."

51
Friday, June 14
Evening Party

Once Kendall and Jane had escaped from the human crush back at the main house and were now standing, or wobbling, on the grassy savanna of the Billings Estate, Jane looked out and down the extremely long, steep stretch of green turf that eventually disappeared into utter darkness and then reappeared where the moonlight shone on the lawn as it leveled out and merged with the pier and dock below. Behind them a band on the wide, open veranda was playing a batch of baby boomer throwback tunes that sounded like Tijuana Brass and some old Sinatra melodies. When "Strangers in The Night" started up, Jane almost collapsed into a fit of laughter.

"Hey, Jane, it looks like neither of ush is in any shape to shtand up much longer, so I have The Perfect Idea, and I know you're the kind of gal who's going to love it and shay YES!"

Obviously Kendall was still on some kind of a buttered roll, and Jane was inebriated to a blood alcohol level that had flushed her face an unhealthy rosy color and left her limbs in San Francisco. So why not go for Mr. *(Ha ha ha ha!!)* Rochester's "Perfect Idea"?

Kendall turned to face Jane directly. "I propose that we do something inshane but fun! Like when we were kids. We're going to lie down on the grash and lock our arms in a hug, short of. And then we're going to kick off and roll down the hill together to the bottom. Trusht me. It's the eashiest way to get down to the dock so we can check out the phosphoreshents."

"Don't you have stairs to the dock, Kendall?" Jane asked, more than a bit confused and now teetering wildly with inebriation.

"Do we look like shtairs material to you, Janie Eyre?"

Oh no...he's slipping into his novel idea again...better go along with his suggestion of rolling downhill together like some kind of Siamese snowball. This was, Jane hoped in a mental haze, her thinking straight for once.

....

They began picking up speed by the fourth turn of their personal rotisserie on the grassy hill, and Jane now knew intimately what the phrase "hold on for dear life" was meant to express. She didn't mind that she and Kendall were horizontal now, more or less chest to chest, locked together at their arms and "down there" so to speak, and flying downhill at thirty miles per hour. It wasn't like it was X-rated or anything. It wasn't like they were on the sex tape together! As long as Mrs. Billings didn't see them disappear down the hill like two drunken hot dogs bunned together, what did it matter? Jane was only doing her investigative job and trying to get some results.

But the questions started flying. "Eeewww, Kendall! I can feel sticky things on my face and legs. What if I'm getting a bunch of slugs on me?" Jane yelled.

"Why would I slug you, Jane?" Kendall yelled back at her. "What kind of a man do you take me for?"

The torque of the two sauced cigars was accelerating and now they were avalanching down the Billings chute in one huge blur, with shots of light streaking before their eyeballs every time their heads whacked the ground.

Jane was starting to get truly pissed. "Look the fuck at what you've conned me into doing, you insane idiot!" she was shrieking. "That's the kind of man you are!"

"I'm glad I'm calming you, Jane It's great that you think I'm a kind man!" Kendall was sounding pleased.

The reason the two petrified twinkies were yelling their heads off in total miscomprehension was because with every revolution downward, Kendall's superior size and weight were causing a misalignment of velocity that left him on top of Jane a second longer than when Jane was zipping by on top of Kendall, such that he heard far less of what she was trying to say, and when she was saying it, her phrasing was getting cut off in distorted dangling participles and misplaced adverbial clauses.

On top of all this, for the split second when their tumbling ears made impact with the grass, all they could hear was something like "shawarma." So whatever they were saying or hearing, it was repeatedly punctuated by "shawarma." And then there was the twirling, skyrocketing dizziness and disorientation that were turning Jane and Kendall into two useless totem poles in a vertical log drive.

Meanwhile, Jane was unsuccessfully trying to bury her face in Kendall's neck, though she was wishing it were Konstantin's neck, so she could ward off the blades of grass that kept going up her nose, and she was absolutely certain her face was all smeared in green. She didn't have a clue how she was going to de-nub all the teeny, weeny barbs of lawn debris that were really starting to dig into the stretchy knit of her little black dress, which for all she knew had now rolled its way up over her butt and waist to park itself right below her breasts. She could hardly feel those anymore anyway because Kendall was so damn heavy when their rolling thumped him on top of her, she was sure he had reconstructed her chest size from a BB cup to an A minus cup in a few quick rotations.

Once they reached level ground, Kendall began yelling. Jane could hear Kendall was on Cloud Nine because of all his yelling. Yelling how he hadn't had this much fun since he was a kid and a horse he was riding took off over a field and Kendall dropped his reins and grabbed the horse's neck, staying there tight while the horse stretched out flat, totally galloping its heart out. TOTAL FREEDOM! That's what he had felt as he and Janie were spinning downhill at the speed of light towards the ocean's edge. EUPHORIA WAS HIS NAME! And Janie Eyre was such a great bud to come along for the zippy jelly roll ride. He couldn't get over it! ALL OF IT!

....

"Just look at the glow slipping through your fingers, Janie!" Kendall was bent down on the dock with Jane and taking aim at the sea below. "Watch me as I thrust my arm through the water. Look at that phosphorescence. Will you look at that?!" A million shimmering dots of bluish white light rose out of the ocean as Kendall's arm pulled the water drops upward. The shape of the glowing water looked like a fluorescent curtain of dense neon dots being stretched to the sky.

"I just love this phenomenon, Janie! Don't you?" Unfortunately, Kendall's enthusiasm was not rubbing off on Jane. And he seemed fixated on calling her Janie permanently, as though the real person wasn't present. Jane was starting to feel disconnected from him, the phosphorescence, and the insanity they'd put themselves through ever since they started getting hammered in the library. It was all getting to be unbearable. And she was afraid she was about to toss her thirty-six ounces of mint juleps all over the dock.

That's when Kendall's gusto cranked up and he jumped up with it. But now he was coughing...slowly at first, and then more convulsively. He was suddenly all over Jane, hugging her, and crying, then coughing and squeezing her until she could hardly breathe. He seemed like yet another person, the third iteration of Kendall Billings in one night. Jane was overcome by Kendall's height and sudden dead weight. And nauseous as she felt, exhausted from acting like a corn dog frying all the way down hill, still she wondered if she should be doing the Heimlich on Kendall to clear whatever seemed to be choking him, just as they both hit the water.

Her body sliced downward into the chilling depths. Underwater...underwater. Flailing was the first reaction Jane had after her body settled beneath the turbulence. Then she pulsed her arms up and down, to pull her body towards the surface. Where was Kendall? He wasn't bobbing up like she just had. Where was he? It was too dark to see him. And she had too much alcohol in her blood stream to see straight or to dive back under to search for him. Panic had arrived.

Jane started calling for help...wildly, and that's all she did, calling repeatedly, repeatedly, until she saw people turning on additional lights to the gangway and dock and running down the steep flight of stairs with its multiple landings and turns. The rescuers came into Jane's view more clearly as the seconds passed. Zara, her brother, Kazimir; Zeke, Maggie, and others. Storm was nowhere to be seen. Jane felt a pang about his absence. But she let go of it quickly.

"Kendall's in the water! We've got to pull him up!" Jane cried out. Someone shined a huge flashlight and Zara and Kazimir jumped towards what seemed to be Kendall's shape. Zeke jumped in as well. Jane was completely shattered now and shaking and yes, she finally crawled up onto the dock and puked into a towel that someone handed her. But what about Kendall? She couldn't believe he was not popping back up. What had happened? *What had happened?*

Kazimir and Zara finally got hold of Kendall, and Zeke helped to move them along as they neared the dock and climbed up the dock ladder while hauling Kendall's body with them. Jane could both understand and not understand why Kendall was acting so limp and out of it. What had come over him? She couldn't bear an answer. She was trying to shut out the reality and stare at the same time.

Dr. Leckman had somehow transmogrified from party onto dock and people were now saying, "Stand back. Give the doctor space."

Maggie was holding on to Jane and helping her move towards the gangway and away from Kendall's commotion.

Dr. Leckman felt for Kendall's pulse where there was no longer one to be found; he made a mental note of Kendall's bluish lips and the time of death.

52
June 15
Past Midnight

Beep. "Jane, it's Storm. Call me if you can."

Beep. "Jane, Storm here. Call me on my cell."

Beep...hang up from Storm's number.

Beep...hang up...ditto.

Maggie and Jane had driven together to Jane's house to try and decompress after the horrifying finale of the party. Maggie's mother was happy to look after Maggie's son until Maggie would return home in about an hour. She wanted to be sure Jane was stable and heading to bed soon.

"Looks like I should call Storm, even though it's past midnight. What do you think, Maggie?" Jane wondered.

"Four messages sound like he does want to hear from you. Why don't you give him a quick call? And then I really think you should go to bed, Jane. You've been through hell tonight."

"Makes sense," Jane said, feeling massively drained of her usual spunk and go get 'em.

"OK, since you might be on the phone a while, I'll head home now. I just wanted to be sure you're all in one piece. You are, aren't you?"

"Who can tell, Maggie? I guess I'll know tomorrow. I feel horrible about Kendall. You know he was crying towards the end. I don't know what was going on with him. It's making me feel so sad. It's all so insane. Oh, God...."

"Take a deep breath, Jane. I'll probably be up for another half hour at home, so call me if you need to, OK?"

"OK, Maggie. Thank you so much for being there. You've had a rough night, too. It's unbelievable."

After Maggie left, Jane sat and took in the peace of the deep silence. She didn't hold back the tears. She knew she was too tired to try and analyze all that had happened, but she was totally mystified and couldn't stop thinking about Kendall. She couldn't make sense of his insane behavior and she thought she overheard someone say on the dock that he was an experienced swimmer.

So why drown? He wasn't entirely plastered when he was focused minutes before on the phosphorescence. And earlier, when she first caught up with him and Zara at the bar station, he had seemed his usual self. Nothing overt at that point. What happened after that?

She traced through her memory to recall exactly what she had seen. When she had looked back at Kendall as she headed to the library, Zara gave him something, and then Kendall started to talk to the bartender. So what did Zara give him? Was that significant? His conversation with the bartender might have been to ask for the infamous pitcher of mint juleps. She wished that detail, for one, had never happened. Oh...it was too much to figure out. It was too much to shovel through right now.

She laid down on her sofa and was about to call Storm when the phone rang anew. "Jane. Finally. Are you OK?"

"Oh, Storm. What a night. Yah, I'm OK. But what happened to you?"

"Hold on, Jane. I'm going to go into the garage and continue talking from there. Hang on."

She heard him walking along, door opening, then closing, and he was with her again.

"It's kind of a delicate matter, Jane. My wife, Natasha, is, well, let's just say she's unhappy that I've been racing off to St. Frewin's these past few weeks. When she saw me grabbing my suit for the party, she started asking questions, and one thing led to another. I'm sorry to bring you into this, but I wanted to explain why I never showed up. Anyway, Natasha decided she needed me to be at home tonight, and I thought I'd better stay put and spend some time with her. But your emergency medical dispatch service on the island called in the death of Kendall Billings to our headquarters and then headquarters called me. I just knew you were probably in the thick of it, because of the sex tape and everything. Jane, I'm really sorry."

"Storm, it's OK. You're OK. Don't beat yourself up about this. What happened is a total nightmare, but when you hear the details, you'll see it probably would have happened even if you had been there. I mean, maybe that's not 100% true...."

Jane thought back to her and Kendall's turning themselves into a human tenpin and rolling down the nearly vertical bowling alley from hell, and well, it's possible none of that would have occurred if Storm had been in the library with them in the first place, and what about her triple dip into the mint juleps? Maybe Jane wouldn't have imbibed all three of them if Storm had been there. And the whole phosphorescence science project...maybe they wouldn't have gotten that far and ended up in the soup. But that was a lot of "maybes."

"Well, Jane, it's late and Homicide does want me on the island on Monday morning to mop this up, so we'll have time to go through everything then. But in one sentence, can you tell me what happened to Kendall?"

"I don't know, Storm. I'm baffled. He went nuts on me in kind of a creative, zesty way...that's how I can best describe it. He wasn't like that earlier in the evening, but suddenly he was on fire. I couldn't believe it."

"Jane, could it be drugs?"

"What? Oh, God. I'm so thick. That didn't occur to me...but then, everything was happening so fast."

"All right. You better get some rest over the weekend, Jane...you'll need it for Monday."

53

Monday, June 17

Jane, Zeke, and Helen were commiserating over the events of Kendall's demise when Storm arrived at the Public Safety Office. The tone among them was quite somber. A Questionable Death had landed yet again on St. Frewin's and while its arrival was their official business, everyone was tired of playing host or hostess.

"We've scheduled a meeting with the Billings family at their home, Jane. If you're ready, we should head over there now," Storm advised.

Jane all but broke down crying when she and Storm walked into the Billings residence, whose ostentatious displays of wealth and absurd taste Jane had no time for today. Just under sixty hours ago, Kendall had been alive and Jane had been plastered. What happened to Kendall was 125% her fault. Deep down, that was the conclusion she had reached over the weekend while obsessing about Kendall's fate, which was now wound up in Jane's fate, too.

A house maid directed Jane and Storm to the main parlor and announced their arrival. Zara and Mrs. Billings, *and* Lieutenant Adderley looked up from their own discussion and greeted the two officers.

Jane wished Storm had warned her about her superior officer from Major Crimes Unit-Central being in attendance. Storm must have known. They may have even taken the ferry over together. What was the big secret?

"Jane, please tell us what happened between you and Kendall the night of the party," Lieutenant Adderley asked, once Jane and Storm had found their places on heavily brocaded chairs, closing the circle of five seated people. Jane went step by step through everything she could remember, including Zara giving something to Kendall at the bar station.

Next Zara asked if she could speak. Adderley gave her the floor. She wore a beautiful yellow floral cotton dress...not one square inch of black on her garb. If she meant to give away her emotions, she had certainly succeeded.

"I want to clear up one thing Jane mentioned. When she saw me handing something to Kendall, it was an aspirin...because he told me he had a headache. Nothing more than that. Now, Jane, you mentioned Kendall started coughing and maybe even choking once you were on the dock. You say it seemed serious?"

"Right. We were standing on the dock, and Kendall was very excited to show me the phosphorescence in the ocean. But then he began coughing and sort of gagging, and before I could do anything, he collapsed onto me and we both fell in the water."

Zara looked satisfied. "Well, it sounds to me like my husband had a coughing or choking spell, something not unheard of—not that rare, and when he and Jane fell into the water, Kendall must have drowned due to his coughing spell. Does that make sense? Lieutenant Adderley? Detective Nosmot?"

"But wait a minute, Zara," Jane interrupted. "It's true Kendall was coughing hard, but right before we fell into the water, he just, he just became like dead weight...I'm sorry. I don't mean to say dead weight, but he sort of crumpled, and that's why we fell off the dock. In other words, I thought something had suddenly happened to him, in addition to the coughing."

Zara was looking at nothing in particular on the walls around them at this point. Mrs. Kenmore Billings had been quiet until then, but she now stood up to gain command of the conversation. "I will put this as simply as I can. My son has died, and I will be requesting an official autopsy. Zara may challenge me on this, but where there is doubt or uncertainty, I trust an autopsy will give us important information as to why someone in the prime of his life, as Kendall was, should suddenly assume an entirely different personality and die from coughing or choking or drowning. We don't have all the answers. I intend to get them."

Jane was impressed to see Mrs. Billings in action like that. Hard to believe that Jane might be jumping under the covers and becoming strange bedfellows with Mrs. B any minute. But it was true. Jane also had too many questions to vote in favor of rushing to bury poor Kendall. Or worse yet cremate him. It seemed to Jane that Zara was trying to move things along too briskly...just a coughing spell she said, just a casual drowning—God bless this one; and now we're done. For all his shortcomings, even if he had been an oversexed hotelier, Kendall deserved better than Zara's seemingly hasty adieu.

Lieutenant Adderley took over the reins. "I'd like to clear up a few details here, ladies. Under the law, a sudden death such as Kendall's often triggers a mandatory autopsy, unless the decedent had known health issues or other factors that could explain the timing of his death. In Kendall's case, I understand—as Mrs. Billings said—he was in the prime of his life. Therefore, the State Medical Examiner will be called in to determine the cause of death. I hope that isn't too difficult for you to handle, Zara."

"Not at all, Lieutenant Adderley. I just hate to see unnecessary effort and expense in a relatively basic scenario. And I would greatly prefer if Kendall didn't have to be cut open. It's an emotional thing, I suppose." Again, Zara remained composed and rather flat in her tone.

Jane thought it was the strangest, most griefless delivery she had ever heard. And where, by the way, were Zara's tears? Or at least the blotchy, drained-eye look of a brand-new widow under peculiar, tragic circumstances. Zara looked just fine to Jane...not a drop of sorrow in those green eyes in that smooth face. And she wore her thick chestnut brown hair loose and free...no tight, formal French knot for this new dowager.

Storm brought up another practicality. "If there are any insurance policy issues or investment beneficiary issues related to Kendall's passing," he explained to both Mrs. Billings and to Zara, "an autopsy will be a great help for bureaucratic questions. And I'm sorry to raise the topic, but we need to know if drugs were involved."

Score One Big One for Mrs. Billings. She smiled at her daughter-in-law and the guests and said, "Well, if we have that settled, I'd like to offer you some tea and cookies. Our ladies in the kitchen just made some delicious Eastern European fried dough knots sprinkled with powdered sugar—we call them crullers in our house. You can't pass that up now, can you?"

It was so "Jane" to drill down to what was really going on here. She had picked up on how miffed Zara was at the direction Kendall's posthumous fate was going. Zara did not want the autopsy that Kendall's mother had just secured. It was classic mother-in-law versus daughter-in-law politics. Who knew better how Kendall liked his pancakes? What kind of shirts he preferred? Should we bury him fast, or autopsy him slow?

Jane's silent vote for Mrs. B's insistence on an autopsy was also a vote for Jane. The coroner would discover what really did Kendall in, which would absolve Jane's guilt. And in case Lieutenant Adderley had it up his sleeve to reprimand Jane's professional negligence with something stronger than a blow torch, she'd be off the hook when the cause of death

(Drugs? More drugs? A flaccid epiglottis?) turned out to be a factor entirely out of her hands.

Delicately stuffing one of Mrs. B's fantastic crullers into her mouth, Jane warded off a sneeze as some of the powdered sugar went up her nose and then excused herself for a few minutes, after asking if she might see the library one more time...it was such an impressive collection. She hoofed it over to the fateful room and headed to the shelf where Konstantin had tucked in the book of poetry. Jane found the volume and flipped quickly to the small napkin still lodged inside on page 44.

> *Drink to me only with thine eyes,*
> *And I will pledge with mine;*
> *Or leave a kiss but in the cup,*
> *And I'll not look for wine.*

A baseball bat whomping Jane behind her knees could not have been more effective. The "chi" in her core was about to explode. Lucky for Konstantin he was nowhere in sight—Jane was all ready to have his babies...theoretically. And where did that leave warm (make that lukewarm) and bulky (he really needed to lose weight) Storm Nosmot? ...With his wife, Natasha...safe at home...married and untouchable to Jane....

"Jane...Yo, Jane. We're heading out now. You all set?" Storm had caught up with Jane at the library and was bumping into her meandering thoughts.

"Oh, Storm...sure. All set," Jane said as she quickly re-shelved the poems. "I was just dilly dallying in here." She rejoined Storm in the hall and they began walking out.

"I haven't had a chance to update you about the forensic team's car inspections and the alibis we've gathered from Anna Stedman's childhood friends," Storm started in. "I finally spoke to Josiah Orbeton last week about his visit to

St. Frewin's around the time of the murder. He had alibis for most of his time here. And when he wasn't out and about with specific people during our murder time frame, he reported he was asleep at his mother's home. His mother also would have been asleep, so there's nothing to deny or support his claim that he was in bed.

"It's the same story with the other men...Sonny Mannix and Connor Mulroy. And that's what you found with Zeke's situation. Everyone had an alibi until they were asleep in bed, and then there was no one to confirm the sleeping. For what it's worth, Zara vouched for Kendall," Storm said.

"Well, at least we've talked to all of them. And what about their cars? No blood, right? Or I would have heard about it sooner?" Jane asked.

"Right...clean...every car. Or normal messes in some cases, but no signs of a violent encounter or bloodshed. As we suspected, but disappointing all the same," Storm confirmed.

"So that's where we're at. I don't know what else we can do at this point, do you?" Jane said despondently.

"Afraid not, Jane."

54

Monday, June 17
Afternoon

Jane was alone at Public Safety when the call came in. Helen and Zeke were on a mission to collect the municipal paperwork that would permit Public Safety, on behalf of the decedents' estates, to bury the ashes of both Ruth Farrow and Shirley Jensen in St. Frewin's community cemetery. Jane paused for a second to consider the number of bodies piling up during her tenure. Was anybody keeping count? Would it be a black mark on her curriculum vitae?

"Hi, Officer Roberts?"

"Yes, Jane Roberts speaking."

"This is Sergeant Anderson from Wheatshare, Iowa. We have some interesting news for you about Ruth Farrow's mail. We heard from the Administrator of Ruth's Estate. It turns out Ruth sent in applications to both 23andme and AncestryDNA. I've got the results right here on my desk if you'd like to hear them."

"Definitely, Sergeant Anderson. Please continue," Jane said.

"OK—the family tree is what I think will interest you. It turns out Ruth's parents were not Benjamin and Jean Stedman. Apparently Ruth was adopted by the Stedmans at birth. Her biological mother is a woman by the name of Helen Orbeton. And along that family line, there's a Josiah Orbeton, who appears to be a half-brother to Ruth Farrow."

Jane was silent because she was speechless. After a moment or two she said, "Well, Sergeant Anderson. Could you hold on please?" Jane put her head in one hand, with the phone in the other. What was going on here? Helen hadn't said a word! So many questions came rushing into Jane's brain, she decided she had to hang up with Iowa for now and get back to them later.

"Um, Sergeant, something's come up in the office. I'm going to have to call you back later, OK? But please fax me those DNA results, if you could."

"Sure, Jane. I'll take care of it right away. Nice talking."

Jane put down the phone. She couldn't begin to put all the pieces together from this new revelation. She wasn't even going to try. First she had to talk to Helen and hear what she had to say. First things first. The rest would fall into place.

....

"Helen," Jane said as she walked over to the receptionist's desk later that morning and looked at Helen Orbeton with entirely new eyes. "Could we talk outside? Maybe walk a little on the old woods road? Not for long...just a few minutes."

"Sure, Jane. I hope everything's OK. You've been through an awfully lot lately."

"All's good, Helen. I just want to talk a bit. Zeke can cover for us in the meantime. OK, Zeke?" Jane called out.

"Right-O, Jane! Carry on," Zeke yelled back from his desk.

The two women set off on the path. Jane had run through her mind how to begin a conversation about the fact that her receptionist was most likely the birth mother of a recent murder victim, who may or may not have been guilty of a car crash that killed seven people seventeen years ago. Could there possibly be an appropriate opening line? Jane decided to take the course her father would have taken...straight to the point, but calmly. Calm would be important here, more effective. The fireworks blasting off inside of Jane would be inappropriate now.

"Helen, this is so awkward, but I need to talk with you about Ruth Farrow. The Iowa police called this morning. It turns out Ruth had her DNA tested and the results just came back."

"Oh, Jane. I was wondering when this moment would come along. I know what you want to ask me," Helen said, her eyes burdened with sorrow as she looked at Jane. Then she started to break up, quiet cries sneaking out of her while she tried to steady herself.

"Helen, I hate having to go into any of this. Are you OK with talking about it?"

"It's OK, Jane. There never could be a good time for all this heartache," Helen said, trying to pull herself together.

"There's been so much tragedy," Jane said, "and so much of it has been yours, which I never knew until now. But I do need to get things straight. When did you first realize Ruth Farrow was your daughter?" Jane asked as they tramped along on the soft mass of copper-colored pine needles at their feet.

Helen began her story in a shaky voice. "I really had no idea it was Anna until the Iowa news came in about her identity and the parents' names. Those tragic homicide photos of the black-haired woman didn't click at all when I saw them."

"I'm so sorry, Helen, for what you've gone through these past few weeks. I wish you had said something. I can also understand why you didn't, but your discretion is amazing."

"You know, Jane, there were a hundred times I thought I should open up, but then I thought it would only add useless drama. And Zeke told everyone who Anna Stedman was, once we heard from the Iowa police. So it seemed like we had what we needed as far as her identity. I didn't really have more to add, not even about the old car accident. And to be honest, it would have been very hard for me to go into my past in front of all of you."

"I understand, Helen. It's just so profound. You've had something like a triple trauma played out over thirty years...giving up Anna at birth, seeing Anna injured in the car accident, and now Ruth's death."

"And you know, Jane, so many questions are coming at me at once. Would it be different if I were pregnant with Anna today? I can't tell you how bad that's been eating at me. And you have no idea what a horrible impact that car accident had on my Anna." Jane could hear the growing pain in Helen's voice.

"She was the apple of everyone's eye...not just mine from a distance. The Stedmans raised her to be a wonderful girl, who would have become a wonderful person, except for that nightmare accident. It nearly killed her, Jane. And it ruined her inside and out. She was never the same, from what little I heard once the family moved away. Ruined for life is what it was, even though she lived to become a functioning adult. And what if I had kept her from the start? Should I have owned up to my fault and taken the consequences, but kept her? Could I have somehow saved her from her fate?"

Jane could see Helen straightening up, but the tears started to resurface. "Everything has changed so much in this world, Jane. Women are having babies left and right now without a care as to whether they're married, or whether they even know the baby's father. But when I was twenty-five, it was still such a disgrace, on St. Frewin's anyway, to have an illegitimate baby...particularly if you were married."

"You felt you had to give the baby away?"

"You never met my late husband, Jane. He was a good man. I couldn't see hurting him or maybe ruining everything we had. He was away doing special ops training in the Iran-

Iraq war, and I...oh...well, I guess I can tell you what happened. I fell in love with another man. And then one thing led to another. I think it surprised even me, odd as that may sound. And before my husband returned to the States—believe me when I say I meant him no harm—it's just that I got pregnant and basically had to stay close to home once I started to show. I took our son, Josiah, with me and went to live with my sister on the mainland a few months before the baby came."

"But you were able to find a good home for your baby?"

"I had been working for Mrs. Herinton, and I told her about my situation a few months into my pregnancy. She was very kind to me and had a really helpful idea. She knew the Stedmans, who hadn't had any luck having children. Mrs. Herinton felt they were decent people, so she suggested she could talk to them in confidence and find out if they would like to adopt my baby."

Helen took a deep breath. "Anyway, it all worked out, and I gave my child away to her new parents before my husband returned. It broke a part of my heart forever, Jane. It was so unbearable for so long, but I felt I had no choice. You're probably thinking I'm selfish."

"Helen, I can't judge you. Each of us has a life that unfolds in ways we never anticipated. And you've been through so much pain with all of this...."

"I'm trying to take one day at a time and accept what's happened. Part of me will be relieved when you finally discover who murdered Ruth, but I'm probably also afraid to find out. Do you know what I mean? We're such a small community here. It's excruciating to think that someone needed to kill this person I gave birth to. It's so senseless!" Helen looked up towards the clouds and the sky. "Also, Jane, at this point, if you feel I should leave work, I will."

"No, not at all. That's not necessary, unless you want to, Helen. In terms of the Farrow case, I don't think any of your personal history needs to come out for public consumption. But do you mind if I clear your situation with Storm? It will be in total confidence. Personally, I think you should stay on."

"I definitely want to help, Jane. I owe it to Anna and Ruth, so to speak. Go ahead and check with Storm. I trust the two of you."

"I appreciate that, Helen. And strange as this may sound, hearing about your love for someone else in your marriage has opened some kind of door for me. I haven't gone into my divorce with you. I never felt like you needed to hear my ranting because it's all so tiring and tired...divorces are a dime a dozen, right? But listening to you just now adds a new dimension. I mean, my husband got caught up in another woman and I was so crushed by my discovery and the damage, and now here we are ending our marriage."

"I'm sorry to hear that, Jane," Helen said, looking at her sadly. Her face was lit by a shaft of sunlight coming down through the pine trees overhead. There was no slut or whore that Jane could see. It was only Helen.

"You've described how falling in love with someone else is simply a possibility in life. Hearing it from you makes it more believable...and bearable." Jane closed her eyes momentarily. "It's not necessarily a heartless betrayal. Or not meant to be. The falling in love, crossing that line, can be there without an intent of betrayal. It's a shift of focus at the time. Maybe you don't fully realize or admit to yourself what a huge shift you're undertaking. It just happens." Jane stood there quietly.

Then she looked at Helen. "What kills me is wondering if the shift can really come out of the blue, or if there is already a wedge—even the tiniest of wedges—that is cleaving away at an otherwise comfortable marriage. But then I have to remind myself, my marriage was not comfortable. It was a mistake. In your case, you kept your marriage. I don't think I'll dare to ask you right now if you've kept your other love."

"No, Jane. Let's save that for another day," Helen answered wearily.

With that, the two women turned back towards the Public Safety Office as if it were just another day, almost. But somewhere in the back of her mind, Jane reached for that detail Rajiv had discovered...did he say a partial match with Ruth's DNA? Of course it was a partial match...of course it was. It was Josiah Oberton.

55
Monday, June 17
Late Afternoon

"Oh, Rajiv. This is exactly what I didn't want to hear. You really can't certify a match between the sweatband DNA and Kendall's DNA?" Jane let out a groan and leaned back in her office chair. Kendall's life had slipped away before her eyes and now the possibility of his murderous guilt followed suit.

"Sorry, Jane. Science has spoken. I can't twist the facts."

"Never mind. The poor man is dead now anyway. How about the other men's DNA? Any luck with those?"

"Well, it turns out not all is lost. I've found the human tied to our partial DNA match on the sweat band. It's Josiah Oberton, Jane. That's based on both the DNA profile you faxed me and Josiah's own DNA results."

"What do you know," Jane said, probably too matter-of-factly. She should have sounded more surprised, but she wasn't. She quickly whistled to give her reaction a little more punch. She didn't admit she already knew because she didn't feel right going into Helen's history for now.

"You don't sound any too stunned, Jane. That's not like you," Rajiv teased.

"Oh, sorry. It's been a long day, Rajiv. Too much happening here. In fact, I better hang up and call Storm now to report your findings to him. But thanks for everything. You've done a fantastic job for us," Jane added as they said goodbye.

....

"Basically I feel like my head's about to explode with all these details coming down," Jane was reporting to Storm, once Helen had left for the day. "Today we received DNA results from Iowa that show Helen Orbeton is the mother of both Anna Stedman and Josiah Orbeton. I spoke to Helen and she confirms it all. Can you believe it?"

"Getting complicated, isn't it?" Storm said.

"And I just got off the phone with Rajiv, who concludes the partial match of DNA found on the sweatband is, indeed, Josiah Orbeton. He really is Anna Stedman's half-brother. This is based on Josiah's own commercial DNA tests and Rajiv's analysis of Josiah's latest DNA sample. Rajiv is certain Josiah wore the sweatband at some point.

"So what do you make of it, Jane?" Storm asked.

"Well, I'm starting to wonder if Josiah Orbeton and Anna Stedman hung out together more than anyone has reported. I mean, could they have been intuitively drawn together as teenagers who unknowingly shared the same mother? And along those lines, was Josiah driving the car with Anna in it when the old accident occurred. He may be the one we're looking for, Storm."

"Or he may not be the one, Jane," Storm cautioned. "We don't really have enough evidence to haul him back to Maine at this point."

"So let's have the police in Josiah's town speak to him again. They can ask him about his friendship with Anna Stedman. Isn't that worth a shot?" Jane pressed.

"Go for it, Jane," Storm said. "We've got nothing to lose." After a moment, Storm kept talking. "There's one major hurdle we still have to get over. Forensics found no evidence in anyone's car...no sign of blood. So where's the bloody clue? What are we missing in the big picture?" Storm fumed.

"Look, if we're right—if Dr. Kerner is right—that a car was probably used to move the body, then where is that car?" Jane asked. "What do people do if they need a car...and they don't want to use their own car? They rent one, yes? Or they borrow one, right? A rental or a borrowed car—that's what we're missing, Storm!"

Jane was beginning to feel the heat of the chase again. "I'll start calling the rental companies first thing tomorrow morning. I am not going to let this car get away from me, wherever it is."

56

Tuesday, June 18
Morning

"Jane, what the hell is going on with Solstice Spree this year, if you don't mind my asking?" Sonny Mannix, the Maine State Ferry captain on duty, was spouting into Jane's phone. "We have got reservations for cars and foot traffic piling up this week like we've never seen in the history of St. Frewin's Island. Can you, as Public Safety Officer, tell me how we're supposed to handle this kind of volume without mashups galore?"

Jane sat there, phone to her ear, perplexed at the call, the questions, the fact that Sonny Mannix was angry at her at all. "Run that by me again, Sonny?" she asked.

"At least the DOT has finally had the brains to release two more ferries to shuttle all the insane traffic you're going to get for Spree this year. Now, I'm not saying it's not a good thing budget-wise, but it's not a good thing. It's going to be a traffic jam out there with all these additional boat crossings. Plus I hear Abe Jenkins is doubling up his water shuttle fleet with subcontractors to cover his increased load. So, I'm gonna ask you a second time, Jane—What, in the name of Sweet Mother of God, is going on?"

Jane sat back from the salty captain's spewing eruptions and finally put two and two together. "Oh, God, Sonny, we have Samantha Lloyd and my sister to thank for this. I thought it might create all kinds of hysteria. And now you've confirmed it."

"Why would Sam and your sister be guilty of jamming our ferry schedule to high heaven? Who is your sister anyway? What could she possibly have to do with all of this?" Sonny was now roaring.

"Sonny—I'm going to tell you this in confidence, though from the sound of it, there is no more confidential any longer. You may as well hear the worst of it. My sister, Desdemona Spode, is here visiting from L.A., and she's serving as the Master of Ceremonies at this year's Solstice Spree and I told...."

"Huh? You're kidding. Hot Damn, Jane! You're pulling my leg, right? Desdemona Spode? THE Desdemona Spode? She's your sister? Whoa, whoa, whoa. Wait till I tell the guys! Our ferries are definitely going to be swamped. Now I see the light. Holy Shit, I've got to figure out how to juggle my crews so I can get to the opening ceremony of Solstice Spree. It's going to be a challenge, but if I can just rearrange my crew chart here, I bet I can...."

"Sonny, sorry to interrupt your rescheduling, but how do you know my sister?" Jane was doing this to herself. She knew better, but she just had to ask. "Why do you suddenly want to attend Solstice Spree along with obviously thousands of other people who never thought about St. Frewin's Island in their life?"

"Jane. Your own sister? I mean, you must know. She's quite the celebrity in, well, shall we say, a certain world of film. And I'm a big fan of hers!"

"Oh, please. You, too, Sonny? Is no man immune to my sister's charms and talents? This Solstice Spree has gotten way out of hand. Thanks to Samantha's wild-eyed planning, the island is going to be overrun by all kinds of horny bastards and deviants."

"Oh, Jane, lighten up a little, will you? What are you? Too good for sex? Maybe you're the deviant. What's the problem with a little porn in your family tree? Are you too evolved to stomach sassy intercourse for entertainment? Really, Jane. Try joining the human race, for God's sake."

After Jane wound down from the highly-charged conversation, she quickly dialed Storm to make sure he had a way to get to St. Frewin's for Solstice Spree. She had invited him, Finn, and Rajiv to join in the festivities, but now she was afraid they would be stranded on the mainland. Who knew this year's attendees were going to swell into something akin to Woodstock or Mardi Gras? Jane berated herself for her lack of imagination and her inhibitions.

"So, Storm, it's going bonkers out here. Tons of people have reserved space on the ferries and the water shuttle. Did you make plans for you and the guys to get over here for Solstice Spree?"

"You bet, Jane. We're all set. The minute Finn heard Desdemona was going to MC the Spree, he got right on the job and made all the reservations we needed."

"Well, how many reservations is that, Storm? I thought you and Finn and Rajiv were it."

"Oh, not just us, Jane. Up to fifty percent of our staff put in for a vacation day for this Friday. And when Lieutenant Adderley heard the news, he hopped right on board...he says he's followed Desdemona Spode for the past three years, believe it or not."

Jane just about chucked her phone out her office window. Finn hadn't followed a word of her stern lecture about keeping quiet about Desdemona's career. And Lieutenant Adderley? But, so soon after Sonny Mannix's scolding, Jane took a deep breath, and another, and thought about her yoga goals. Let go of the stress...breathe in, breathe out; diaphragm in, diaphragm out. She knew she had to get it off her chest...get over the hump of Desdemona humping all those guys in all those porn films. It was adult entertainment. It was a reality. Jane didn't have to take offense.

So what if it was an unfathomably WEIRD component in Jane's personal life? Tolerance was going to be a challenge, but it was time for Jane to learn some Tolerance...she was going to shut up and put up, but GOD DAMN THAT FINN! God Damn Him. Hah! She knew exactly what she would do for revenge. It wasn't violent. But it would be satisfying to Jane. And it would be funny. Why not? Finn had it coming to him. Someone had to start him on the path to clean living. Christian morals and family values—that's what he needed.

"OK, Storm. Glad to hear you're all set. See you at the Spree on Friday!" and Jane hung up.

Her brain started pouncing and snarling at her, and she rushed to crunch the numbers of visitors they could expect for Solstice Spree. Jane suddenly envisioned mounds of bodies in sleeping bags, piles of discarded pizza boxes, empty plastic water jugs, apple cores, and candy wrappers. She grabbed the phone again and rang up Samantha.

"OK, Samantha. This whole Desdemona as Master of Ceremonies was your brilliant idea, right? So please tell me, are you equipped to make and sell food to all these porn addicts who are about to descend on St. Frewin's Island for the Spree? Has your planning committee ordered enough port-o-potties to accommodate the hordes...and not just any old port-o-potties, but the ones that are child-safe so kids won't fall in and get buried in a can of crap?"

"Take it easy, Jane! We're good. We're OK. When Nathan and I were out sailing the other day, I told him all about our expansive plans, and he proved to be such a gentlemanly savior, I can't praise him enough."

Jane looked around for the best place to puke as Samantha waxed on about Nathan this, and Nathan that.

She was going to have to have a talk with Samantha about Nathan's upcoming wedding bells, feeble though they might be.

Sam's report kept glowing. "It turns out Nathan has this cousin who supplies all kinds of party gear for huge corporate events along the coast, including really high-grade poly-johns. Nathan said he'd be happy to cover the bill to have his cousin provide our event with twenty-five high-grade poly-johns, plus enough TP for thousands, and a crew to set everything up and then haul the crap away once we're done. Is that not the sweetest offer you have ever heard?"

Jane had to stop trying to gag herself and focus on answering Samantha...with Tolerance. Jane swallowed her pride and exclaimed "Why Samantha...you and Nathan have made my day. That's fantastic! And about the food for all these people sleeping overnight or day tripping...you're all set on that, right?"

"Again, we're golden, Jane. I've had Torrance Balankoff assisting me on all the details. She's great, by the way. Kind of unconventional in some ways, but a really good organizer. We got the Town to up the number of food vendor permits this year, so we'll have more than enough chow for sale to all these hungry visitors. And Torrance negotiated with the island conservation corps to organize as many volunteers as we need for general clean-up during the day and the day after. They know we're going to give them a nice fat donation once we divvy up the hefty charitable contributions we'll be able to pull in this year. So it really is all coming together like a charm."

"I am so relieved to hear all of this, Samantha. I had no idea how happily out-of-control this event had become, but it sounds like you're covering all the angles. I'm very proud of you."

"Jane, I'm good at this stuff, and we've been lucky so far. You've got to trust that most of us are capable adults...we can depend on each other and we can get things done. And your sister has been a dream. She's all set to deliver the opening presentation. And she's even prepared herself as the female understudy for the role of Julibyte in Speedo Shakespeare—as a back-up for Zara Billings, just in case. So, it should all go according to plan. No more worrying, OK?"

57
Monday, June 18, Afternoon
and Tuesday, June 19

"I'm sorry Officer Roberts, but we have no auto rentals under any of those names for the past year." After thanking the supervisor, Jane clicked the phone and checked off another name...Sunnycars. She had never heard of the outfit. Alamo, Thrifty, Hertz, Avis, Ace, Enterprise, Easirent, National, Budget, Dollar...none of their supervisors had found anyone on Jane's list of potential suspects in their computer banks.

Jane laughed at her next and last attempt...Rent-A-Wreck. Inspiring. She dialed their number in Biddeford...definitely a long shot. No logic in their location concerning Jane's search. But maybe someone in coastal Maine would go to the trouble to rent a death mobile all the way down in southern Maine.

"No, Ma'am. None of those names comes up on our rental records," said the woman on the phone.

"You know, let me ask you something," Jane said to the Rent-A-Wreck clerk. "Where could someone rent a car in the State of Maine that wasn't a national car rental agency, or even a statewide rental business? Have you ever heard of local car rental companies? Hope that isn't a stupid question."

"No, no. Not stupid. Let me think. I know down here in our city there's maybe one or two really local spots that will lease out cars...like car repair places. But have you thought to ask any car dealerships? I think some places rent out cars so you can try out a car, or rent a car for business or holiday travel, something like that. Maybe check them out."

"I didn't know that," Jane said. "Thanks so much for the tip! Oh, and one more thing. Do you know how many dealerships there are in Maine by any chance?"

"Let me look quick on the computer." The clerk ratatatted the keys, they both waited while a million routers sent info packets hopping all over America, and then the clerk came back with an answer. "This news article says there are 115 dealerships in Maine."

"Oh good," said Jane. "That shouldn't take forever. Thank you for your help."

"And don't forget the used car dealers, Ma'am. They probably rent, too."

Jane sucked in her cheeks and popped them out. This was going to be a chore. What a pain. Detective work at its driest. But she could do this. Work was work.

She hopped on the ferry to the terminal on the mainland and searched on the waiting room computer for new and used car dealerships in an ever-widening circle radiating out from Abenaki County. Then she took the ferry back to the island and began forging her way through the dealerships.

....

Palmyra was her next stab...Roy's Used Car Sales in Palmyra. Maybe Roy, or his wife, or his son would be Jane's lucky strike?

"Hi! Is this Roy's Used Car Sales?" Jane asked cheerily, coaxing along her enthusiasm for the mindless task.

"You dialed the number, didn't ya?" the elderly female voice croaked back.

"So this is Roy's," Jane concluded. She began her spiel. "I'm calling from the Public Safety Office on St. Frewin's Island. We're trying to track down a car rental this past May. Would it be possible for you to check your May records for about five names?"

"What makes you think, young lady, that I got all day to do that?"

"Well, it's only five names, and I hope it won't take too long...Mrs. Roy, is it?" Jane asked. "We're working on a murder case and you would be doing us an important civic favor if you could."

"Murder?! Are you pullin' my leg? Here you are, Missy— a total stranger. And you're expectin' me to find your murderer? I ain't gettin' caught up in no murder, Missy. I don' want some jackass killer comin' round to grind up my grankids into mincemeat 'cause their granma's doing her civic whatnot. You can hang up right now, or you can ask me another question," came the old woman's vinegary reply.

Jane heard some sudden rustling and clanking of the phone and another, seemingly saner voice came over the line. "Hi, pardon my mother-in-law. She was just helping to man the phones while I dealt with the kids. May I help you, Ma'am?"

Jane calmly repeated her request.

"Yes, certainly, I can help you with that. Please give me...Oh, Cherryty! Put that cell phone down! Don't you dare go near the toilet with that! Cherryty, no! Just a minute, Ma'am...."

Jane heard the mother-child brawl commence and escalate. Over the phone line came the heated skirmish— child screeching, toilet flushing, mother massacring child due to cell phone thrown into flushing toilet, mother hustling child away, mother returning to Jane's call.

"Now where were we, Ma'am? Sorry about all that. Why don't you run those names by me slowly and I'll check them as you read them."

....

"Now, you know it's been more than two weeks since May, Officer Roberts. So chances are any car rented in May would have been returned by now and I would have seen what shape it was in." Harry Mann himself of Harry Mann Pre-Owned Cars was lecturing Jane on the line.

"I realize my inquiry is somewhat awkward, Mr. Mann," Jane hastened to add.

"Awkward? Sure is, Officer Roberts. We must seem to you like the kind of hick place that rents cars to murderers all the time," Mr. Mann said. "And when people return those cars all soaked in blood and guts, you know how we clean 'em up good?"

Jane held her tongue.

"We rip the whole fuckin' inside out. I mean what the hell are you drivin' at, Officer Roberts? If someone's taken my inventory and turned it into a casket, don't you think I would have called the police? I think we're done here."

....

Jane's next call was to "Dick Lovett / Deals on Wheels" in Etna. "Thank you for checking all the same, Ma'am," Jane said after the clerk found no pertinent rentals in May. "May I ask what Etna is known for these days?" Jane was curious. She wondered who even went to Etna.

"Oh, you'd be surprised, Officer Roberts. Our big focus is spiritualism."

"No kidding. That's amazing. How does it work? If I showed up in Etna, how would I pursue spiritualism?" Jane really did wonder.

"You should look up our town on the web," the clerk answered. "In fact, later this summer in August we're offering a week-long seminar with classes that might interest you. I could put you on our mailing list. We've got 'Being One with Spirit: Taking Mediumistic Abilities to Next

Level,' and 'Your Role with Animal Companions: Who Choose Who?' and so on."

" 'Who Choose Who'?" Jane asked. "Don't you mean 'Who Chooses Who'? Or maybe 'Who Chooses Whom'? I'm just thinking of subject and verb agreement and objective case pronouns."

"Ma'am...I can't really answer that for you. We aim for a higher realm here; we're not too worried about words, you know? Maybe you'd like to talk to one of our mediums or healers? Maybe one of them could conjure up your car rental for you?"

....

And so it went...for hours. The random tetchy exchange bobbed up at times, which suggested to Jane that some people had actually had experiences renting cars to homicidal maniacs. But for her specific search, no luck. No luck anywhere within a seventy-mile radius from the mainland ferry terminal for St. Frewin's Island. Jane decided to stop there. Helen could take over and make more calls the rest of the week.

58
Friday, June 21
Solstice Spree

"It's great to see a presentable version of Desdemona in action," Jane whispered to Maggie and Torrance, as they waited for the Master of Ceremonies to announce the winners of this year's Chef Competition. "When she first came on stage for the Opening Welcome, with all that sunlight behind her creating a halo around her body, she looked like a Madonna or our Lady of Lourdes, don't you think?"

"Or even Botticelli's 'Birth of Venus,' but with clothes on, of course," Torrance added.

"Yah. In that beautiful Renaissance gown, Desdemona really clicked," Jane went on. "I even think the transcendent glow of her image has had a calming effect on the crowd. How else do you explain her controlling this sea of male lechery all around us? They're like lambs right now, nestled in with their sheepy Mom."

"You could be right, Jane," Maggie said. "It's amazing we're not hearing hooting from the younger guys and whistling from all the older gents. Maybe there are enough women and children here to help keep the testosterone in check."

The three women looked across the mass of humanity that had assembled, at complete strangers smiling at one another, at the wonder and amusement playing out on people's faces over how such a bizarre set of circumstances could combine to transform one day into a really great day. And so it came to pass that the Ginger-Headed Goddess Sister, now metamorphosed into the Ginger-Headed Earth

Mother Goddess, drew in all sincere participants and island residents, day visitors, and debauched male tribes close to her heart and bestowed upon them peace on the longest day of the year.

....

"And now for the favorite moment everyone has been waiting for!" Desdemona called out to the crowd. "Samantha Lloyd has just handed me the envelope with this year's winner of the Solstice Spree Chef Competition, focusing on foods based on historical figures or events. And here we go. OK, let me see," Desdemona paused, reading over the contents of the envelope. "What do you know?" she said, stretching her beautiful, long, bare arms out to her audience. "It looks like our esteemed panel of judges could not zero in on any one top winner, so we have a winning sex...tet...oops, did I say that? ...We have six winning chefs with the following blue-ribbon entries. We'd like whoever was behind each crowning achievement to rise as you hear your creation named, and please join me on stage for the awards presentation. Here we go:

> *Custard's Last Stand!*
> *Roman M-Pie!*
> *Attila the Bun!*
> *Dessert Storm!*
> *Julius Cheesewiz!*
> *And Cleopaté!*"

Happy chefs giddily began making their way up to the stage for their moment of recognition. Laughter and cheering poured out from all directions and the clapping turned from random to rhythmic.

Bystanders could overhear confusion among some of the older set. "I don't get it. Do you, Stan?" Wilbur Moody was looking at Stan Helmstadt with a blank face as people around him exhibited a variety of reactions...outright chuckling, quizzical looks, or total non-comprehension. "What's Custard's Last Stand all about? What could that taste like?" Mr. Moody said.

"Look, Wilbur. All those winnahs have funny names. Just think about it. Cleopaté...that's a joke on Cleopatra. Pâté is something you can spread on crackahs...sometimes it's got livah in it," Stan explained.

"Well, I don't know about no liver spread, Stan. It sounds like fancy food. And you know me, if the Missus can't find that there Cleopaté at Walnuts, I'm probably not eating it. We stick to Walnuts for our fancy party stuff."

"Do you mean Walmaht, Wilbur? It's Walmaht!"

"Yah, that's what you call it."

People got a further hee-haw out of the winning prizes as Desdemona daintily handed to each of the beaming chefs a rolling pin with two round scouring pads stuck on one end. Jane thought that was a risqué stretch for Samantha and her committee to go public with rewards so phallic in appearance, but that was Jane's problem.

Samantha took center stage next and assured the crowd that before Speedo Shakespeare commenced, there would be a half hour break, during which time interested parties would have a chance to mingle with Desdemona for autographs and selfies, and various DVDs would be available for purchase to support the Solstice Spree charitable causes.

Jane pondered whether she might have a melt-down over this part of the events, but she marched herself back towards Tolerance—again—after Maggie reminded her of all the municipal benefits. "Jane, just think of the recycling program and how Desdemona's helping to raise money towards an improved separation facility at the dump to benefit the environment. It'll be such a step forward!"

59

Friday, June 21
Mid-Morning

Officer Kaylee Dayton sat at her computer, intensely scanning through CCTV footage at the Maine Drug Enforcement Agency's headquarters in Augusta. She had a knack for reading the footage, her superiors had noticed, and her seventh sense couldn't simply be chalked up to her youthful eyes and fresh enthusiasm.

"Well, this is interesting, Sergeant Arey. Do you remember those new CCTV cameras the Agency installed for the China White sting operation down near Route 16 in Central Maine? They had some kind of glitch and were out of synch during May? The tech guys finally cleaned up the data and now we've got visuals for that specific location." Officer Dayton moved her mouse to sharpen a certain image on her computer screen. "Most of the action involves our known suspects, but in late May, you should come look at this woman. She seems out of place. Doesn't she appear quite upscale...more than middle class maybe?"

Sergeant Arey walked over to Dayton's desk and peered at the woman captured on the screen. It was her excellent posture and how confidently she held herself that set her apart from most of the other players caught in the Maine DEA's digital spider web at this site. The woman was filmed walking into the package store on the side street, and once inside, a second camera showed her asking the cashier a question, then handing some money over to a second man, who in turn, gave her a very small package...sufficiently incriminating details to support bringing the lovely looking woman in for questioning. Her license plate was clearly discernible from yet another CCTV eye outside the package store. By the time Officer Dayton's lunch break rolled around, she had organized all the information her superiors needed to hand it off to the DEA's Regional Task Force covering Abenaki County. They would take it from there.

....

The Central DEA Sergeant responsible for relaying sting operation findings for the coastal region was talking over the State police radio system to his colleague Officer Tuttle of the MCU, which covered the DEA Regional Task Force for Abenaki County. "You're telling me about fifty percent of your force is simultaneously out on an unpaid free day today, and that about fifty percent of your force is spending that free day on St. Frewin's Island?"

"Roger that," said Officer Tuttle.

"Am I dealing with a coincidence of mammoth proportions, Officer Tuttle?" asked the DEA Sergeant.

"I guess you could say that, Sir. And it'd be awfully redundant to send additional officers to pick up your suspect. There's already more than enough off-duty manpower out there to arrest the entire population of the entire island. I'll call down to their Public Safety Office, and their staff will alert some officers to take care of the task. Not a problem."

The Central DEA Sergeant hung up the radio from his conversation with Officer Tuttle and looked at his colleague seated nearby. "You heard all of that, right? Did any of it strike you as a breach of duty, or somewhat errant? What is going on on St. Frewin's Island that we don't know about?"

....

"Hey there, Mrs. Orbeton. This is Officer Tuttle from the DEA Regional Task Force. Any chance I can talk to Lieutenant Adderley or Storm Nosmot?"

"Well, Hi, Officer Tuttle. We haven't seen you out here for quite some time. I guess that's a blessing—no offense to you," Helen chuckled and smiled into the phone mouth piece. "None of the force are here right now. I can run over to the Solstice Spree celebration and deliver your message to them if you'd like."

"Thanks, Mrs. Orbeton. Yes, this is very important. Please tell Lieutenant Adderley and his crew that the DEA needs a minimum of three officers to transport Zara Billings to the Regional DEA office in Graniteville as soon as possible. Zara Billings is a prime suspect, and she's considered a serious flight risk at this time, so she should be escorted with caution. And one more thing, Mrs. Orbeton. We've alerted the Chief Medical Examiner's Office about this situation. They concluded their findings on the autopsy of Kendall Billings late this afternoon. Lieutenant Adderley and his crew should give the Medical Examiner a call right away."

"Will do, Officer Tuttle. And I do hope you get a chance to catch a ferry to the island before summer's over. Bye for now." Helen shook her head as she stuffed the DEA notes in her pocket and headed out the door to track down the officers.

60
Friday, June 21
Early Evening

It wasn't every year that the New England weather patterns cooperated with the timing of Solstice Spree. In former summers, hammerhead thunder clouds had blown at times, drenching the wobbly Speedo Shakespeare sets, or pelting Lady Macbeth on the head with violent batches of hail. This June, however, a gentle southwesterly breeze flowed warmly into the golden light of early evening…the perfect aura and tone for "Romeo and Julibyte."

Ooohs and aahs trickled from the audience as the curtain arose on St. Frewin's very own Zara Billings, resplendent as Julibyte in her gown of fine linen and silk organza, her chestnut hair piled high, her green eyes awash in sorrow over her missing love:

Romeo, Romeo, WIFI art thou Romeo?
Deny thy father and refuse thy DOMAIN.
Or if thou wilt not, be but sworn my love
And I'll no longer be a CPU.

While Julibyte lamented, Romeo silently appeared on stage, hidden from Julibyte off to one side, where his Renaissance version of a laptop sat atop an ornately carved pillar. Romeo's alter ego (Stan Helmstadt) was up on a ladder over Romeo's head, waving huge flashcards to illustrate what Romeo was typing away on his laptop, as he input his search terms into a search engine. Stan waved a flashcard: "Who's Julibyte?" And another: "Where's

Julibyte?" Followed by…"Julibyte—images" and then…"Julibyte—White Pages?"

Helen Orbeton quickly walked over to Storm and Adderley and quietly delivered the DEA directive. Storm and Adderley separated and discreetly gave a sign to several of their colleagues as Julibyte continued with her aches and pains…

'Tis but thy MEMORY STICK that is my enemy:
Thou art thyself, though not a MEGABIT.
What's MEGABIT? It is nor KILOBYTE nor GIGABYTE…

As Julibyte called out her woes, six men calmly began to approach the stage, casually, but methodically, as though Shakespeare himself had penned their stage directions. Julibyte seemed caught up in her pertinent swoon, but something was ratcheting her voice higher and higher, with a growing strain of hysteria…

Nor TERABYTE nor ZETTABYTE
nor any other YOTTABYTE
Belonging to a MOTHERBOARD.
O be some other HOME PAGE!

As the plain clothesmen approached the bereft Julibyte, she began sidestepping them, inching away from all these knaves who would close in on her in vain. For some reason, the law enforcement knaves themselves suddenly seemed caught up in the hypnosis of the drama, and instead of rushing at Julibyte, they too began to mimic her sidesteps as she dodged them more and more frantically on the stage, with her monologue becoming more heightened and shriller….

What's in a DOMAIN? That which we call a CHIP

LOBSTERS WITHOUT BORDERS

By any other name would smell as PHISHY!;
So Romeo would, were he not Romeo call'd
Retain that dear perfection which he owes
Without that title. Romeo, doff thy HARDWARE!

Julibyte was now emoting like fireworks...a true Thespian to the end with a thorough delivery of her frenzied lines:

And for that FLOPPY DISK, which is no part of thee,
TAKE ALL MY COOKIES!!#$&~%(!!

In one precarious, flying leap, Julibyte did a broad jump off the stage and tore through the throngs, racing away from the officers, who were quickly coming to their senses and piling in after her. They closed the gap and narrowed in on their prey, but Julibyte wasn't a Capulet for nothing. She dug into the deep pockets of her Renaissance gown, turned her head sharply towards one of the law enforcement knaves, and doused his face with SABRE 3-in-1 pepper spray.

The crowd was aghast, as they saw the wild-eyed Julibyte sprinting off through the far fields, her beautifully coiffed tresses now tumbling down...her diaphanous gown being torn from her sleeves and skirting by the thorns of wild roses, all the while the police were following in hot pursuit.

The stunned audience looked to one another for an explanation, to figure out how cops got into a Shakespeare play. "Well, I don't know what the world is coming to!" Trudy Moody exclaimed. "What just happened up there, Wilbur?" He hesitated, speechless at first. "It's just a new-fangled thing, Trudy, Honey. Don't pay any attention to that chase scene. Those cops are going to bring Julibyte back to her Romeo 'cause you can tell he's having a hard time finding her."

....

The next day, as the ferry powered up and churned forward, a superior summer day in Maine opened wide to the passengers on the top deck. The sky was reaching clear over to Spain, with mashed potato clouds flung across the infinite blue. Pure bleached sunlight struck the ocean surface in every direction, conjuring up images of tiny white-hot butter pats jiggling atop the choppy, metallic blue sea.

The talk on the ferry was everything Solstice Spree. Rubbing elbows with Desdemona Spode of course! And what good, clean fun it had all been, nonetheless. But what about Julibyte on the run from the law—would they ever get the full story on that?

A few visitors pointed their binoculars towards St. Frewin's Island as the ferry shoved its way through mild swells, slowly passing alongside the island cemetery. Unbeknownst to the ferry passengers, Ruth Farrow had finally been cremated, and since there was no one in Iowa to return her to, and no known relatives anywhere really, the Town Office had consented to the burial of Ruth's ashes on St. Frewin's Island.

The ferry riders could see a lone woman with a scarf on her head, and she was weeping and kneeling before what looked like a very small, very new grave, blanketed in peonies. Although the onlookers could not hear what the woman was saying, perhaps some of them could imagine what she felt, because they, too, had felt the same at some point in their lives when pain and the passage of time refused to uncouple themselves. *Dear God, I'm releasing her to you...to the air, to the sky. I don't want to let her go. I hate letting her go...even now after all these years.*

After the grieving woman had departed, some lingering passengers peering at the receding island saw a man in a white truck drive up and walk over to stand quietly before the same headstone. A ferry passenger happened to train his binoculars at the truck's license plate. "Look at this," he said to his friend. "I think it reads 'DR. VET.'"

257

61
Tuesday, August 20

It wasn't only Jane who was dreading the "Cold Case Recap" meeting scheduled that August day at the DEA Task Force Office in Graniteville. Storm's fifteen years in homicide hadn't produced any miracles for him concerning Ruth Farrow. Finn stuck by his sense that Ruth had been the victim of a random person on St. Frewin's Island with a bent for evil—someone who had no prior history with Ruth and never would be found. Rajiv felt frustrated that all the DNA forensic tools in the world hadn't helped him reach a useful conclusion.

Jane held her breath, hoping maybe the homicide team could squeak under the wire with a "Luke Warm Recap" because although Ruth Farrow's murderer remained unknown and at large, the homicide team had a suspect in hand for the death of Kendall Billings. Zara Billings—following her fleet-footed efforts to elude Adderley and his men—had finally been cornered and escorted down to the Regional DEA Office for an interview on her possible role in her husband's now firmly-established death by fentanyl-laced heroin.

No amount of questioning was able to determine if Kendall had taken the China White of his own accord, or if Zara had helped the fatal dose along its way and into his system, but Zara was definitely booked for possession of an illegal drug. And the Assistant Attorney General was working up a creative murder charge in the vein of "*res ipsa loquitor*"—the trusty Latin term for "the thing speaks for itself": But for Zara's purchase of the deathly drug and supplying the drug to Kendall, or giving him the drug without his knowledge, Kendall might still be alive today to bail her out.

Mother-in-law Billings certainly wasn't about to foot the bill, and Zara's cash flow was tight at the moment. She had been patiently sitting around in jail until she could figure out how to post the $1,000,000.00 bail slapped on her, given the very nature of her role to some degree in Kendall's death and her mad flight as Julibyte during Solstice Spree.

When Lieutenant Adderley walked into the Cold Case meeting, everyone shook off their disappointment over their lack of results and came to attention.

"So, here we are," Adderley began, not glaring at them, but looking rather lackluster. "No closer to the truth than the day Ruth Farrow was murdered. What do we know, Storm?"

"We know the state of Ruth's body when she was found. We can conclude she suffocated as a result of the lobster in her throat and the stones up her nose. And we learned from law enforcement in Iowa, where Ruth lived and worked, that Ruth had changed her name. She was christened Anna Stedman and lived on St. Frewin's Island for a short time until her family moved to the mainland.

"Anna's family would return to the island in the summertime, and during one of those visits she had a car accident that resulted in the death of a family of seven. She herself sustained serious bodily injuries, including severe amnesia, which never cleared sufficiently for her to recall her accident.

"Her family moved to Iowa following the accident and went to court to change Anna's name to Ruth Farrow. In late May of this year, Ruth's Iowa employer sent her to St. Frewin's with some colleagues for an R&R retreat, and she was murdered sometime in the evening hours of May 23 or the early morning hours of May 24. That's where our trail runs cold."

"Finn, Rajiv, Jane, do you have anything to add to that?"

"We searched Ruth's hotel room and found nothing of consequence," Finn said. "We interviewed and researched Ruth's colleagues, the Inn owners and staff, as well as the few people on St. Frewin's who had known contact with Ruth, or who had known Ruth, that is, Anna Stedman, as a youngster. We were unable to isolate any suspect in the end."

Rajiv gave his input. "Our department investigated samples collected at the murder site, but we came up empty-handed, given the heavy rainfall the night of the murder. In addition, we searched the home of Nathan Herinton, who socialized with Ruth Farrow during her last week alive, and we analyzed a foil-wrapped piece of partially eaten fried chicken found near the crime scene.

"We also checked the DNA of anyone known to have had contact with Ruth Farrow during her visit, and the DNA of the now adult friends of Anna Stedman from when she visited the island as a teenager. Our findings confirm Ruth had sexual contact with Nathan Herinton. Zeke Pendleton was the person who happened to drive by the crime scene and toss leftover fried chicken out his car window on the day the murder occurred—apparently a coincidence."

"You're all comfortable with that coincidence?" Lieutenant Adderley looked at the four of them. They nodded in assent.

"Jane Roberts located an old evidence package from the archived files on the Anna Stedman car accident," Rajiv continued. "This evidence package contained an old sweatband, which we assume came from the car Anna Stedman was driving at the time. With this sweatband, we were able to isolate DNA that had a partial match to Ruth

Farrow. Josiah Oberton's DNA profile proved to be the partial DNA match with Ruth Farrow."

"A partial match, you say?" asked Lieutenant Adderley.

"Yes," said Rajiv. "Additional information reported by Iowa law enforcement confirmed that Josiah and Ruth were half-siblings. Other than these details, we found no other definitive matches due to the age and partial disintegration of various DNA detected on the old sweatband, and the lack of DNA at our own crime scene."

"I'd like to add," said Storm, "that Josiah Oberton was further interviewed concerning the sweatband found in the old evidence package. He admitted to knowing Anna Stedman during their childhood—a fact which his mother Helen Orbeton has noted numerous times during our investigation. Josiah, however, has no recollection of being in a car with Anna and no memory of any sweatband in an accident."

"Jane?" Lieutenant Adderley looked at her, Jane noticed, without his usual inchoate, reprimanding glint of the eye.

She momentarily pondered a mental image of Adderley rivetted to Desdemona's top selling "The Lord Is My Shepherdess" or "Little Jack Horny," and she wondered if she could or should maintain any respect for this man. But she knew she had to. It was the way of the world. Solstice Spree had been a blunt revelation about people and their inner workings.

"Yes, Lieutenant Adderley. Along the lines of my hypothesis that an old friend of Anna Stedman's may be the murderer, forensics found no evidence of our crime in the cars of Anna's male teenage friends, who are now adults, both on and off the island. No traces of blood or bloody blankets or personal items belonging to Ruth Farrow. And everyone appears to have alibis up to the time they went to bed the night of May 23rd. I also researched car rental companies and dealerships under these people's names during our time frame and found no pertinent rentals. That's within a seventy-mile radius of the mainland ferry for St. Frewin's."

Jane put down her notes. "But despite our lack of any proof or supporting information, I still believe there is more to the old car accident than we know. I would go so far as to say I think whoever was driving the car that killed the family is still out there. That's the murderer we haven't found yet."

"Jane—I have to hand it to you. You are dogged." Finn could not hold his peace. "You crawled out on a limb and you've stayed out on that limb. Not that it matters much at this point. We're so in the dark, this isn't a cold case. It's freeze-dried."

"You know, Finn," Jane smiled angelically as she spoke. "If I weren't such a lady I would say your brain is so straight and narrow, I bet you must tuck it into bed every night inside a condom. But I'm not going to stoop to such talk."

"Enough, people," Storm shut it down. "Enough." He'd seen this stage before, unfortunately. There was nothing to celebrate, no raising a toast for having worked hard to put Justice back on her throne. When his crew was frustrated by a lack of victory, more often than not, their bickering remained. Storm also knew Jane and Finn had fundamental character clashes. They lived in alternate universes.

Storm glanced at Jane. She caught his eyes. She could see there was something positive and also a need in his look, but she knew there was probably nothing either of them could do about those feelings. All she could hope for was another case together in the near future. His guidance had been generous these past months, like a father or a brother.

Rajiv leaned in towards Jane. "You know, I've been thinking. What if I tossed in the towel and moved out to St.

Frewin's to open an Indian restaurant? That wouldn't be the end of the world, would it? Even if my parents might have twin heart attacks. Why shouldn't I start day-dreaming about it?" Jane was about to give Rajiv the thumbs up when Lieutenant Adderley spoke.

"All right. Thank you all for coming in today for this wrap-up," Adderley was dismissing them. "If anything new comes to light out on the island, you know to call us, Jane." Adderley shook their hands and headed out the door to his next coastal cold case wrap-up in another room down the hall.

"By the way, Jane," Finn said as he moved close to pinch her arm while they were exiting the building with Storm and Rajiv. "Very funny and so kind of you to gift me a starter subscription to PUREFLIX."

Jane put her hand on Finn's arm and looked him deep in the eye. She hadn't seen it coming, but she was seriously tired of their dog fight...done with it. "You know, Finn. I have a creative idea. How about a permanent truce? Let's be civil from here on. I'm going to try my darnedest. What do you say?"

Finn glanced down at his feet and Jane could have sworn he was blushing. He looked at her and smiled. "I admit I'm always thinking you're the kind of person who needs a good hosing down, Jane. But maybe I should just accept you. So, sure, let's give it our best shot."

"I may even ring you up for a drink sometime when I'm on the mainland, Finn. So now you're officially forewarned!" Jane felt a small, unexpected wave of goodwill.

She then thanked all of them for their help and wished them well. "Come to St. Frewin's any time!"

62

Late August 2019

Zara sat with her head down, hands gripping her cheeks, elbows scrunched into her ribs, feeling cold and alone, and haunted by her very own recent choices. Her anger and pain and her burning need for revenge or some kind of punishment had totally blinded her sanity. She had purchased the drug and handed it to Kendall. And now he was gone forever. And she was imprisoned in the Maine Correctional Center. Where they only allowed female inmates four white bras, four pairs of white underwear, and four blue shirts, which had to be worn fully buttoned and tucked into one's pants. Just two blankets and one tube of lip balm—squeeze type only. And the barber limited all haircuts to a "basic design."

Nyet, Nyet, and Nyet. This dinky little State of Maine prison system was not going to swallow up Zara Ivanov Billings. Her ancestors' Russian blood would have none of that. She was going to tackle all the inane requirements in the "Female Prisoner Handbook," even if it meant petitioning the governor relentlessly.

What Zara needed was advocacy. Time to get rolling and take action. She was going to call her friend Chanson Pratt for the one fifteen-minute personal phone call Zara was allowed per week.

....

"Chanson! You've got to help me get things straight here at the prison. This can't go on!" Zara poured out her panic to Texan semiconductor, multi-millionaire Salem Pratt's wife, who was still at her summer house on St. Frewin's Island. "We have to come up with a plan to save me now!"

"Hold on, Zara. Just listen for a few minutes. I want to tell you what I've been up to. I don't know if you know I'm on the Board of Directors at "J. T. Karl's Wild Open." They're looking for a really edgy, fresh angle to their marketing and they're about to begin strategizing for their Spring 2020 Catalog."

"What's that got to do with me, Chanson? I need your help here...not with J. T. Karl's!" Zara moaned, watching her fifteen minutes blow away. The nearby guard assigned to inmate phone time shot a quick frown in Zara's direction.

"OK...so listen up, Zara. At our marketing conference later this week, I'm going to push the idea of J. T. Karl's Wild Open featuring *you* as the lead model in their Spring Catalog. A convicted felon would be a first for them. Look at what a great run *Orange Is the New Black* has had. And it helped launch a societal focus on women in prison. You're not the only person who's felt compelled to kill off her spouse. And now the country is interested in helping those people get back on their feet. I also have a concept for a line of female-prisoner-inspired clothing that I'll present to the company. If I can convince the Board and the marketing group that you'll be the perfect face for their Spring campaign, I can't imagine you won't get better treatment at the prison, no matter if it's not fair to your fellow inmates. If you're going to be the centerpiece for J. T. Karl's merchandise, you'll have to look fantastic, head to toe—hair care, facials, manicures, all of that. So bear with me, Zara. Be patient. I'll talk to you at your next allotted phone call. OK, Honey? Hold fast."

Zara wanted to cry, but she just stood there with the phone in her hand, frozen by this bizarre news. All she managed to blurt out before her line cut off was "Oh, Chanson! I would kill to get into that catalog!"

....

"Wilton, let me show you pictures of Zara Ivanov Billings on my cell phone. And when you meet her, you'll see exactly what I'm talking about." Chanson Pratt was doing her best to mesmerize Wilton Savoy, J. T. Karl's Marketing Chairman, over lunch at an elegant inn near the store's headquarters.

"Here," Chanson said as she handed her phone to Wilton. "Look at these shots. Zara is a gorgeous chestnut-haired woman with those long Slavic eyes from the steppes of Eurasia that turn a thousand heads. She's the top of the Euro-trash heap! I bet you'd be able to sell anything she puts on."

"Criminally negligent manslaughter, you say?" Wilton stroked his green bowtie and looked at Chanson with an enormous amount of what could only be termed dubiousness, marching across his weathered face. He began eating his salmon filet with care.

"Yes, Wilton, but it only adds to Zara's mystique and allure that she's been convicted for the death of her husband. I know, I know," Chanson said, putting her hand up in a stop sign. "You're going to have outrage and arguments among your marketing and advertising people. But you want to be a pioneer, don't you? You want to be groundbreaking, yes? Murder is riveting, Wilton. And that sense of playing with fire means you'll have all kinds of curious public thumbing through your Spring Catalog—existing buyers and new buyers. You know how people want to escape the quotidian...they want to think they're making outré fashion choices. If a woman can say, 'I'm wearing the pants of a murderess'—what a blast of noir cachet!"

Chanson rested her case and her elbows on the thick white tablecloth before her. She loved a white tablecloth setting...it was textile's bastion of civilization. And surrounded by sterling silverware—long-tined forks and knives with substantial, heavy handles. None of that blunt modern flatware that didn't feel good in your hand or your mouth.

Wilton smiled at Chanson. He could never resist the bat out of hell in her ideas.

Chanson paused to quench her thirst. "One more item I'd like to run by you. What would you think of creating a female-prisoner-inspired line of clothing? A hip institutional look to bring self-esteem back to inmates, or to cultivate what self-esteem they've managed to hold on to, on their way to the lock-up. I'm thinking with this concept, you could position J.T. Karl's Wild Open to be in the right time, at the right place—to give a boost of redemption to this traditionally shunned population. You could pitch the line to the general public as well. Zara could be your torch bearer."

"She's in the slammer for how many years?" Wilton asked in a way that showed Chanson he might actually be calculating his long-term profit margin...and possibly warming up to the toys in her attic. He hadn't said no yet. He could never say no to Chanson.

"Fifteen years," Chanson said breathlessly, her juices of persuasion pumping hard. "Think of the foreign potential, Wilton. Zara is part Russian. Haven't you wanted to conquer the Moscow and Leningrad markets for a long time? Throw in Siberia, too! She's the perfect key to opening all those doors. She's fluent in Russian...marketing videos would be a cinch...no dubbing needed."

"How do you propose to convince the State authorities to make this Zara available for J. T. Karl's purposes? And how does she stay in good shape in the can? She's not in there to have a good time, you know," Wilton said.

"You're asking the deep questions, Wilton. You are a genius!" Chanson winked and clinked Wilton's martini with her wine glass. "Yes, obtaining permission from the proper channels has also been on my mind. I called around and discovered a curious chain of authority. Makes no sense to me, but apparently the inmates are officially recognized as 'personnel' of Maine State law enforcement while they're incarcerated. The jurisdiction over these prison personnel rests in the hands of the Head of Human Resources at the Maine State Police."

"The Head of Human Resources? It sounds kind of loopy, Chanson. But I'm following you. Keep going...though I think I know where this is going...."

"Exactly. So let me elaborate. Accommodating prisoners while they're being featured in major ad campaigns is not something the Head of Human Resources has a lot of experience with...obviously. By the way, the woman at the helm is a Mrs. Harriet Buxton. No one you know?" Chanson asked.

"Actually, Chanson, I do know Harriet. Or rather my wife knows her. She's a close friend of my wife," Wilton said.

"Really? Well, thankfully Mrs. Buxton is also a good friend of Winnifred Billings, who is a longtime summer resident on St. Frewin's Island. I've known Winnifred for years. She's the former mother-in-law of Zara Billings. I'm telling you all of this because Mrs. Billings was willing, albeit grudgingly, to play diplomat. At first, I encountered an absurd, protracted standoff with this Harriet Buxton. She's a battle axe stuffed to the gills with nuclear warheads, Wilton! We did finally, though barely, bundle together a solution after Winnifred Billings interceded on Zara's behalf."

Wilton found his head wagging in step to the tune of Chanson's verbal choreography.

"Can you believe Harriet Buxton actually told me that unless J. T. Karl's Wild Open agreed to include her in the Spring Catalog with a contractual sign-off by her of the final copy, she would deny approval for Zara to work with J. T. Karl's? And on top of that, Harriet Buxton assured me she would alert the Maine State Revenue Services to take a closer look at J. T. Karl's tax filings for the past five years unless the company complied with her demands. The nerve of that woman! If I ever cross her path in person, she won't forget it."

"Chanson, we're not actively looking for trouble here, are we? I mean the Zara concept, while potentially a brave new world, is rather dicey. And suddenly we're duking it out with head honcho Harriet, who may be walking on the thin ice of extortion. And now you're telling me we can't have Zara without including this Head of Human Resources of the Maine State Police in the Spring Catalog? I don't know. I just don't know. I haven't seen Harriet in ages. Do you have a recent picture of her you can show me?"

"She would probably look a sight better with a make-up stylist and a hairdresser," Chanson suggested as she handed her cellphone photo of Harriet Buxton to Wilton.

"My God, Chanson. J. T. Karl himself is going to fart in his grave if we run with this woman! Harriet's looking like a cross between Bozo the Clown and Count Dracula these days. Really, are you serious?"

"Our hands are tied, Wilton, if we're aiming to secure Zara for this project. I wish we could downplay Harriet by sticking her in the ads for slippers or camp stoves for retirees."

"And what do you think Harriet would say to that?" Wilton asked with raised eyebrows.

"Well, you're right. She specifically insisted she be featured in the high-end clothing lines. And she won't back down."

Wilton laughed out loud and took one of Chanson's hands in his two palms. "When have I ever been able to say no to you?" he murmured as her civilized toes, beneath the white tablecloth, began wiggling deeper between his thighs.

63

Wednesday, September 4

"Oh, my back. These mattresses weigh a ton of bricks," Maggie said, huffing and puffing as she and her assistant, India, hefted yet another old box spring out of a guest room at the Grand Harbor Inn and into the hallway for the maintenance men to remove.

"I know I say this every time, but be careful with these beautiful wide-plank pine floors and the wallpaper, India. I just couldn't find enough drop cloths to protect every inch." The women slowly lowered the box spring and leaned it against the wall.

Maggie was replacing the mattresses throughout the Inn and had closed the business mid-week for two days in early September so she could concentrate on the Inn makeover, now that the summer rush had dispersed. She wanted to head into the fall season with a fresh new start to shake off all the drama and trauma of the past year.

When the two women walked into the next guest room, they both took in an extra lungful of breath as Maggie brought up what they were thinking. "Here we are in Ruth Farrow's room. You know, India, I don't really think I have her to thank for my owning the Inn now. But I guess her death did start a very bad ball rolling for Kendall and Zara. I'm just grateful I was able to take this place over from Kendall's estate. And Abenaki County Bank has been so supportive. Did I tell you about my cute lending officer?"

"Hah. You've told me about him five times. And I can't imagine St. Frewin's without this elegant, historic inn, Maggie," India said. "I just know you're going to survive and thrive. The whole community is behind you."

They began tugging the puffy white duvet and sheets off the bed and set the linens aside on one of the two chintz upholstered chairs in the room. Next they stripped the quilted mattress cover from the mattress. Maggie folded the bulky cover and put it on top of other linens. Then she and India tackled moving the mattress out into the hall. Something fell out with a clunk.

"What is that? And where did it come from?" Maggie asked as she and India put down the mattress. She looked more closely at the frame and suddenly saw a cut in the mattress upholstery.

"Looks like a book," India said, bending down to pick up the object that fell out of the mattress. She and Maggie stared at the red book in India's hand. "My Diary" was embossed on the worn cover, which was closed with a simple lock.

"Son of a gun? What is this? Whose is this?" Maggie wondered aloud. "Oh, Lord, what if it belonged to Ruth Farrow, India? Oh my god...this is unreal."

"Somebody certainly went to a weird amount of effort to hide this thing. But Maggie—we are going to call Jane right away and let her know. Or better yet, you or I should drive it down to the Public Safety Office immediately."

"OK. I'll call Jane's office now. If I can't reach her, I'll leave a message and drive over there and maybe ask the Town Office if they know where she is. Don't let that diary out of your sight. I think it makes sense to keep it here where we found it. And don't open it until Jane decides what to do. She may want to call her bosses on the mainland. I'll be back as soon as possible," Maggie said as she left the room to head downstairs. She made a quick call to the Public Safety Office and left a message for Jane that she was driving over to see her.

Once Maggie was gone, India sat down in one of the chintz chairs in the bedroom and took the diary in hand to examine it more closely. There was nothing special about it on the outside—just a fake, red leather cover with a cheap lock. India could only imagine what they might find within. And imagine is exactly what her mind began to do as the minutes crept by. She looked at the pros and cons of not opening the book. She tried to pry the cover up at the corner, to peek into the pages, but the diary was too fat and stiff to budge. She wiggled the lock a bit, but was afraid to break it if she tried too hard.

India finally stood up with the book and went downstairs to get a paper clip in the front office. She tried several maneuvers until she succeeded in getting the clasp free from the lock on the diary. India was not going to look back. She ignored the question deep in her brain about her many fingerprints now on the book. She was going to read the diary quickly to find out whatever she could.

She flipped towards the last entries and quickly began scanning the handwriting. She didn't want Maggie to pop back in and find India riveted or cringing over the contents. She didn't want Maggie to know she'd opened the book at all.

India began with the first part of the final entry.

64

Wednesday, September 4
Afternoon

"Hey, Zeke...how's it going?" Maggie asked as she stepped inside the Public Safety Office. It looked like Zeke was the only one around at the moment. "I wanted to have a chat with Jane. Do you know when she'll be back?"

"You may have a bit of a wait, Maggie," said Zeke. "Jane's off to the south side of the island to have a chin wag with someone who called in a complaint. I don't know who the caller was. But Jane should be back in about a half hour."

"OK, that's fine. Maybe I'll just wait here a bit."

"Is there anything I can help you with?" Zeke looked ready as ever to spring into action as he turned towards Helen's desk to get paper and pencil that were near her phone.

"Oh," Maggie sighed. "India and I think we may have found..." she started to explain, but then something held back her tongue. "Oh, never mind. I can sit and wait for Jane. It's silly really. We think we may have found some old documents about the island's first policeman while we've been cleaning up and clearing out old junk in the Inn's attic. I wanted a break from all the dust. I'll just sit tight until Jane gets back, if that's all right."

"Righto—no problem." Zeke paused a moment, took in Maggie's hesitation, and then opened his mouth for a huge yawn. "Actually, Maggie, I'm feeling a tad knackered. Some of us guys were out late last night drinking. Could you please let Jane know I had to leave a little early? It's nearly 4:30 PM anyway. Ta ta."

Once Zeke was out of the building, Maggie waited a few minutes and then stepped outside to stroll around and to pull together her thoughts as to why she had hesitated to tell Zeke about the diary.

They still didn't know who murdered Ruth Farrow. And according to Jane's comments the night of the Billings' party when Maggie was assigned to talk to the old timers about Anna Stedman's car accident—and thanks to that notorious sex tape—the two people the police knew of who talked to Ruth while she was on the island were Nathan Herinton and Kendall Billings. But they couldn't be suspects in the crime or there would have been some action against them. Obviously that didn't apply to Kendall now.

Jane also said she was focusing on men who knew Ruth when she was a teenager. That could be any number of guys who were from St. Frewin's. Again, no one had been arrested yet for anything, but that didn't eliminate them absolutely. So Maggie decided Jane was the only person she should tell about the diary.

Maggie headed back to the office and continued to wait for Jane. Finally, the door to the office opened and Jane walked in, quite surprised to find Maggie. She began to tell Jane about the diary, when Jane interrupted her a second. "There's a few messages on the phone," Jane said. "Let me just check them." Jane hit the play back button for Maggie's message. Then Jane hit the second message. "Jane! It's India!...."

65
Wednesday, September 4
Afternoon

India read along in the last entry, not believing what she was reading, hardly aware that her hands and breath were lightly jittering as if breakdancing at a cellular level.

My Diary
Thursday, May 23

No one is going to believe this when I tell them. All this stuff in my head, all these awful pictures of a car crash—I know they mean something. I'm starting to know what they mean. We're at some picnic table, lots of us. It's so beautiful, lots of trees, grass, fields, sunlight all around. I think it's some kind of big, happy family lunch near a flower garden. The table is piled high with lobster, baked beans and ham, potato salad, blueberry pie. People are talking to me like they've known me all my life, and I feel so good around them. Here are my Mom and Dad and they have lots of friends, and I have friends my age.

But then the really sick and bloody part is coming in clearer now. I hate it when my brain jumps to that. I want to run from it, or scream it out of my head. But what's crazy is that it's here. It's HERE ON THIS STUPID ISLAND! I mean it's stupid, because I just want to get back to Iowa. But it's so happy in my vision, and I think St. Frewin's Island is the place in my head. It's like maybe I'm really from here, and now I'm back here. But then, in my vision everyone is staring at me while I'm so out of it. Everything hurts in me and I'm lying on grit and broken glass on the ground. And people keep saying "What has she done? What has she done?" And there's some moaning and crying and people rushing around. They sound like I've done something wrong. Something really horrible. And I'm like, Holy Shit, I can't talk, can't move, or hardly breathe through my fucking nostrils, 'cause they're so full of blood and everyone's blaming me for something? Isn't anyone going to help me??

What's going on in these visions that makes me the bad girl? What happened to the guy driving our car? Where is he? Who is he? He was right in the car with me. I can almost see him now, laughing to someone on my cell phone, he's laughing and not looking at the road and I'm yelling at him to watch out, and suddenly we're smashing totally hard into something big and black right smack in front of us. I remember kids, lots of little kids I can see through my car window. And then a HUGE EXPLOSION OVER AND OVER. What the fuck?! What's happening? Where is the MF'er who did this to me, to all these kids? Go ask HIM what happened...NOT ME!

Oh God, these visions...so sweet one minute, and killing me the next. I know I've got to get help...before it's time to pack up and leave this weird scene. So I started hitchhiking to the police station this afternoon. I knew I had to go talk to the police on this dinky island. If they don't know about the old car accident, no one will. That's when I hooked up with this really great guy...he's pretty cute. Lots of black hair, and I bet he's English...like from England. Like Hugh Grant, but with dark hair. Cha cha!! He stopped his car and offered to take me where I was going. I told him I wanted to find out some info at the police station. And like he says to me, "You want to talk to a Bobby?" Is that English or what? Funny...way out here on this island.

While we drove along, I told him all about my visions, and the car accident, and how creepy the whole damn thing was. And do you know what? He said he grew up here and he knows THE EXACT SPOT WHERE THE ACCIDENT WAS! And he can show me and maybe it will help to clear my head. And then he said I could go see the coppers at the nick on Friday and figure things out. Ha ha!! Is that lucky or what?! And he can pick me up, "his mate," later tonight, after his dinner and a meeting he has to go to. He said the meeting might go on for a while, so he'll come by for me around 10:00 and meet me up at the beginning of the entrance road to the Inn. And then he says to me, "Well, got to bugger off now." Oooooo...I love how he talks! So I'm going to get to play Detective in my own life tonight! Am I one hot shot Private Eye, or what? Cheerio!

66
Wednesday, September 4
Early Evening

India was so shocked, she felt like her lungs were caving into a black hole. Zeke, of all people! Funny, sweet, Britty Zeke. But she simply could not take time now to fathom her dread. She had to focus, before things got worse. She looked towards the huge glass windows in the Inn living room, with hopes of seeing Jane and Maggie driving up. Instead, she saw Zeke turning in with his Mini Cooper and preparing to park. OMG. OMG.

India raced over to one of the wing-back chairs in the living room and stuffed the diary under the bottom cushion. She then rushed to the front desk phone and dialed Public Safety. No answer, yet again. India gasped and left a three-second message: "Jane! It's India! ...At the Inn. Come now! I think Zeke is the murderer and he's heading into the Inn right now!" She hung up before he could see her and forced herself to look like a routine Inn Assistant tidying things up at the end of the day.

"Cheers, India. How's it going?" Zeke poked his head through the front door and sauntered into the Inn's generously wide and elegant entry hall.

"Zeke—What a nice surprise! What brings Romeo to the Grand Harbor Inn so late in the afternoon?" India was scrambling to think of topics of conversation to capture and nurture Zeke's attention, to hold him at bay until Jane and the rest of the world, *please God,* could get to the Inn and tie this guy down for good.

"Well, I'm certainly no longer trying to track down Juliet, or Julibyte, that's for bloody sure," Zeke said with a laugh.

"I must say, Zeke, you were very funny up on stage when all the chasing started. You jumped up and started hiding behind parts of the set, then sticking your head out suddenly and looking so startled. It was hilarious. Where do you get your talent from?" *Please God, please God. Where's Maggie? Where's Jane? What else should I do with this cold-blooded killer until they get here? I can hardly stand up, let alone carry on a run-of-the-mill conversation with this monster!*

"Ah, the psyche of an actor. It's in me blood. It's part of my heritage. But let's talk about you...and Maggie, India. I'm actually here to pick up whatever it is you and Maggie found today...she said something about cleaning out the attic, and wanting to show stuff to Jane. Does that make sense?"

"Oh, yah...it was just some old stuff, like you say." India tried to dismiss the idea casually, not knowing what the hell Maggie had said or meant.

"You do know what I'm talking about, don't you, India? Tell me what you two found."

India was brainstorming like her life depended on it, which she figured it did, and she knew she didn't know what Maggie had said, so India had to divert Zeke with something more enticing.

"Oh Zeke, let's talk about that later. It's not all that interesting. But it is past 5 PM, so surely it's time for a Scotch?" India broadcasted her biggest, whitest smile in Zeke's direction. "We have some fantastic Talisker Exclusive Single Malt at the guest bar. I can sneak us both a glass...just make yourself at home on the sofa in the living room and we can chill out a bit." She grabbed an especially large glass for Zeke. She had to try and keep him happy.

Zeke was thinking it might be worth a superior whiskey to be patient and reel India in a little slower until she told him what they found and handed it over. And if he didn't succeed, or if Maggie returned, no harm done. It was just good old Zeke making his rounds. "Sure, India. I'd be chuffed to bits to have a taste."

India managed to navigate Zeke, their two drinks, and her internally combusting self onto the large, lovely sofa in the living room, where she knocked back her Talisker with a flick of her wrist. She encouraged Zeke to do the same. And then she whirled on top of him! Astonishing herself as much as Zeke, and smothering his eager face with her long blond hair, throwing in whoops of laughter for good effect.

India hoped God would forgive her. She had run out of topics. Her mind was a total blank...that would, of course, happen when someone was looking face down at a killer, well, OK, alleged killer—but was India worried about legal niceties? She had to make the moves on him, until Jane and Maggie could get their damn asses over here. Where the hell were they, anyway? Were they crawling to the Inn?

Zeke thought to himself he was a bit sloshed, and it looked like India was feeling hot. Why not shag her before he started to pressure her a little more to spill the beans. A shag was a great way to get pumped up for a little grilling. Why not?

Zeke breathed in India's scent. He absorbed her weight on top of him. He was marveling at his tallywacker gaining incredible length and volume. Zeke suddenly felt the bullish surge in his spine. He reversed their bodies and straddled himself over her welcoming, bare legs and those strawberry creams, which, whew!, had gloriously burst forth from underneath her blouse. Tally Ho! What did you know? He and India were practically starkers, and now he would butter her up so she would reveal what Maggie was so crazy to show Jane.

India's head and shoulders were colliding into the arm of the sofa in a concentrated rhythmic mode, as the St. Frewin's Island Fiend took his good old time with his cannon shot.

She wanted to concentrate on positive thoughts while the villain of death was pounding her innards. If only she could keep him occupied long enough for the LAW TO ARRIVE...WHERE WAS THE LAW? LAW? BETTER ARRIVE ANY MOMENT NOW!

India understood she needed to stay on Zeke's good side and support his efforts, so she started seething with carnal noises. While she was pacing her orgasmic fake, she noticed an incredibly massive cob web at the end of the picture window curtain rod. They really have to get rid of that disgusting bug nest first thing tomorrow, assuming of course she would still be alive tomorrow to tackle her to-do list.

And what about the poor gorgeous sofa getting trashed by all their jiggling and thumping? India didn't want to think of the dry-cleaning bill for the sullied upholstery. What if Maggie took it out of India's wages? But India reasoned that surely she was not the first to have floundered into spontaneous, erotic behavior on this particular couch, as she ruminated on those who had come before her, so to speak. Including Kendall Billings, no doubt!

"Uh, uh, oh, yes, yes...this is it. This is it!" Zeke's voice was hoarse, almost rasping, as he collapsed on top of India. Much to India's shock, she was starting to feel far, far more sexual percussion than she ever ethically intended to, and a huge electrical serpent jolted through her body while she desperately suppressed every square inch of her vocal chords. After all, she thought she had given Zeke more than enough entertainment here while she was patiently waiting for the slowest rescue operation on earth to arrive. The last thing she wanted was to give him the satisfaction of hearing her satisfaction.

She was quick to open her eyes when Zeke began bearing down rather hard on her neck with both palms. "Enough of the charades, India. Just tell me what you and Maggie found.

You found something about me, didn't you?" His voice was unusually deep.

Before she could react to throw him off, unbelievably, out of the cringing corner of her eye, India saw movement behind her felonious Romeo. JESUS, MARY, AND JOSEPH! Maggie and Jane were standing there, vigorously shushing India with their index fingers over their lips as Dr. Leckman silently closed in on Zeke's spermy zenith and jabbed his shuddering raw hide with a syringe full of just enough ketamine to put him out of commission until they could all figure out what the hell was going on.

67

Wednesday, September 4
Evening

"For Fuck's Sake! What took you guys so long?" India was shoving her way out from under Zeke's slumped body. She attempted to pull herself together, grabbing for her shirt. "I've been here for over an hour with that maniac. I could have been killed! Or God knows what...." She must have looked like a wreck, and she knew it. She started crying. "Sorry. I'm so shook up. Please don't look. I've got to get to the bathroom."

"Here, I'll go with you, India," Maggie said, and the two women left the room.

"So, Jane," Dr. Leckman began. "Like I explained on the way over here, Zeke will be under for about a half hour. Since the Public Safety Office has no cell, we can bring Zeke to the animal recovery room at my clinic. He can sleep off the drug and stay locked in there until tomorrow. You and I can take shifts to keep an eye on him." Dr. Leckman turned Zeke over, put his clothing in order, and resettled him with his back on the sofa.

Jane needed a minute to take it all in. Had this really happened? She was having a hard time coming to grips with the bizarre nakedness and insanity that had just come to a close.

Her oddball Office Manager was lying there in a stupor, good as guilty for the murder of Ruth Farrow, which somehow probably tied him to the old car crash victims as well. Or innocent until proven guilty, though guilty Jane was sure Zeke must be.

She shifted emotional gears to deal with the new reality. "OK, I called Storm earlier from my office and let him know our plans. He'll be over on the first morning ferry with some attending officers to take Zeke to the mainland for questioning. I guess all we do is wait until they show up. Unless you can think of anything else, Doctor?"

"I'd like to call Helen Orbeton. She'll probably want to see Zeke tomorrow before Storm takes him away. Maybe we can convince her to bring us some breakfast," Dr. Leckman said with a grin.

"And what about dinner right now?" Jane asked. "Can we stop at the pub on the way to your clinic and get some take-out? Maybe Maggie and India are hungry too?"

Maggie had returned to the Inn living room in time to hear Jane's suggestion. "I think, Jane, given all that's happened, India and I will throw some food together here and just lay low for a few hours."

"But," Maggie added as she walked over to one of the wingback chairs, "India remembered to ask me to give you this." Maggie reached into the cushion and handed Jane the little red diary. "Keep it safe."

68

Thursday, September 5

"Zeke's definitely chock full of explanations," Storm reported to Jane by phone when he and another fellow detective took a break from questioning Zeke at the Abenaki County Sheriff's Office the next day. "And naturally he's saying he didn't do it."

"Well, no surprise there. They all say that. Ah...jeez, Storm. Is this pathetic or what? It's too much to process...the idea that Zeke has killed...and more than once actually. But all the evidence lines up, right? Ruth Farrow's diary, and the DNA results from that chicken bone matching Zeke's DNA?" Jane looked down at Zeke's paraphernalia on his desk while she and Storm were talking. Who would have imagined Zeke was the one?

"That's what you and I think. But here's the thing, Jane. Zeke keeps asking us why we think he would kill Ruth. He says he works in law enforcement." Storm looked down at his cold coffee. The paper cup was beginning to go slack.

"Well, that's certainly no defense," Jane said dismissively. "Did he ask for an attorney yet?"

"He's in the process of getting one now. I'm sure we'll be challenged on all of this, as usual," Storm said. "Zeke also points out he has his grandmother to worry about, and he's got to take care of his new kittens. Why would he abandon them he says? And he has no idea who did it."

"Obviously he's going to try and wiggle out of this, Storm. That's typical. His grandmother and kittens are reasons enough for him to want to get rid of Ruth Farrow— before she could tell the whole world that Zeke had been driving the car that killed that whole family. She could have ruined his life. And there's nothing to support that he's being honest about any of this. I mean, look at his bizarre personality...forever talking like he's British. That's always struck me as très weird, even if he claims his Englishness, whatever we call it, is due to being brought up by his grandmother. Like he has to hide who he really is. It seems logical to me now that he's the murderer...he's been living behind a mask for years."

Even as she spoke, Jane reflected on how often she was irritated by Zeke's persona, and all his kinks and his meditation gear, and maybe that was why she wasn't keen to defend him. She would probably burn in Hell for that kind of attitude, but she figured Hell wouldn't arrive any time soon.

On top of that, she was furious at Zeke for playing them all like a fiddle, partaking in most homicide meetings, hopping around at the white board to take notes, recalling the island history of the car crash, setting up that altar in memory of the dead, giving Jane only half the story when his fried chicken was found. *Yes!* Zeke duped them all, which is why she was a tiny bit willing to see him go down for the death of Ruth Farrow. Was that a horrible kind of moral laziness on Jane's part? Possibly. But right now, she could not stand back enough from the case to separate her feelings from the facts.

"And Storm, does he have an alibi? How does he explain Ruth's final diary entry?" Jane carved another chunk from the piece of blueberry pie on the plate she was holding and slipped it into her mouth.

"It's kind of curious. Zeke admitted he wasn't quite sure how to deal with Ruth Farrow. When they first talked, with her black hair, he hadn't been certain she really was Anna Stedman...after all these years and no idea what had happened to her. And the more she spoke, he realized

Anna, if that's who she was, did not recognize him. So, Zeke says he never got the chance to visit the site of the old accident with Ruth. By the time he got out of his meeting, he decided it was too late to go driving around. He says he caught up with Ruth at the Inn and simply drove her to the site of the old accident. He left her there, and drove home. Just like that."

"So why the heck didn't he tell us about Ruth at our first homicide meeting after we found her? Why didn't he come out with this when I interviewed him about his fried chicken found at the crime scene? How can we believe him after he's stayed mum from the start?" Jane's frown was multiplying all over her forehead.

"Believe me, Jane. I asked the same questions you're asking. You can talk to him yourself, if you want. Who knows if he's telling the truth? Anyway, he told us he didn't dare say anything about meeting Ruth, because he could see it would make him look really bad."

"Do you think the crime scene investigators will find any useful evidence in Zeke's car or at his house?" Jane wondered.

"Nothing's turned up so far. And for the last piece of this puzzle, I asked Zeke about India and what the hell that was all about. He says when Maggie came to the office looking for Jane, she seemed to have some news she really didn't want to tell Zeke. He panicked that India and Maggie had found something that would somehow incriminate him. When he went to the Inn to try and find out what India knew, he got a bit tipsy on the Talisker she gave him. And she threw herself on him, so he went along with that he says. At the end, he admits he was trying to use some force to get her to tell him what they found. But he was drunk and acted too aggressively. And that's when you and Maggie and Dr. Leckman showed up."

"So where's the Attorney General's office come out on all of this?" Jane wondered.

"Funny you should ask. We're not in the clear yet. The AG assigned to the case is still looking at both pieces of evidence. He's not 100% confident that he has sufficient facts to prove Zeke murdered Ruth Farrow. He's not even sure he can convince a judge to keep Zeke locked up until his grand jury proceeding."

"Storm, smoke is starting to pour out of my head," Jane said in exasperation. "The general public out there thinks most district attorneys can get a ham sandwich indicted. What makes this AG so special that he can't even get bail denied?"

"Well, he feels he needs more than the diary entry and the leftover chicken. When Zeke's attorney gets wind of those details, he'll come down hard on the AG's ammunition. He'll argue the diary record falls far short of proving actual murder...and the tossed chicken was simply casual and inadvertent. We need to come up with more evidence, Jane, and fast. If our case is too thin, Zeke could go free altogether. The pressure's on."

"All right. All right, Storm. As you know, nothing turned up during my car rental research. So we've got to think through everything from the start and find the gap in the murderer's work. There's got to be a gap somewhere."

"Well, good luck trying to focus, Jane, and let me know if you find the gap. I'll concentrate on it, too," Storm added.

"Maybe," Jane suggested, "you can walk the AG through our working hypothesis again—to be sure he gets it. First: Years ago Zeke was the driver talking on the cell phone, and Anna was the passenger. Zeke slammed the Stedmans' car into the car of the family with five kids. And somehow, Zeke was able to get out of the car and flee the scene entirely, without witnesses. Second: Now, years later, he happens to meet Anna, now Ruth, who records this in her diary. Zeke freaks out that she's going to remember he was the driver in the fatal crash. So he arranges to meet her again at night, takes her to the scene of the old car crash, kills her, and leaves behind his half-eaten chicken—or maybe he tossed it earlier in the day. We don't know."

"That's another thing," Storm said. "According to Zeke, he had absolutely nothing to do with the old car crash."

"Well, Storm, like I said earlier...of course Zeke's not going to admit he's guilty."

"Anyway, your timeline is what we've figured so far. The fatal car crash is too old to do anything about, so that's a dead end. But it doesn't matter. Assuming we can somehow bolster the AG's case for the grand jury, Zeke may eventually be locked up for a very long time. So, Jane, you or somebody just got yourselves three kittens and a grandmother."

69
Monday, September 16
Two Weeks Later

"Hey there, beautiful. Whatcha doin' still hangin' out at Public Safety when you should be headin' home to cook suppah?" Jane looked up from Helen's desk and saw Bernie Pushaw swaggering into the main office with his usual paunchy jaunt.

It was not Jane's place to ask why Bernie didn't try cleaning his filthy work cap from his job at "Environmental Fields," the municipal septage recycling compound on the north end of the island. But God if he didn't look like a middle-aged greaseball. A nudge wouldn't hurt, would it? "Hey there, yourself, Bernie. Good to see you. From the looks of your hat, you've been working too hard. Maybe time to throw it in the wash?"

"Come on, Jane. You know I'm busy all day long, shiftin' shit and shiftin' sin from them waste drums into them fields. When I'm up to my neck plowin' that crap into compost, how's a clean hat gonna help me?"

"You make a good point." For the past two weeks, Jane had been staring at her office whiteboard plastered with smudged case notes, curling stickies, and meandering arrows. She was trying to channel Zeke's murderous mind, to attempt to discern the missing Master Clue before his lawyer got him out of jail. Where was the blood evidence? Where was the answer? Bernie's invasion did not help her concentration, but Jane was willing to humor him. "So, Bernie, what's up?"

"I just saw your truck in the parking lot and figured I'd drop in to say Hi. How come you're sittin' in Helen's place? She quit or somethin'?"

"No. Helen just left a little early today. Her son, Josiah, is back in town for a quick visit. I'm wrapping up some paperwork."

"You know, I gotta tell you, Jane," Bernie said as he twirled a toothpick in his mouth. "It ain't no wonder what's goin' on with Zeke. The whole damn island is talkin' about how he fucked up for good this time. And I for one am not surprised one bit. Not at all."

"What do you mean, Bernie? Why aren't you surprised that Zeke is in so much trouble?"

"Well, Jane, it's like this. Not a whole lot's goin' on up on the north end around Environmental Fields. Not a whole lot of traffic. Me and Jason Coombs are about the only ones out there day and night workin' with the crap, you know? And what did Zeke, the Wonder Boy, do early this spring when he thought nobody was lookin'? He went racin' around up there in this old, mustard-colored Ford mustang like a bat outta hell. Like he thought he was Jimmy Dean or somethin'. And it weren't even his car! It's a dead man's car. I call that illegal."

"Could you run that by me again, Bernie?" Jane asked in surprise.

"Zeke was tearin' a blue streak on the roads in a dead man's car. Not too often, mind you. Just once in a while, but I seen 'im. I know it was him." Bernie gave Jane his ole piercing stare.

"Whose car is it, Bernie? What dead man? Could you show me the car? Like right now?" Jane said in a hurried, worried voice.

"Sure thing, Darlin'. Captain Pushaw at your service. You wanna hop in my truck? Or you wanna follow me in yours?"

70
Monday, September 16
Fifteen Minutes Later

Jane slowed down her truck behind Bernie as he pulled his truck into the yard of Warren Gould. She realized this was the place where Zeke had used the hair-dryer to thaw Warren Gould's frozen corpse off his barn floor this past winter.

"Out back this way, Jane. Watch for ticks when you're walkin' through this brush," Bernie cautioned as he headed towards an old shed located beyond the house and the barn. "It's gettin' all overgrown and weedy and them buggers'll suck you dry."

The soft scents of Indian summer and wild grasses blew into their faces as they tramped down to the shed past asters and goldenrod. There was something about a field that could surround you with its sweet warmth and peacefulness and hold you close to the earth. Jane looked out towards the ocean and could feel the sense of security settling over her.

When they reached the shed, they found the door unlocked. Jane peeked inside and laughed at her apprehension. She had almost expected to see dead bodies swinging from the rafters, but there was none of that. Just like Bernie had said...a very shrill hot-yellow Mustang sat inside. Beyond the car was a wall made up of two large doors that could swing open to bring the car in and out. Funny the hobbies and passions people have Jane was thinking as they neared the car. Even if she had been into cars, she never would have chosen such a gaudy color.

"Warren loved this baby all right," Bernie cooed as they stood before the hood and looked through the front window into the pale blue interior. Jane started to respond as they peered towards the back seat, but instead she gasped.

They both jumped the moment they understood what the abrupt change of color meant. Brash, incongruous splotches of dull maroon and pale brown had ruined the sky blue of the back seat. Jane rushed to open the back door. But reason froze her.

"I've got to call headquarters right away, Bernie. This may well be the part of our crime scene that's been missing. And you and I can't touch a thing or we'll go messing it up. Sorry to be so abrupt," Jane added as she guided Bernie back towards the shed door.

"No problem, Jane. It don't take ole Sherly-Locks to guess that's a hell of a lot of blood that ain't supposed to be there. A shit load of blood, Almighty. Let's hustle over to Environmental Fields and you can call the cops from there."

The abrupt, dense smell of gasoline hit Jane's stomach. Motioning a silent "shh" to Bernie, she reached to open the shed door for their exit. Locked. They both turned towards the large doors on the other side. And saw Josiah Oberton, who had appeared from nowhere. He put down a gasoline can and looked at them blankly.

What? What's Josiah doing here? How can this be? A gasoline can? The questions flooded Jane's mind.

For a few seconds, no one spoke until Bernie let loose a long-winded gurgle of flatulence. He bent over with a hearty guffaw. "Pardon me, Ma'am and Sir. Must be those baked beans the Missus served up last night." He broke the next layer of ice just as effortlessly. "How you doin', Josiah, my boy! I was jus' showin' Jane this treasure o' Warren's. She's a beauty all right."

"Is that so, Bernie?" Josiah said, slowly walking towards them.

"Josiah, hi. How are you? Helen mentioned you were visiting." Jane's pounding heart muffled her hearing. She felt like her hands were about to fall off.

"That's right—just a quick trip. And Bernie—if it's OK with you, I need to talk to Jane alone. You should be heading home now anyway...it's getting late."

"No problem, Josiah. Good to see you. And don't you two go joy ridin' in this princess here without me. Heh, heh," Bernie chuckled as he patted the hood of the Mustang. He gave Josiah and Jane a salute and headed towards the large doors and out of the shed.

Josiah rushed towards Jane as Bernie left the shed. Josiah didn't waste time grabbing her and shoving something hard into her ribs. "No funny stuff, Jane Roberts. Not a scream," he whispered.

"Is that a gun?" Jane was horrified, and angry. Fed up with all the bullshit that had surrounded this case.

"You're an idiot."

"Josiah, what's going on? What's with the gun? I was just about to leave." *Oh, God. I need a weapon......*

"Don't play dumb, Jane. You know everything now. Don't tell me you don't get it. You've seen the car. You see me. You've figured it out...finally. And now you're going to act like a hostage and we're going to take some cash out of your bank account."

"Josiah—I'm don't know what's going on here. I'm happy to help with money, but maybe you want to talk things over first?" Jane asked. She had to have answers. "And don't forget...there's a cap on how much I can take out of the ATM." *I need a weapon.*

"Just shut up."

They heard Bernie's truck take off. Josiah kept the gun against Jane and pulled out a pack of matches from his pocket with his other hand. He handed Jane the matches.

"Before we go, you get to be my accomplice, little Miss Wonder Shit. Once we're outside, I want you to light a match and throw it to the ground, right near the entrance."

Josiah began marching the two of them out of the shed, into the growing dark.

"Why a match?" Jane said.

"What do you think? To torch this place. And then we're going to take your truck to the mainland and head straight to a machine. Once you get me some money, I'll let you go and leave for good. Don't try any tricks."

"Can I take a pee first right outside? Before I light the match?" Jane asked. "I'll be quick. I've really got to go. Sorry...."

"Jesus, Jane. Hurry up," Josiah said. "My gun's pointing straight at your ass."

Jane hoped to buy some time—precious moments so Bernie could get help somehow, somewhere? She yanked her pants down. She could smell the gasoline fumes rising up from the ground.

"Whatever happened with Ruth, Josiah? Can you tell me that much?" *OK...this might work, if I hold it just so...I may have my weapon....*

"You don't need to know any more from me, Jane."

"Well, I have to hand it to you. You had us all fooled. We were sure Zeke was guilty."

"Yah, the dumb ass. He proved useful in the end."

"How so?" Jane asked, pulling her pants up.

"Do you know how fucking annoying you are? Light the goddamn match before I shoot you!"

"OK. OK, Josiah. You're so impatient. What's the big hurry?" She began lighting one match after another, each match dying a sputtering death, fluttering useless towards the grass.

"You're dicking around, Roberts. Keep trying the matches."

"Josiah, do you realize who you killed? Did you know Ruth Farrow was Anna Stedman? And she was your half-sister?"

"What? You bitch! Cut it out. Cut the bull shit. Light the matches!"

Jane had unsettled him. *Good.*

"Sorry to screw up your plans, Josiah, but these matches are not behaving like you want them to," she said. "What we need is to light a piece of cloth or something and then drop it on the gas and run like hell. Here, I can use my handkerchief…it's right in my pocket." *I don't know how I'm going to do this, but I am going to do this. I've got to get this motherfucker under control.*

Josiah pointed his gun at Jane's hand as it wiggled into her pocket. He didn't want any funny stuff. Jane took out her handkerchief.

"See, here it is." She waved the handkerchief towards Josiah in the fading light. *I'm not going to yell; I'm not going to say a word.*

AAAAAGGGGHHHHHHHH!

When the hanky floated past Josiah's eyes, he didn't see the truck key hidden beneath. He didn't know to react when Jane drove the sharp end of the key into his neck. But Jane could see that he felt it.

And he lost it. Like a swollen balloon popping its bloody contents. Josiah's red, red blood drenching Jane's fist. His shrieks drenching her ears.

She knocked the gun out of his hand and grabbed it off the ground. He was staggering and screaming. Too stunned to touch the key.

Jane tore off to her truck, pulled out a pair of handcuffs and a rag, and raced back to Josiah. Shocked and stumbling, he did not resist when she yanked his hands together and cuffed them towards his front.

Josiah's shirt was soaked in blood. Jane was gummy with red. "Don't touch that key, Josiah. Leave it in. You'll bleed less. Just leave it in. Here. Hold your arms up and press this rag hard against the wound. I'm taking you to Dr. Leckman right now. He'll figure it out. He'll help you."

They heard the grinding sound of a large vehicle as it turned into the Gould property. Jane tugged and nudged Josiah towards her truck. The headlights from the newly arrived vehicle lit their way. Bernie Pushaw stepped out of the driver's cab of his septage truck and into the light to greet them.

"Will you look at that...Public Safety Officer Jane Roberts in her finest hour," Bernie said.

"Bernie, would you please get over here and help me put our friend in my truck so I can get him some medical help...NOW? QUICKLY?"

"Sure thing, Jane. And I brought along my shit spreader just in case you wanted to coat this maniac with a shot of poison chocolate." They hauled Josiah towards Jane's truck and deposited him horizontal into the cargo bed. Jane stuffed some folded canvas under his head.

"Won't be necessary tonight. But very handy, Bernie. I'm impressed," Jane said.

"Yes, Ma'am. I do what I can. Bernie Pushaw is WEAPONIZED!"

"You sure are. In fact, take this gun and go sit with Josiah in the cargo bed. Make sure he stays put until I get us to Dr. Leckman's, and don't touch that key in his neck. OK?"

71

Friday, September 20

Storm leaned back in his chair at the Public Safety Office table. Jane sat there looking tired and deflated, as though defeated by the price of victory.

"Jesus, Jane. I have to hand it to you. You brought him in. You really brought him in."

"Yah...huh. What a scene. But what a tragedy too, Storm. Now what? What about Helen? We have another nightmare, even though Josiah's been caught."

"Look, a lot of people may suffer when someone is murdered. You can't make it right for everyone."

"I get that. But I'm really worried. I don't want Helen to leave. And I certainly don't want her to feel like the mother of a monster every time she walks out her door. I like working with her. She's a big part of this office. I need to tell her that...again."

"Maybe a raise would help?" Storm said.

"A raise? Storm, Helen's lost her daughter. She's all but losing her son. You think money is the answer?"

"I admit there's not much heart in the suggestion. But why don't I at least run it by the higher-ups?"

"Fine." Jane looked around the room and let out a huge sigh. "We might as well try. And everyone's absolutely sure Helen did not know a thing about Josiah's role in all of this, right?"

"Right."

"And Zeke...what about Zeke? I really need to do some damage control where he's concerned. We put him through the ringer, Storm."

"Jane, sure, you can go see Zeke...any time. Make amends. But would you please stop talking for a moment? I came all the way out here to tell you the whole story in person, so that's what I'm going to do, OK?"

Jane nodded.

"Josiah admitted to everything. After a summer party all those years ago, he drove off with Anna Stedman in her family's car. Just a spin around the island. He was at the wheel, like you hypothesized. And he was on Anna's cell phone when the accident occurred."

"How did he get away?"

"Josiah said he himself had no idea why he wasn't seriously injured, but he was able to get out of the car, and he ran. Took off. Totally freaked out and scared to death."

"Did Finn hear about these details?" Jane said.

"You're not gloating, are you, Jane?"

She shook her head no.

"So, this past May, while Josiah was at the pub, he noticed a woman with black hair. He didn't think he knew her, but her face seemed familiar. And then he said he began to feel haunted...that face. Could it be Anna Stedman? The more he looked at her, the more he felt sure it was his friend from years ago. And he panicked. He said he became very angry and focused and he knew he had to do something about her."

"How did he ever snare the poor woman?" Jane said.

"He said the first night he saw her, he left the pub, waited in the pub parking lot, and followed Anna and Nathan Herinton back to Nathan's house. Josiah parked and waited near Herinton Drive. Later he followed the couple when Nathan brought Anna back to Grand Harbor Inn. Same thing the next night, Thursday."

"By then he must have made a plan," Jane said.

"Right. By the second night, he realized he had to do something, in case she created trouble for him. Especially since he had no idea what she was telling people. He was obsessed with keeping her quiet. So he got his tools together beforehand, including the lobster. After he saw Nathan and Anna arrive at the pub the second night, he raced over to Warren Gould's house. Zeke had told Josiah and other friends about the Mustang in the shed. The keys were hanging on the wall for anyone to use. So simple. Josiah put his tools in the Mustang and drove back to the pub. And again, followed Nathan when he returned Anna to the Inn later that night."

"Wait a minute. If other people knew about the Mustang, how come someone didn't discover the bloody mess before we did?" Jane said.

"Easy. Josiah kept the car keys and locked the shed so no one could get in. The night of the murder, he parked off the road and away from the Inn driveway entrance and sat there rehearsing in his mind how to draw Anna Stedman out to the car. Then, to his surprise, he saw Zeke pull up to the beginning of the driveway and park. And there she was, Anna Stedman, walking towards Zeke and getting into the car.

"When they drove off, Josiah followed behind them, slowly. He could see where they ended up, right near the scene of the old car accident. Josiah was certain this was no coincidence and he was now totally compelled to get rid of Anna.

"When Zeke left her on the road and drove off, Josiah knew this was his answer. He watched Anna look around for a bit and then begin to walk back to the Inn, and he drove up to offer her a ride. He stopped his car and got out. They began chatting.

"Anna, now known as Ruth Farrow, introduced herself and started to talk about the old accident. Josiah told her he grew up on the island and knew about some of the details. He drew her in with those details and offered to show her a map. To better explain what had happened.

"He went to retrieve his map from his car trunk, but he really went for the map *and* his hammer. While they studied the map, he hit her on the head with the hammer. And you know what he told us? Anna had looked up at the full moon and her last words before he struck were, 'This is all so beautiful. I kiss the night.' "

"Are you trying to make me cry, Storm?"

"So listen. He hit her on the head. She fell, and he hit her again. He tied her hands and hauled her into the back seat. Then he drove over to our crime scene and carried her into the drop spot. She started to come to, so he grabbed some stones and stuffed them up her nose. Then he went back to his car for the lobster. And he finished her off, just the way you found her."

"I'm so tired of homicide. I don't think I can take much more."

"You're a Public Safety Officer, Jane. You've got to be able to handle this stuff."

"I'm mostly interested in the 'safety' part...not when things go haywire."

"You'll get used to it."

"I hope not," Jane said.

72

Mid-October

Everyone's emotions were popping up and down on the rigid gray folding chairs, like ice cold water sprinkled into a very hot frying pan. A respectable number of island residents had actually chosen to attend the Community Policing Presentation at the Town Hall. Major Crimes Unit-Central arranged for the event to inform people and put their ragged nerves to rest after the murderous uproar that had unfolded on St. Frewin's Island over the past summer. Officials felt the interested public deserved to hear the final truth on the deaths of Ruth Farrow and Kendall Billings and the incarceration of Josiah Oberton and Zara Billings...or at least a digestible version.

Wilbur Moody invited his cousin Hansen Moody to ferry over for the anticipated event, and they and Trudy Moody were seated with Stan Helmstadt and his wife, Frieda. A few of the Semiconductor neighbors who lived near Stan's dairy farm were seated in the row in front of them.

"I am sure we are not going to hear the whole story," Trudy declared in a loud whisper to her husband and crew. "Word's out that an awful lot may have gone on between that India Barton and our fake criminal Zeke."

"Trudy—pipe down and let the officer fill us in," Wilbur reprimanded his wife. He was all ears right now. And the look on his face said he was tired of his wife trying to run every show, especially when she was in the audience.

"So what's the latest with your snarky ex, Jane?" Samantha asked Jane, while they waited for Storm Nosmot to take the podium. They were sharing a row with Nathan

Herinton, Torrance, Torrance's husband, Bazyli; Maggie, and Maggie's favorite new loan officer, Ryan Young.

"Hah! I can hardly even remember the man," Jane said with a big smile on her face. Thank God for divorce—a harsh tool, but a civilized tool. 20-20 vision had finally settled in her heart, and she was glad to be free—like she'd never been married. "And since you and Nathan seem to be in the thick of it, I'm happy for your sake, Samantha, that he called off his wedding plans to whoever his fiancée was. Did you hear that Rajiv quit his job at the State lab and he's planning to open an Indian restaurant over here?"

The air took on a sudden hush and a quick shifting of legs and clearing of throats as Storm adjusted his microphone before the crowd, ready to straighten out the explosive facts and help St. Frewin's Island back on its feet again.

"Good for Rajiv! And how is Helen Orbeton doing, Jane?" Samantha whispered. "That poor woman has had enough tragedy for two lifetimes."

"Helen is a strong person. I think she'll survive Josiah's troubles," Jane said leaning in close to Sam. "But she needs a break from the office for a few weeks. I told her to take a vacation. And she has Dr. Leckman at her side...officially, that is. You know, don't you, that he was the father of Anna? OK. We better shut up."

"Yah, the whole island knows by now. Life's crazy!" Sam and Jane both sat up straight as Storm began.

"Thank you all for attending today's meeting. Major Crimes Unit-Central wants to express its sincere appreciation to St. Frewin's Island for all the kind support it provided our officers over this difficult past year. I'd like to summarize our findings and take about ten minutes for questions at the end."

After Storm elaborated on just enough details to give the audience a satisfying version of the truth, he finally reached the fate of Zara Billings and Josiah Oberton. "We want to conclude with an update on the status of the charged parties. Zara Billings pled guilty to the criminally negligent manslaughter of her husband, Kendall Billings, by fentanyl overdose. She will serve a sentence of fifteen years at the Maine Correctional Women's Center in Windham, with a possibility of probation. If any of you want to communicate with Zara, we have her contact information on the table in the entry hallway.

"As for Josiah Oberton, the statute of limitations has expired for his role in the fatal car accident seventeen years ago. So even though Josiah admitted to driving the car that killed the Webber family, the old accident had no role in his sentencing. However, Josiah did plead guilty to the murder of Ruth Farrow and has been sentenced to twenty-five years at the Maine State Prison in Warren."

Storm switched topics. "Concerning Zeke Pendleton, Major Crimes Unit-Central wants to emphasize that Zeke had nothing to do with the two murders we investigated. He is entirely innocent of any crime. Zeke plans to wrap up his role at the Public Safety Office and pursue a new career managing an animal shelter on the mainland. We wish him all the best.

"Finally, we'd like to recognize India Barton, the assistant manager of Grand Harbor Inn, for her calm, intelligent handling of a possible suspect during the investigative phase of this case. She successfully managed to engage this suspect in conversation until Officer Jane Roberts was able to arrive on the scene.

"I should add this suspect was later found to have no involvement in our case. Nevertheless, India deserves our appreciation. And if India doesn't mind standing up, we can give her a big hand now. India Barton...yes, there she is."

"A hand, my foot!" said Trudy Moody, sizzling at her husband while she barely flapped her palms together. "I tell you, human nature just doesn't work the way Storm Nosmot says. A woman thinks a man is a murderer and she's gonna just sit there and yack away with him for over sixty minutes? You can call me a monkey's uncle!"

"You're just letting your mind run down the gutter, Trudy," Wilbur scolded his wife. "What else in God's name was India supposed to do with a possible killer standin' right there in front of her?"

"Use your imagination, Wilbur! Where has your antenna for hanky panky gone to, I ask you?" People nearby saw Trudy starting to flush rosy and get a bit sweaty over this little spat of theirs.

"Now, Trudy,"...Wilbur looked at Stan Helmstadt for moral support and found none. "If your 'magination's runnin' hog wild and you are sittin' there officially thinkin' that poor India now has the spam of the devil in her, I am ASHAMED of you, Honey. Honestly ashamed. You heard the officer. Zeke Pendleton is not a murderer."

"SPAM of the devil, Wilbur? SPAM? If you had made it past fourth grade, you would know it's 'SPAWN' of the devil, Wilbur!"

Storm began taking questions from the floor, focused largely on how Zara had killed Kendall and what would happen to Josiah in prison. Frieda Helmstadt, Stan's wife, tried to divert Trudy's eruption in front of the Texan semiconductors toward calmer ground. "Do you know," she leaned forward to Salem Pratt's wife, Chanson, "we got a letter last week from our insurance company asking if we wanted Terrorism Insurance. Imagine that! On this little island. What do they think? The Russians are coming?

Heavens—the Russians already own quite a few homes on St. Frewin's Island."

"But, Frieda," Stan piped up. "Don't you think we oughta get some of that terrorism insurance? I don't want nothin' to happen to our cows."

"Stan, of course we don't need it, and neither do the cows! The only way you are ever going to see a terrorist is if you go to Hannaford and some jihadist is there tryin' to buy, I don't know what all they eat...maybe pita bread?" Frieda looked at people staring at her and decided to shut her mouth. She was making nearly as much of a scene as Trudy Moody had.

One of Salem Pratt's house guests nudged him and whispered "What was all that ruckus about spam and that pretty young woman India?"

Salem leaned close and said, "I'm guessing it's Frewinese for 'sex.' "

73
The Afterlife

> *"...from morn*
> *To Noon he fell, from Noon to dewy Eve,*
> *A Summers day..."*

—PARADISE LOST
John Milton

This is it. Obviously. I, Ruth Farrow, am dying. Keep things simple, right? ...Especially now. I am dying. My body is so out of whack in this mud, I can't close or open my mouth, and my nose is all plugged up. I can't breathe. But my mind is my own. I can tell you I am delirious and gagging—you probably already know that. Everything is humongo clear to me now. I see that entire day of the last day of my normal teenage life, when everything began to go to shit. I have been going downhill ever since, but I was the last to know.

All the faces of my once perfectly happy life as Anna Stedman are zooming past my mind. It was JOSIAH, my FRIEND, Josiah Oberton! It was him all along! He was driving the car. He was on the cell phone. He smashed us and that poor family to smithereens. But he had a miracle going for him. He WAS the miracle.

That bastard never said "Anna, are you OK?" He never yelled, "Let me help you!" Not one square inch was he truly hurt. He just crept out of that wrecked car and never looked back; he didn't care about me; he cared less about that family. He was gone like a spooked deer, slipping through the trees to nowhere, to nothing. Accident? What accident? He hadn't been in any accident. He didn't know anything about it except what he heard and read.

And now? Look what you've done to me. This is the end zone. I get it. I finally get it. Way back then, you left me all alone at the crash, to turn into the walking dead. Now you've stuffed me until I really am dead. Kind of overkill, don't you think, Josiah?

And you don't know this, Josiah. Because you're still alive, you asshole. But when we die, the mind lives on for a few more minutes. We're given enough time for One Final Happy Thought. No way are you going to smother my last thought, which is a thought of love.

My life is going to end with the memory of my wonderful Aunt Helen. We're leaving that summer lunch on St. Frewin's Island, and Aunt Helen comes over to us to say goodbye. She has been so nice to me and my parents all along...reading books to me and going on walks with me when I was a kid, bringing us peonies and raspberry pies, telling us funny jokes. Her eyes are nearly crying as she gives me the biggest hug on earth, close to her heart, and she whispers to me, "You'll always be our pride and joy, Anna!" I love her! And I tell her so.

Carol Chen lives in Camden, Maine. She is nuts about peonies, Chinese plums, her dogs, and laughing over dinner with family and friends. LOBSTERS WITHOUT BORDERS is the first Jane Roberts Mystery.